DEROS

"Fr. Jake Austin, the hero of Vanek's promising debut and series launch, returns to his hometown of Oberlin, Ohio, in 2002 to take up a temporary post at a Catholic hospital in nearby Lorain—an assignment that coincides with his high school class's 30th reunion. In high school, Jake was a football star and rowdy. He later became a medic in Vietnam, eventually a doctor, and finally a priest. At the reunion, Jake reconnects with such people as police chief Tremont 'Tree' Macon, a former football pal; old girlfriend Emily Beale, whose blindness comes as a shock; and Emily's acerbic ex-husband, Everett McDermott. The reunion quickly goes from bad to worse: at the banquet, the speaker collapses, another is attendee is poisoned, and a threatening note seems to target Emily. Late that night, someone shoots Everett at his home, leaving him in a coma. Full of conflicting emotions, Jake has a lot to cope with in a mystery that's as much a character study as a whodunit. The title is an acronym for Date of Expected Return from Overseas—the relevance of which isn't immediately obvious. Readers will look forward to seeing more of Jake."

—Publishers Weekly

"Interesting, nuanced characters in a finely wrought setting."

—Laura Lippman, New York Times bestselling author of Wilde Lake and the award-winning Tess Monaghan series

"John Vanek guides the reader through the seldom-seen worlds of both medicine and the priesthood. His years as a physician at a Catholic hospital make him the perfect creator of this literary mystery set in a small college town, but few physicians can manage prose as well as Vanek does."

—Sterling Watson, author of *Suitcase City* and *Fighting in the Shade*

"A riveting tale of mystery and murder. Superb storytelling with a deft touch by this talented author who keeps ratcheting up the tension until the explosive ending. A fast read, but the characters linger in your memory."

—Ann O'Farrell, author of the Norah's Children Trilogy

"John Vanek brings small-town Oberlin, Ohio to life. Locals will recognize familiar people, places, and threads of Oberlin history woven throughout the story as Father Jake Austin reconnects with his past and gets caught in a web of deadly vendettas."

—Liz Schultz, Executive Director of the Oberlin Heritage Center

DEROS

DEROS

Date of Expected Return from Overseas

A FATHER JAKE AUSTIN MYSTERY

JOHN A. VANEK

coffeetownpress

Seattle, WA

coffeetownpress

Coffeetown Press
PO Box 70515
Seattle, WA 98127

For more information go to: www.Coffeetownpress.com
www.JohnVanekAuthor.com

Cover photograph of the Jewett House by Ed von Hofen
Permission granted by the Oberlin Heritage Center
Cover design by Sabrina Sun

DEROS
Copyright © 2018 by John A. Vanek

ISBN: 978-1-60381-619-9 (Trade Paper)
ISBN: 978-1-60381-620-5 (eBook)
Library of Congress Control Number: 2017954660

Printed in the United States of America

Acknowledgments

———•———

I AM EXTREMELY grateful to my wife, Geni, and to Jessica and Randy Dublikar, Jen and Matt Vanek, Father Thomas Winkel, Sterling Watson, Laura Lippman, Michael Koryta, and Dennis Lehane for their help and encouragement. Special thanks to Abe Spevack, Ann O'Farrell, Susan Adgar, Barbara Schrefer, and Lee Summerall for their brutally honest critiques over the years. Thanks also for input and support from: Maureen and Mark Johnson, Kathy and Emil Poporad, Jim and JoAnn Gavacs, Mary Winter, and the Pinellas Writers. Pat Murphy and the Oberlin Heritage Center provided guidance and critical access to Oberlin's historical records. Any factual errors or exaggerations are purely those of the author. Finally, I wish to thank the tireless team at Coffeetown Press for guiding me through the morass of the publishing world: Jennifer McCord, Catherine Treadgold, Becca Eskildsen, and Aubrey Anderson.

The two short poems that appear in the story, "Squall" and "Twenty-One Guns," were originally published in my book of poetry, *Heart Murmurs: Poems*, and are used with permission from Bird Dog Publishing.

Short quotations from Thomas Merton are used with permission of The Thomas Merton Center, Bellarmine University. These originally appeared in *Learning to Love*, edited by Christine M. Bochen (HarperCollins). I also wish to spotlight these other fine books, which helped me bring the historical aspects to life. I highly recommend them:

The Things They Carried, by Tim O'Brien
The Town That Started the Civil War, by Nat Brandt
Out of the Night: The Spiritual Journey of Vietnam Vets, by William P. Mahedy
John Mercer Langston and the Fight for Black Freedom, by William Cheek and Aimee Lee Cheek

Author's Note

———•———

IT TAKES A village to raise a child, but it took a small town to raise this novel to life and bring it into your hands. You are now its foster parent, and I hope that you come to love it too. If you do, please tell your friends. Word of mouth is the lifeblood of independent presses and their authors.

DEROS is a work of fiction. Oberlin, Ohio, however, is real and similar in many ways to countless American towns. I have rendered its physical description and history as accurately as possible.

I practiced medicine for years at hospitals throughout Lorain County, including St. Joseph's Hospital, which I resurrected for the novel. It closed its doors in 1997. In addition to treating patients, I also taught interns and residents, many of whom were foreign-born, far from home, and living in dormitories adjacent to the hospital as depicted in the story. The hospital snack shop was modeled after one operated by the sightless at Strong Memorial Hospital in Rochester, New York where I attended medical school.

I wanted to portray Father Jake Austin as a spiritual man, but with ordinary human flaws and failings that we all possess.

Although he is a fictional character, aspects of his personality and struggles were modeled after two Catholic priests who became my close friends and confidants. When I first met them, I expected the usual stereotypes, but when their Roman collars came off and we relaxed with a few beers, I found that they were wrestling with the same emotions and concerns that most of us share. One of these priests confessed his attraction to a young nun. Call his love unrequited; he called it hell. I watched this righteous man struggle courageously with his commitment to his vows. This became the inspiration for Jake and Emily's relationship in my novels.

It seems as if child molesters, charlatans, and thugs dominate the headlines these days, while those who sacrifice personal needs for the sake of others are seldom thanked, let alone celebrated. Besides spinning a good yarn, I hoped to honor all those who pit their will and faith against their human frailties and daily temptations, not just in the clergy but in all walks of life. As Father Jake says in the story, people aren't born priests. And as Oscar Wilde said, "Every saint has a past, and every sinner has a future."

The characters in this novel are all fictional except for Pat Murphy and the late Gene Presti, my friends and well-known citizens of Oberlin, who allowed me to include them in the story for the sake of realism. The remainder of the characters, settings, and all the events are entirely the product of the author's imagination.

Prologue: The Quarry

———•———

Saturday, July 1, 2002, 10:00 a.m.

THE CHIEF OF police, Tremont "Tree" Macon, parked his cruiser next to the coroner's meat wagon. As he unfolded his six-foot-six-inch frame like a jackknife from the driver's seat, a television van roared up, spewing gravel and filling the air with dust.

Tree spat on the ground, expressing his disgust with police scanners. He wasn't fond of reporters either.

A young woman with a microphone stepped from the van, glanced at him, and yelled, "Hurry, Darth Vader's here!" Her cameraman leaped out of the van's door like an Army paratrooper, his video camera whirring.

Macon spat again. He had always been partial to the nickname, Tree. It suited him. Being called Darth Vader on account of his size, deep voice, and skin color, however, just pissed him off—and few people dared to call him that to his face.

He waved off the reporter's questions and trudged up the dirt path, feeling every one of his forty-eight years. Streamers of yellow crime-scene tape whipped and snapped in the wind. He signed the logbook, slipped on latex gloves, and weaved around evidence markers until he saw the county coroner near the edge of the sandstone quarry.

Dr. Gerta Braun's white hair and crow's feet revealed her age, but only hinted at her toughness. Bright hazel eyes peered up at him from her weary face.

"Morning, Tree. We have a female, mid-twenties. She's been dead a couple of days, long enough to bloat her like a tick. The kids over there were partying." Gerta pointed with her body-cavity thermometer toward two teens being interviewed by a policewoman. "After drinking some of Daddy's vodka and making out, they jumped in from the ledge for a swim and discovered the body. The blonde felt something touch her thigh. She thought her boyfriend was getting frisky, so she reached for him and accidentally pulled our victim to the surface—gave her a hand, so to speak—resulting in instant sobriety and an abrupt end to romance."

Tree returned the coroner's sad smile. He hated gallows humor, but sometimes it helped to make the horrors they saw bearable. He and Gerta had both been doing this job longer than he cared to remember.

"Accidental drowning, Gerta?"

"Definitely not, Chief. Somebody dragged her to the quarry from the south parking lot. She lost a shoe along the way. The tire iron and car jack tied to her ankle weren't heavy enough to weigh her down after the bloating started. She'd probably already begun floating up from the bottom when the kids dragged her to daylight."

Tree sighed. A homicide. So much for his weekend off. Murders were rare in Oberlin, Ohio, and his sleepy little town wouldn't get much rest after this hit the evening news.

The air was thick with bottle flies, dive-bombing his face and buzzing his ears. The coroner seemed not to notice. Swatting them away, Tree breathed through his mouth to lessen the pungent odor of decay. He gagged anyway. Each breath tasted like a copper penny wrapped in raw ground beef—the flavor of death. He was pretty damn sure it would cling to his tongue for days.

The coroner handed him a small jar of Vicks VapoRub to mask the smell. He closed his mouth, put a dab on his upper lip, and inhaled cautiously.

"Did she have any ID on her, Gerta?"

"Nope." She gestured toward the water. "God knows what sank to the bottom."

"I'll call for scuba and have a diver check it out."

Tree waved to a crime-scene tech making a slow sweep around the quarry's edge with a metal detector, then he circled the body from a distance. A drop of sweat rolled past one eye, and he wiped his forehead on his shirtsleeve before removing a small spiral-bound notebook from his pocket and logging his findings in a shorthand only he could decipher.

The victim lay on her side with one hand raised as if waving goodbye. Her face was partially covered by long, slimy hair that looked like black seaweed. She was petite, a pixie of a woman. Her slender arms and legs suggested emaciation, and her waist must have been tiny before the bloating. Marbled blue-gray skin almost obscured a tattoo of roses encircling her right biceps, the pink buds climbing from her elbow to her shoulder like a trellis. A small flap of waterlogged flesh had peeled away from her plum-colored lips. Even distorted by decay, however, she looked vaguely familiar.

"She's skinny as shit, Gerta. I'm thinking druggie. Was she a shooter?"

"No needle tracks. We'll know more when the tox screen's back. It's not likely she's a junkie, the way she's dressed. The gown's Versace, and her high heels are Manolo. Expensive stuff. She must have been very pretty before the decomp. Could be a top-shelf hooker, I suppose."

He nodded. "Any sign of a struggle?"

"She doesn't have defensive wounds. I'll scrape under her fingernails and see if she clawed some DNA from our perp."

Tree made a second lap around the body, scribbled more notes, then used a twig to move the woman's hair away from her face. A strand fluttered in the breeze, giving the illusion that a flicker of life remained.

Nature was merciless after death. The woman's mouth was open, as if her life had ended mid-sentence. Decomposition, accelerated by the water and warm weather, had caused her eyes to protrude like ping pong balls, producing a ghoulish stare. He followed their gaze across the murky quarry toward eternity.

Rifling through the Rolodex of wasted faces in his memory, he came up empty, so he reversed the logic. How would this pixie have looked if she were heavier? Then it hit him.

"Oh, sweet Jesus! It's Joanetta Carter."

"You know her, Chief?"

"Yeah. I collared her for misdemeanor possession of weed and let her off with a warning, 'cause my wife knew her. That was several years and thirty pounds ago. I wonder why she lost all that weight."

"Could be she graduated from the minors to the big leagues—coke, speed, smack. Too many visits to the all-you-can-ingest/inhale/inject buffet. Or she bought into that heroin-chic bullcrap the fashion magazines are always selling." The coroner inspected the woman's mouth with a small flashlight. "No dental erosions to suggest bulimia. I'll review her medical records and see if she had a history of anorexia, cancer, or drug abuse."

"What's your best guess at cause of death, Gerta?"

"I don't guess, and I didn't bring my Ouija board. When I finish the postmortem, you'll know for sure. There're no knife or gunshot wounds, but check this out ...." She pointed to the victim's upper chest. "It's some sort of tiny puncture, just below her clavicle. There's a matching hole in her dress with a blood stain around it, indicating she was alive when it happened."

"An ice pick?"

"The wound's the right diameter, Chief. It could have collapsed a lung, though I can't feel any air crackling under her skin. When I—"

A loud whirring sound drowned out her words as a news helicopter banked in, circled the quarry, then hovered above them like a huge metal dragonfly. The sudden vertical wind flipped the pages of Tree's notebook.

"Son of a bitch!" He punched the button on his radio. "Get that frickin' whirlybird the hell away from my crime scene before I trash the First Amendment and throw someone's ass behind bars!"

Mid-morning and already the inside of his head was beating out a steel-drum solo. He closed his eyes, pinched the bridge of his nose, then refocused on the body.

"Damn. I'll have to tell my wife. They were in a book club together—a bunch of ladies who read romance novels." He took a final lap around the body. "Joanetta graduated from Oberlin College. Bright kid. What a waste."

"Some lives are so sad and short, Tree, you wonder why God even bothers."

"Amen, sister."

"Don't know if this helps, but I found this around her neck. If it's real, we're talking big bucks."

She handed him a plastic evidence bag containing a ruby pendant set in gold. He flipped it over and read the inscription: "To JC from EM."

Nice to catch a break in a case once in a while. Maybe this bauble would be his good luck charm. Joanetta worked at Everett McDermott's collection agency in town.

"Helps a lot, Gerta. It tells me robbery wasn't the motive." He returned the pendant. "And gives me probable cause to interrogate the crap out of a real scumbag. Keep me posted. I'm gonna have me a chat with Mr. Repo Man."

Chapter One

———•———

Saturday, July 1, 2002, 11:00 a.m.

SHE LOWERED HER tray table and her fingers brushed my thigh, lightly and just for a second. My muscles tensed. She smiled and did that thing with her hair, flipping it away from her face. She was centerfold material. Full lips, high cheekbones, long-stemmed neck—and young, early-thirties, at least fifteen years my junior.

I let my eyes roam from tan legs, to full breasts, back to green eyes.

Bad idea. This could only lead to trouble. The airplane rumbled through turbulence as if God agreed. I lifted the shade and shifted my focus to the clouds floating past my window.

Although coach class offered little room and there was an obese man in the aisle seat, she seemed to be leaning against me. I was flattered by her attention, but distracted by a pounding in my forehead—probably *guilt* enlarging in my brain like an aneurysm.

I rubbed my eyes and massaged both temples, trying to shake off the throbbing pain.

"Headache? Want some aspirin? Something stronger?" she asked, her hand lingering on my arm. "I have an entire drugstore in my purse."

"No, thanks. I just hate flying."

"Who isn't afraid since the attack last year? I was in the city when the Twin Towers …." She looked away and took a swig of her drink. "My god, those planes! I was so scared. Still am. I'll never forget that day."

Neither would I. September eleventh had been both my forty-seventh birthday and the birth of America's somber new reality. I suspected that the near future would be as dark for the country as my time in the Army had been for me, but kept my thoughts to myself. The last thing I wanted to discuss with this woman was war, especially one with religious overtones.

She raised her cocktail, her second since takeoff. "Sometimes I need … a cup of courage or two when I fly," she said, her machine-gun banter beginning to misfire. "I spend more time on planes than at home. I'm Tanya, by the way."

"Jake Austin. Nice to meet you."

What I really hated wasn't flying, but this woman's constant chatter since the moment she took her seat, as well as being confined in this narrow, winged tube, unable to move. Ever since that day in Vietnam years ago, tight spaces made it hard for me to breathe.

I went silent, hoping she'd babble for a while at the fat guy in the aisle seat.

"So, you're headed to Cleveland, Jake?"

"Oberlin, actually. I grew up there and haven't been back in decades."

"Yeah, I know the place," she said, her voice a breathy flute solo. "West of Cleveland. Cute town." She raised her plastic cup. "A toast to your homecoming. I wonder if it's true what people say. You know. You can never go home again."

"Good question. I guess I'm about to find out." Oberlin conjured up no warm, fuzzy feelings, and was the last place

I wanted to be. "And lucky me, I arrive in time for my high school reunion. Fate has a really warped sense of humor."

"Reunion, huh. Is it a biggie? Twentieth?"

"I wish!" I pointed at my hair. "The gray doesn't lie. It's my thirtieth, I'm afraid."

"A little sugar mixed in with the spice. Not such a bad thing." Her flute music danced in the air with a hint of her perfume, something earthy and alluring. She drained her drink. "Can be kind of sexy."

So this was the siren song that sailors heard before crashing onto the rocks.

"Will there be any old flames to fan at the reunion, Jake?"

Turbulence again shivered the plane, as Emily's long, auburn hair and cameo face flashed in my mind. The mere thought of her still hurt. I willed her image away.

"No old flames. No sparks. Only ashes." Tanya was fishing for personal info, and I needed a diversion. "What brings you to Cleveland?"

"Drugs." She placed her lips close to my ear and whispered, "I sell drugs. Told you I had a purse full." She waited a beat, then added, "I'm a drug rep for Ely Lilly. But marketing prescription drugs used to be a lot more fun. Now, all the travel makes me," she examined her empty cup, "I don't know, tired and lonely."

She raised a tan, well-muscled arm and pushed the call bell to summon a flight attendant. A pale band of skin encircled her ring finger.

Recently divorced or separated and adrift, maybe on the rebound.

As Tanya ordered her third Scotch and soda, I let my eyes wander over her again.

"Want another drink, Jake?" She winked. "I'm buying! It's on the old expense account."

I glanced down at my ginger ale, wanting to lace it with a double shot of bourbon, but I sure as hell didn't want to squeeze my claustrophobic butt into the plane's tiny restroom.

Besides, I'd need all my wits about me when I got back home—as I needed them now. Even dead sober, I was sliding down the silky slope of her green eyes.

"I'll nurse this one awhile, Tanya, thanks."

"Your loss." Maroon fingernails raked through her wheat-colored hair. "So, what do you do, Jake? Where do you work?"

She was still fishing. I took a small sip, buying time.

"In a hospital. I'm starting a new job." A half-truth, and as close as I cared to get to a lie. I should have stopped this charade, but part of me didn't want the game to end. I hadn't played it in ages.

"Which hospital?"

"St. Joseph's in Lorain. It's not far from Oberlin."

"St. Joe's? That's one of the hospitals I service. Maybe I'll see you there. Let me guess." She pursed her lips as if trying to solve an algebra problem. "I think … you're a heart surgeon. Am I right?"

Was the question personal, or was she simply selling product? It didn't matter. I wasn't taking the bait.

"Nothing that exciting. I'm only a helper bee, trying to relieve suffering like everyone else. Now, if you'll excuse me …."

I turned my attention to the cloud tops, hoping she'd get the hint.

The flight was full, the air stifling, and the small air vent in the console above nearly useless. Sunlight poured in the window, frying me in my black shirt and slacks. I drew the shade down and rolled up my sleeves.

"What a cool tattoo!" Tanya studied my forearm. "What's it mean?"

Don't go there! I slammed my mouth shut before the answer could leave my tongue.

"It's so unique. It's got to mean *something*, Jake."

She was as relentless as a hound dog after a bunny.

"Nothing important."

"Snakes and dragons? Come on, give."

"It's shorthand for my youth."

She tilted her head. "And?"

"The serpents and staff represent the caduceus. I was a medic in the army, a lifetime ago. The dragon symbolizes Vietnam."

"And the K.B. and H.N.?"

"Close friends." I was trapped between Tanya and the miniature window with no chance of escape. "Friends I couldn't save."

"I'm so sorry, Jake."

I adjusted the air vent, leaving her apology dangling between us.

She yanked the *SkyMall* magazine from the seat pocket, opened it, and flipped through the pages.

For the first time since takeoff, Tanya's chatter ceased. I savored the silence—briefly.

"Vietnam's such a hot travel destination now." She pointed at my tattoo. "My cousin went last year and said Saigon was lovely."

My smoldering headache suddenly burst into flames. I jerked my arm away. *Enough!*

"It wasn't a damn resort back then! Trust me, no one I knew wanted to vacation there. I did my time in a hellhole called Cu Chi, not exactly a tropical paradise."

I raised the window shade. The Cuyahoga River slinked along below us like thick brown sludge. Cornfields coasted by, sliced into a giant yellow-green checkerboard by a crosshatch of roads. I could almost hear the wind whistling through the stalks.

The intercom announced our descent into Cleveland Hopkins International Airport. Seats popped forward and tray tables clattered to their upright positions. The turbulent approach muffled conversations. As we rocked and pitched, Tanya closed her eyes and clutched the armrests. I silently prayed an Act of Contrition, finishing as the wheels screeched down, bounced, bounced again, and we braked hard to a full stop. Scattered groans and applause erupted behind us.

We disembarked in silence. At baggage claim, Tanya approached me, a bit wobbly from the Scotch. She handed me her business card with the name of a hotel scrawled across the bottom.

"About before, Jake … I didn't mean to pry. Sorry. Let me make it up to you. I'm at the downtown Sheraton all week." It was more a question than a statement.

I shouldn't have let things get this far. God, this was difficult. As I took a long last look at this beautiful creature, St. Augustine's famous prayer came to mind: "O Lord, make me chaste—but not today."

"I'm sorry too. I really wish …."

I couldn't find the words.

The glow in her eyes flickered and died as she waited for an explanation that never came. She shook her head and stomped to the baggage carousel, passing a gray-haired woman wearing gold-rimmed spectacles, a flowered dress, and holding a sign that read FATHER AUSTIN.

As I approached, the woman greeted me with a thick Irish brogue.

"Is it yourself, Father? I'm Colleen Brady. Delighted to meet you." She offered a firm handshake. "It's good you're here to stand in for Father LaFontaine while he's in the hospital. I'm to collect you and take you directly to the rectory."

I buttoned my shirt at the neck, removed a clerical collar insert from my pocket, and slipped in the white calling-card rectangle. I wasn't used to the Roman collar yet. It felt alien, and particularly tight today.

A few yards away, Tanya watched me. I hoisted my luggage, tipped my head toward Colleen's sign, and shrugged. As I exited with Colleen, Tanya burst out laughing.

Chapter Two

———•———

Saturday, July 1, 2:00 p.m.

L ESS THAN FIVE feet tall in her sensible flats, Colleen Brady perched atop a thick telephone book, barely able to see out of the windshield. If she'd worn a conical red hat, she could have passed for a garden gnome. She flogged her ancient Toyota Corolla like a stubborn mule until it finally reached a 50 mile-per-hour lumbering trot. The engine protested, doors rattled, and semis flew by us on I-480 as if we were parked.

Colleen wore a helmet of short white hair, and her demeanor reminded me of my drill sergeant in boot camp. She met my attempts at small talk with one-word replies and an occasional "harrumph." From what little she said, I gathered that she was the part-time housekeeper at Sacred Heart Church, the only Roman Catholic parish in town, but I didn't learn much else. Given her lack of interest in conversation, I began to wonder if she was really Irish. When I asked about her family, her knuckles whitened on the steering wheel and the Toyota swerved, resulting in a cacophony of horns from the cars around us.

"Jesus, Mary, and Joseph!" Her face flushed red and her brogue thickened. Without taking her eyes off the road, she hissed from the side of her mouth, "If you don't mind, Father, I would appreciate a lack of distraction. You people drive like the demented, and on the wrong side of the road too. I'd prefer to get you to the church *alive*, don't you know."

Yup, definitely Irish. That ended our chat and began a silent thirty-minute drive southwest from the blue-collar suburbs of Cleveland, past farmland, to the Oberlin exit. The Toyota hobbled over potholed streets, past apartments and understated homes, until we entered downtown.

Oberlin hadn't changed much in the decades since I'd been away, and not much over the last hundred years. The architecture remained a patchwork of antebellum and modern, Asian and American, including a mosaic of nineteenth through twenty-first century elements—the end result somehow giving the town a timeless quality.

"Ms. Brady, please drop me off here." Floundering in a sea of memories, I gestured toward the town square. "It's been a long time since I've seen the old girl, and we need to get reacquainted. I'll unload my bags when I get to the rectory."

She narrowed an icy eye in my direction.

"That would be missus, not *miz*." She drew out the word until it sounded like an angry hornet. "I lost my dear husband some three years ago, God rest his soul." She took one hand from the wheel and blessed herself, and the car wandered aimlessly before coming to rest at the curb. "So, reminding me of my loss, Father, is a mite distressing. If it's all the same to yourself, I'll thank you to call me Colleen."

Determination, cloaked in deference. She would definitely keep life interesting.

"Deal. Thanks for the ride, Colleen."

The passenger door resisted. I nudged it with my shoulder, and it popped open with a mournful groan. As my feet hit the sidewalk at the intersection of Main Street and Lorain, my past

rose up to meet me. Part of me was happy to be home again—
the rest sensed loss and sorrow. Warm sunlight caressed my
face like a mother greeting her prodigal son, yet the breeze
swirled around me like the ghosts of my youth.

I closed the door, and the Toyota disappeared in a roiling
cloud of oily exhaust. Nearby, a young woman in a tight
pullover with the Oberlin College logo guided a tour for a
sullen teen and his family. The boy wore all black, except for
bright-red Converse sneakers. His T-shirt sported a toothy fish
and the words SPAWN TILL YOU DIE.

The guide directed their attention to a burnt-orange brick
structure on the corner. "Now that you've seen the college, I
want to give you an overview of the town. This is First Church,
built in 1834. The Anti-Slavery Society used it as a safe house
for runaway slaves before the Civil War."

It wouldn't have mattered where Colleen dropped me off. In
a city founded by ministers for religious freedom, you couldn't
throw a hymnal without hitting a church. My new home at
Sacred Heart was only a few blocks west.

As I waited for the light to change, the guide added, "First
Church is rumored to have had a secret tunnel that slaves
used to evade their owners and bounty hunters. Oral histories
suggest that there were several such tunnels in town."

Heck, according to stories and legends, Oberlin was
honeycombed with shadowy passageways and hidden rooms,
the majority probably fruit cellars or cubbyholes built to hide
moonshine from the Temperance League.

"Oberlin's abolitionists believed that God's laws trumped
the Fugitive Slave Act," she added, "earning it the reputation as
the town that started the Civil War." The teen's parents nodded
vigorously. The young man just ogled the tour guide's legs and
broke into a leering grin, revealing rubber-banded braces on
his teeth.

As I lifted my gaze from the boy's pale face to the stone
facade of Fairchild Chapel, a chill zippered down my spine.

Emily had married Everett McDermott there. I didn't want to be near it, so I crossed against the light, jogged half-a-block down Main Street, and stopped in front of the Allen Memorial Art Museum.

A lone hawk carved circles into a blue chamber-of-commerce sky. Tappan Square unfolded to my right. Stately trees formed a green roof, shading red-brick walkways. A brigade of college buildings stood as silent sentinels along the far border. The lawn had been recently mowed, and the air smelled sweet. Two snow-white squirrels chattered, chasing each other up a tree. When I was a boy, ghost-squirrels had also lived in the square, and I took their continued presence as a good omen and a welcome home.

I ambled south, knee-deep in nostalgia, until I arrived at the Apollo Theater, a landmark since the early 1900s. First-run movies were still inexpensive there, and only two bucks on Tuesdays and Thursdays. I'd spent most of my allowance and much of my youth nestled in its flickering darkness with Emily. We'd shared our first kiss in the back row.

Crossing the street, I dodged two kids on bicycles, remembering the joy of growing up in a small town where two legs and two wheels could take you everywhere.

I glided below baskets of scarlet and indigo flowers hung from lampposts until I reached Gibson's Bakery, where the heady fragrance of fresh bread and doughnuts beckoned like the promise of life everlasting. In that instant, I was twelve again, when joy was as simple as a cinnamon roll drizzled with icing. The aroma drew me with magnetic force through the doorway, hurling me headlong into an enormous man.

Chapter Three

---·---

Saturday, July 1, 2:30 p.m.

I RECOGNIZED HIM immediately. Except for his shaved head, Tree Macon had changed little in appearance since our high school days together. He resembled a middle-aged Michael Jordan. Same height, with the bull neck, broad shoulders, and side-of-beef biceps of the NFL prospect he had once been.

Our collision had splashed much of his coffee onto the white tile floor, chalked a powdered sugar ring on the front of his blue police uniform, and left a doughnut crumbling in his hand. Mirrored shades masked his eyes, but his fury was in plain view.

"Watch where you're going, for Christ's sake! Jeezus! What're you smirking at?"

A young woman near the cash register took her child's hand and stepped away from us.

"Who the hell do you think you are … ah, Father?" His voice softened. "You a priest?"

I stepped forward and straightened my clerical collar. No

one in Oberlin knew I'd become a priest, and I couldn't have been more out of context for my old teammate.

Relishing his confusion, I said, "Well, I'll be darned. Don't *you* fit the stereotype!"

"Stereotype? What damn stereotype you talkin' about?" His jaw clenched. "I already had my quota of racists today. If you're looking for trouble, you found it!"

"Yeah, you know, Officer. Stereotype. Like in cops and doughnuts." I paused. "Don't you recognize your old free safety? I had your back for three years, Tree."

The big man raised an eyebrow. "Never needed anybody covering my back." His face relaxed and his eyebrows realigned. "Nobody ever got past me."

"I see you're still the same humble guy who taped his own press clippings to his locker. All-state defensive lineman, oak-sized limbs, yadda yadda yadda. If your head had gotten any bigger, it wouldn't have fit in your helmet."

"God, I can't believe it. All these years without a call or a letter, and suddenly here you are again! Great to see you, Jake."

"You too. You haven't changed much."

"Few more pounds, a lot less hair." We shook hands. "I didn't recognize you in that outfit. You impersonating a priest?"

"That's funny, I thought you were impersonating a cop."

"*Chief* of Police, FYI." He tossed the remnants of his doughnut into the trash, dusted powdered sugar off his shirt, and furrowed his brow. "So, you really a priest? As I recollect, your class prophecy was 'Most likely to get a drunk-and-disorderly.' Then, without even a goodbye, you're gone. What happened to you after graduation?"

I shrugged. "Like in that Beatles' song, 'The Long and Winding Road,' life took me for one heck of a ride, then led me back home to Oberlin. If you have a minute, we could catch up. Let me buy you some real food."

"Nope, doughnuts. Got to keep up the cop image." Tree guided me to the counter. "Lemme get yours, too ... vow of poverty and all. Not to worry, I get the police discount here. Free."

"Thanks, Tree." I was low on cash and happy to keep my wallet in my pocket.

I let my eyes wander. Had it really been thirty years since I'd been in Gibson's? It was still an old-fashioned general store, with groceries and sundries stacked in the back aisles. The same glass counters lined the right wall, offering ice cream and a variety of nuts. Bread and baked goods filled the counters on the left. A vast selection of wines, however, indicated that the *dry* town of my youth had become *wet* while I was away.

We carried our drinks and food out to a sidewalk table. Four women seated nearby gawked at us, speaking in hushed tones.

"What's that about?" I gestured in their direction. "Why are they staring?"

"C'mon, Jake. Doesn't take a detective to figure that out." He leaned in and whispered, "A priest sitting with a cop? They're wondering which of us is in deep shit."

I pried the plastic top from my Styrofoam cup.

"I'd always imagined you'd be playing pro ball, Tree. How'd you get back here?"

"Blew out my knee sophomore year at Ohio State, and tore my Achilles tendon as a senior. Game and career over." His eyes locked on the horizon. "I considered coaching and teaching phys ed ...." He broke into an easy smile. "Then I remembered what a pain we were in school, and figured it'd be easier to arrest the little troublemakers. I started out as a cop in Cleveland, joined the SWAT unit, but ..." he paused. "What's so funny?"

"Sorry." I reined in my laughter. "You just look like a one-man SWAT team."

"Knock it off, Chuckles." Tree lifted a big arm and feigned a backhand to my face. I flinched. "SWAT stands for Special Weapons And Tactics. But in your case, it means *Slap Wise-Ass Teammate*. Anyway, I hated being a cog in the big-city machine and decided I prefer fistfights to gunfights."

I raised my cup in a toast. "Blessed are the peacemakers."

"I'm a family man now and I enjoy the slower pace of a small-town gig. Fewer calluses on my flat feet, and fewer on my conscience."

Three students with colorful spiked hair and tie-dyed T-shirts sauntered by, carrying picket signs reading STOP KILLING FOR OIL and HONK FOR PEACE.

"Only in Oberlin, Jake. Another bunch of veggie-munching, dodge-ball targets majoring in protests and pot. Guess that's why they call it *higher* education. Those kids would protest sunrise if they thought it would get them laid. Political rallies and flower children still bloom here soon as the snow melts. It's like living in a time warp. Things haven't changed since we were young."

"That's one reason I didn't come home after 'Nam, Tree. I knew what kind of reception I'd get. They probably would've called me a baby killer and thrown sheep's blood or red paint on me."

"Those were … confusing times."

"Yeah, for everyone. For the first time in history, Americans watched their sons die on TV." Old angers rose up like lava. I tried to steady my voice. "But the country couldn't find the guts to go all-out or call the damn war off. Folks here simply placed a scarlet 'V' on our chests and went on with their *Ozzie and Harriet* lives—and left us hanging."

"No question, the bad-old-days. After high school, I was all about crushing quarterbacks, and not much else." Tree nodded solemnly. "I am grateful for your service and your sacrifice … and sorry about my silence back then."

"Thank you, my friend."

I gazed at the town square. A new bandstand had been constructed during my absence. It resembled a giant rickshaw, its oriental motif reminiscent of Oberlin's early ties to the Far East, when the college sent students as missionaries to save the unconverted. Undergrads probably didn't even take a religion class anymore.

I needed no reminders of Asia and returned my attention to our table.

A dissonant chorus of car horns shattered my reverie. One of the tie-dyed kids snatched a dollar donation from a Volvo and trotted back to the sidewalk.

I must have looked confused because Tree said, "Not to worry. They're just *honking for peace* and donating money to the students' anti-war group—which, I suspect, the kids use to buy beer." Tree tapped his badge. "These protests are illegal, but I let it go if they don't obstruct traffic. Usually they're chanting, 'Give a dollar. Stop a war.'"

"Heck, if that worked, I'd empty my wallet and every collection basket I could get my hands on."

Tree sipped his coffee, then said, "So, what the hell happened to you after graduation? Where you been all these years on this long, winding journey of yours?"

Chapter Four

———•———

Saturday, July 1, 3:00 p.m.

I WANTED TO say, "None of your business," but owed my friend an explanation. Where to begin? Grade school, when my father deserted us to blow jazz and cocaine in honky-tonks? Or Mom's subsequent one-way swim into an ocean of alcohol? Tree already knew most of that. Maybe I should start with my taste of Purgatory in Vietnam.

I leaned back, stretched my legs, and closed my eyes. Images danced across the back of my eyelids. *Winding road, my ass.* Who was I kidding? The war had swept my youth away like a cork in a raging river.

"I had no scholarship and no money for college, Tree. When I drew a low number in the draft lottery and knew I'd be called up, I said to-hell-with-it and enlisted." I opened my eyes again and snickered. "My dear old Uncle Sam kicked my butt through boot camp, then decided in his wisdom to make me a medic."

"What's so funny, Jake?"

"Let's put the party boy with a fondness for booze and drugs in charge of the morphine. If you love irony, you can't do better than the U.S. Military. Anyway, they taught me the basics, painted a red cross on my helmet, and flew me to Cu Chi, about seventy klicks northwest of Saigon, for my on-the-job training."

Wisps of clouds laced the sky, but I saw concertina wire, sedge swamps, and jungle vines.

"When the transport plane dropped me in 'Nam, it was like falling down the rabbit hole into Wonderland. Only *this* magic garden was the Garden of Evil, infested with snakes, littered with booby-traps and landmines, and my platoon leader made the Mad Hatter look sane.

"The first month there, Tree, we got caught in a firefight outside this village. Guys were getting hit, and I was the little Dutch boy, sticking my fingers into bullet holes, trying to hold back a sea of blood. We were taking fire from all sides when something came charging at us from the bush. My best friend, Kenny, emptied his magazine and killed a water buffalo spooked by the gunfire. Then, above the chaos, I heard this keening wail from an old woman. She collapsed to the ground next to the water buffalo, cradling the bloody body of her dead granddaughter who'd been herding the beast."

My eyes found a sidewalk crack between my loafers. I'd seen the child a week earlier when we'd passed through the village. Most Vietnamese had yellowed, decaying teeth, but her smile had been bright white, like a beacon in that drab gray-green wasteland. Funny what you remembered. Now, all I could recall were her teeth sparkling through her death grimace. I shook off the memory and drifted back.

"Collateral damage, Tree." I thought of my dead friends and my entire platoon. Hell, we had all been *collateral damage*, even those of us who made it back alive. "Kenny caught more flack for killing the animal than the girl. A gook was just a gook, and no one cared. *That* was the kind of insanity we lived with. Nothing made sense." My voice faded to a whisper. "Ten months later, I held Kenny in my arms and watched him die."

Tree bit his lower lip until it blanched. "Hard to get my mind around that, sitting here watching kids play in the town square."

An errant Frisbee rolled into the street, and a sandy-haired boy, alive with promise and possibility, retrieved it. I knew him. Years ago, I had been like that boy.

Thwop, thwop, thwop. A news helicopter banked over us, the pulsating throb of its blades carrying me back to the war. I could smell festering wounds, hear screaming monkeys and soldiers, and see the face of the man I'd killed—the phantom who haunted my sleep. My fingers found the small crucifix I wore under my shirt. I wanted to tell Tree about that day, to confess what I'd done, but my tongue refused to move.

No. I had said too much already.

"One year after I set foot in that godforsaken country, *poof,* I was back in the States, dirt and blood under my fingernails, and it was all a bad dream. One that never went away."

Tree finally took a bite of his doughnut. "You ever think about dodging the draft back then, going to Canada?"

Words like *cowardice*, *duty*, *arrogance*, and *shame* floated through my mind.

"Sure, I considered it. I was no John Wayne. But when you're young, you think you're invincible and can take the world in a fair fight."

"True. We were all pretty dumb back then, Jake. There wasn't a brain among us."

"My cockiness didn't last. Hell, I was only eighteen, intestines and lives slipping through my fingers." I groped for a logical explanation of the mysterious seismic shift that became my rebirth. "I was alone and scared and … one day I started praying, actually talking to God. I swear there were days He talked back."

"A foxhole convert?"

"You could call it that. It's hard for a soldier *not* to think about death and the existence of God."

The police radio on Tree's belt squawked, but he ignored it.

"Go on, Jake. I'm listening."

My cinnamon swirl rested on the table untouched. I'd lost my appetite, so I pushed it away, then stirred my coffee and chewed the swizzle stick like a toothpick.

"Anyway, you grow up fast in a war. Uncle Sam taught me what I *didn't* want to do with my life, so I used my GI Bill for college, and parlayed decent grades and my medic training into a ticket to medical school. Uncle Sam paid my tuition, and I repaid him with time in the Army Medical Corps."

Although Tree's head snapped up and his mouth opened, he remained mute. I was used to the reaction. My dual professions always shocked people.

"But I ... kept reliving the war, kept searching for answers in the bottom of a shot glass. Vietnam was a fish bone caught in my throat, choking me. I couldn't breathe and needed a way to make up for what had happened. Finally, I turned to God."

"Sorry, I had no idea." Tree shook his head, sunlight gleaming on his shaved scalp. "It's still hard to believe, though. You of all people, a priest?"

"I don't know what to tell you. My medical practice wasn't enough. I wanted, no *needed*, to ease spiritual pain as well as physical suffering. I started going to church again. Maybe religion filled a void, maybe I got *the calling*, but I knew what I had to do. I entered a seminary."

"Healing the here and the hereafter?" A hunk of his doughnut vanished. "C'mon, how can you do both jobs?"

"It happens all the time. Nuns work as schoolteachers or nurses, priests as educators. A few run colleges."

"But combining the priesthood with medicine?"

"That's not uncommon in some Protestant denominations. Oberlin's parish is small, so it won't require much time. And Catholic hospitals, like St. Joseph's, serve the poor and are desperate for physicians. I'm a member of the Camillians, and—"

"Chameleons? What, you change color to blend in?"

I laughed. There was some truth in that. I changed from hospital white to religious black almost daily.

"*Camillians*, Tree. That's the Order I belong to. There are dozens of separate Religious Orders in the Catholic Church, like the Jesuits or Franciscans. Most have different callings and many take different vows. In addition to poverty, obedience, and chastity, the Camillians take a fourth vow of service to the sick. We focus on ministering to the frail and infirm, and work in hospitals and nursing homes worldwide. With my medical background, they were a perfect fit. The Order actually encouraged me to keep up my medical license while in seminary. I'm a *two-fer*. Two for the price of one."

"Whoa, whoa! Back up the bus. *Vow of Chastity?* Meaning *celibacy?* You?"

I thought about flirting with Tanya on the airplane, felt my face grow warm, and nodded.

"Huh. Never would have predicted that." Tree shook his head, pondered this as he chewed, then shifted gears. "So, you back in town to stay?"

Not if I can help it, I thought. It was nice to see my old friend again, but hopefully after a quick trip down Memory Lane I would be back on an airplane, headed far away from the ghosts of my past. There was nothing left for me here.

"Who knows, Tree? I go where I'm sent."

"Well, I hope you'll be at our class reunion tonight."

I saw the blitz coming and tried a head-fake. Hoping to dodge the subject, I pointed at the giant boulders along the edge of the town square.

"Folks still paint messages on the rocks, Tree?"

"Yeah, they're like stone billboards. Hard to change tradition. The city doesn't care, long as they're not obscene. If you stripped away the decades of paint, the underlying stones are probably the size of softballs."

The boulder closest to us had been spray-painted with large

jade letters reading THINK GREEN. Years ago, I had painted
JAKE & EMILY 4-EVER inside a crimson heart on that same
rock.

"Hello, Jake? You still with me? The reunion?"

"Oh, is that today? I don't know. I haven't unpacked, never
RSVP'd. And I have a sermon to prepare. Heck, I haven't been
in touch with anyone since—"

"Since what, Jake?" The last of his doughnut disappeared. He
wiped his hands on a napkin and balled it up. "You mean …
since Emily got married?"

Ouch. A shot to the chest, to the heart. Just as in our playing
days together, the big guy had squared up and knocked me on
my backside.

"I guess I'll never understand what she saw in that guy."

"You should ask her. I'm sure she'll be at the reunion."

"She won't want to see me."

Tree pointed at my uneaten cinnamon bun and said, "You
want that?" When I shoved it across the table, the human
eating machine went to work.

"I wrote her all the time from 'Nam. She answered the first
couple, then never wrote back again. When Mom sent me the
newspaper clipping of her engagement to McDermott, I gave
up and threw my damn pen away."

"You're shittin' me! What'd you expect, love letters? After
you banged Marisa?"

Heat rose in my cheeks. I drained my coffee and crushed the
Styrofoam cup.

"Damn it, Tree! With flag-draped coffins and body bags
on the news every night, I was drunk or stoned half the time
back then, and Marisa … was *willing*." I took a deep breath and
watched the breeze twirl my flattened cup like a pinwheel. The
deep, blistering burn of guilt replaced the flush of indignation
on my face. "I know, I know. I was selfish and cruel."

"No, you were a friggin' hand grenade in those days. You
couldn't wait for Friday nights, so you could crush some poor

wide receiver and stand over his body till they brought out the stretcher. I figured you'd end up in either Army green or prison orange." Tree grunted. "Hell, Jake, you broke Emily's heart. She and Marisa were *friends*. And you were a complete dick."

"Ah, come on! You remember high school. We were hardwired horny. All accelerator and no brakes. It's a miracle we didn't all crash and burn."

The fact that I'd flirted with Tanya on the plane a few hours earlier made me wonder if that urge ever died out.

Tree bared his teeth and spit out the words. "Don't give me that 'everyone else was jumping off the bridge' defense. There's no excuse for what you did. Your argument is inadmissible, and I find the defendant guilty as charged. You were a self-centered bastard and you owe Emily an apology."

We were both angry and had raised our voices. The four women at the next table were gawking at us again.

I leaned forward and whispered, "Damn it, Tree, I was a teenage boy. I wasn't *born* a priest."

He lowered his voice. "No, but you'd become a nasty piece of work by the time you left town." He slowly finished my cinnamon swirl, then added, "Maybe nobody told you. Emily got divorced from that asshole, McDermott." Tree's eyes looked right through me to some faraway place, and he seemed lost in thought. "Speakin' of the devil, I spent twenty minutes today with Mr. Charm."

"McDermott? Why?"

"Let's just say he's a person-of-interest in the untimely demise of a young woman we found at the quarry. Wish I had—"

My cellphone played Handel's *Messiah*. It was Colleen. I needed to select a separate ringtone for her, maybe an Irish jig.

"Father, you'd best be getting here. Confession begins at four sharp."

I thanked her, clicked off, and realized I'd never given her this phone number. She was a crafty woman, and I would have my hands full with her.

"Sorry, Tree, duty calls. I have to walk to the rectory, so I'd better get going."

"No sweat. My cruiser's 'round the corner. I'll give you a lift."

"Cool! Can I run the siren?"

"Collar or no collar, I can see the seminary neglected to address your smart-ass attitude. Guess some things never change."

We stood and began weaving between sidewalk tables toward the squad car.

"Tell you what, buddy. If you skip our class reunion tonight, you'll hear the damn siren when I come to drag your butt to the party."

Chapter Five

———◆———

Saturday, July 1, 3:30 p.m.

WHEN I OPENED the rectory door and walked into the cool of the foyer, Colleen greeted me with a sour expression, her foot tapping out an impatient rhythm.

"The police, Father? I saw you drive in. Trouble already, is it? And you, a man of the cloth."

The woman didn't miss much.

"Relax, Colleen. Chief Macon's an old friend of mine. He gave me a ride." I turned to leave. "I'll be upstairs if you need me."

"One moment there, Father." She walked over and handed me two keys. "To the rectory and the church. You're alone here in the evenings, so lock up tight."

I took the keys as she plucked a sheet of paper from her apron pocket.

"You'll need this too. Your schedule came in the post. Until Pastor LaFontaine gets well and returns, weekday services have been reduced to Tuesdays and Thursdays, and Father Vargas from Lorain celebrates those." She waved the paper, emphasizing each phrase. "You are only responsible for Sundays and Saturday Vigil Masses." Her expression of scorn almost screamed the word *slacker*. It reminded me of the way the nuns used to look at me when I failed to pay attention in Sunday school. "Tonight you assist Father Vargas. Tomorrow you're on your own."

What the heck? *She'd opened my mail.* I was about to launch into a protest, but Colleen raised her hand and continued, "Better hurry or you'll be late for confession. I've placed your things in your room, but I'll not be putting them away for you."

I reached for my schedule, but Colleen held fast, refusing to release it. She trained her eyes on me like the business end of a double-barreled shotgun.

"Oh, and by the way, Father, a young woman came here yesterday asking for you. Tall she was, and thin as a post, God love her. And in wicked form too, with hair as red as the Devil's britches."

I waited. Her silence resulted in a staring contest. I blinked first.

"Does this woman have a name, Colleen?"

"I'm sure she does, though she never thought to share it. She was a mite upset, don't you know, that you weren't here."

"What did she want?"

"To speak with you. Most insistent she was. Said she'd be back."

With that, Colleen gave me my schedule, showed me her back, and marched into the kitchen. I climbed the stairs, shaking my head.

After a quick shower, I began unpacking my suitcases. An old manila envelope stuck to my fingers. It was my version of a scrapbook. In seminary, I'd been instructed to leave such things behind, but I had carried my portable memories for too many years to throw them away. Knowing its contents by heart, I set the envelope on the nightstand unopened, next to my Bible.

After my hectic flight, the quiet of the rectory was a blessing. I slipped on a clean cassock from my garment bag, contemplating Christ's few short years on earth as I secured its thirty-three buttons, a meditation that helped me transition from the secular world to the spiritual one.

I hung my black clerical shirts and pants in the back of the closet, added a couple pairs of jeans and my other civvies, then put my socks and underwear into a dresser drawer. *Done.* With so few possessions, unpacking was quick and easy.

A grandfather clock somewhere downstairs chimed four times. Officially late for my first duty at Sacred Heart, I scurried to the church, relieved that no parishioners were waiting for the Sacrament of Reconciliation.

I entered the confessional, sat, inhaled deeply, and slowly released the air. Since my time in the tunnels of Cu Chi, confessionals always felt like upright coffins, and this one was particularly confining. As the walls closed in on me, I focused on praying the Liturgy of the Hours, a collection of psalms and readings required daily of all priests. I finished with prayers for my departed mother and the two close friends I'd lost in Vietnam. No prayer for my old man. Although I dispensed absolution for a living, no matter how hard I'd tried over the years, I could never manage to forgive him for abandoning my mother and deserting me as a child. God could absolve my father and have mercy on his soul if *He* so desired.

I slid back the wooden panel covering the grilled confessional screen, savored the faint scent of incense, and wondered about the red-haired woman Colleen had described. Why would she seek me out? I had no relatives or close friends in Ohio, and virtually no one knew I'd been assigned to Oberlin. It made no sense.

When no one entered the confessional, I opened a Michael Crichton paperback, which I'd hidden in my cassock. Crichton was another physician who had found his passion in an unrelated field. His fast-paced plot promptly transported me to another world and distracted me from my gathering claustrophobia. As I finished the first chapter, my flock began to wander in.

A child entered the confessional. The boy struggled to think up things to confess. I suspected that he'd recently made his First Communion, complimented his effort in a gentle tone, and gave him one Our Father and one Hail Mary, purely for practice. If he grew up to be anything like I had been in my teens, prepaying penance couldn't hurt.

A slow trickle of penitents followed, confessing the usual transgressions—lust, anger, greed. Most reported venial sins— minor offenses, the theological equivalent of light beer. I'd confessed my share of sins in the past, including a few of the Bacardi 151-proof variety, so being seated on the other side of the screen was a job I took seriously. Hearing confessions, however, could at times be a stark reminder of the darkness of the human heart.

After another brief lull, a man entered the confessional. In a husky smoker's rasp, he admitted to an affair with a married woman. I thought of my philandering old man, unleashed a wrath-of-God tongue-lashing, and dispensed an entire rosary as penance.

After he left, I immediately felt guilty. I'd been instructed in the seminary not to let my personal feelings cloud my decisions in the confessional, but the return to my hometown had resurrected long-buried memories and feelings that brought out the worst in me. All I wanted was to finish my temporary stint in town and get the hell out of here. But if taking out my frustration with my father on this womanizer forced him to reflect on the consequences of his destructive behavior, held one family together, saved one child from being fatherless, then maybe it was worth my lapse in judgment. I hoped so.

The church grew quiet and I opened my novel. Michael Crichton soon had me completely entranced until a woman's soft voice interrupted my reading.

"Bless me Father …."

I waited. "Yes. Go on."

"I don't know how to say this. I …" a catch in her voice.

"It's okay. Just say what's on your mind."

The silence expanded.

"I don't want to drag you into this mess, but I need help. Terrible things are happening. My son …." She mumbled something about danger and innocent lives being at stake.

"Maybe you should speak with the police."

"No! No cops. They'll make it worse. It's complicated. I need *your* help."

Time for a different approach.

"Feel free to tell me anything. Whatever you say is privileged and confidential."

Her only response was restlessness and sniffling. Leaning forward, I caught the faint fragrance of musky perfume but could only make out a shadowy silhouette through the confessional screen.

"Your secrets are safe with me. I'm bound by the Seal of Confession and can never reveal a word you say here."

"I'm so sorry. I don't want to hurt you, I really don't, but there's no time left. It's all unraveling so fast."

Hurt *me*? What? I squirmed in my chair. "Please, trust me. I can help."

"You can … if you want to." Ragged breathing followed a soft moan. "You must!" Her voice became fragile, that of a frightened little girl. "I didn't want to tell you this way …. I stopped by the rectory. There are things from your past …."

My muscles stiffened. My *past?* What the hell?

A jangle of youthful voices echoed in the church. The kids plunked down in the pews nearest the confessional, their nervous chatter and soft commotion continuing.

She fell silent.

"It's okay. Tell me what troubles you. We'll find a way. What is it, my child?"

"That's the problem. My child …." She wept words. "I'm afraid he'll …. No, I can't. Not here. Not like this." A painful whimper. "After Mass tomorrow, Jake."

At the mention of my name, my throat tightened. The confessional door banged open, followed by the sound of footsteps scurrying away. I jumped up, wanting to follow her, but I couldn't violate the privacy of the confessional, especially with several young witnesses sitting nearby.

Cautiously, I peeked out in time to see a tall, thin woman snatch up a young boy from a back pew and sprint from the church, her long hair streaming behind her, as red as the devil's britches.

Chapter Six

---•---

Saturday, July 1, 7:30 p.m.

NORMALLY, I EMBRACED the sublime simplicity of Holy Communion and the joy of Mass. Not true on Saturday. Travel fatigue and the day's bizarre events had blurred my focus and tainted my time with the Lord. I'd almost dropped the Eucharist while removing it from the tabernacle. If I hadn't been merely assisting Father Vargas, I might have completely botched the service.

After Mass, I'd intended to pop open a beer and watch television, but the priesthood can be isolating and the oppressive silence of the rectory made me painfully aware of my aloneness. I wanted to renew my friendship with Tree Macon, and after all that had happened that day, a stiff drink and some mindless conversation were appealing. I was also curious about some of my classmates—well, one in particular. I changed clothes, borrowed Colleen's old Toyota, and drove across town to my high school reunion at the Oberlin Inn.

I was distracted, however, on the short ride. Given what the red-haired woman had said in the confessional, she was hip-deep in trouble, possibly something illegal, and trying to drag me into it. I wanted to involve Tree, but I was bound by the Seal of Confession and unsure how to proceed. I decided to ask the bishop for guidance at our meeting on Monday. As I pulled into the parking lot, a cocktail sounded better and better.

I parked the car, turned it off, and listened to the ticking of the cooling engine and the pounding of my heart.

Did I really want to see Emily again after all these years? Would she unleash pent-up anger and frustration on me, or dissolve into a pool of tears? Would it crush her, or would it crush me?

The Toyota's door opened with a groan. I considered closing it again and abandoning the whole reunion idea, but instead trudged to the ballroom entrance.

My reflection in the glass doors startled me. My civilian clothes, black slacks and charcoal-gray button-down shirt, were nearly as drab as my clerical garb. On the plus side, if I stood in the shadows, no one would notice me.

I grasped the door handle, but hesitated before crossing the threshold from *now* back to *then*. When I finally found the courage to yank the door open, I swam through a sea of middle-aged gray-heads, none of whom I recognized. A few eyes bounced off me without lingering. No surprise. Since graduation, I had been nothing more than a rumor. If my name appeared at all in the alumni newsletter, it was in the "Where Are They Now?" section. I'd spent a lifetime running from the avalanche of my adolescence and had never wanted to be found.

I hadn't RSVP'd for the event, and the woman at the reception desk glared at me. She looked vaguely familiar, but I had no memory of her. I paid with a check that nearly emptied my account. Before joining the Camillian Order, money had never been tight. Now, all of my medical income went to the Church, and I lived on a small monthly stipend. I had no problem with my vow of obedience, but I was still learning to adapt to my vow of poverty. I slipped my checkbook back into my pocket, stuck a name tag on my shirt, and joined the party.

As members of our class trickled in, the ballroom filled with small talk and braggadocio. I observed signs of old jealousies—pursed lips, too-hearty backslaps, and narrowed eyes. Handshakes and hugs unlocked doors that hadn't opened in thirty years. The secret passwords to the past were "Remember when?"

Colorful banners welcomed us home. Vintage 45 rpm vinyl records surrounded by flowers served as centerpieces on circular tables draped in white linen. Old photos and yearbooks lined one wall. Balloons floated overhead in the school colors of red and blue. A life-sized poster of an "Oberlin Indian" occupied one corner of the room. The new cardboard mascot, a politically correct "Oberlin Phoenix," dominated another. How ironic. The school had rebranded itself, just as I had rebranded my life. Maybe tonight I would rise from the ashes of my youth.

In the back of the room, a DJ spun tunes from the graveyard of forgotten oldies. Paul McCartney wondered if his lover would need him when he turned sixty-four. The chronic aching in my knees reminded me that sixty-four wasn't nearly as far off as I had imagined in high school.

Across the room I spotted Marisa Jenkins, wrapped in a low-cut, clinging burgundy dress bisected by a black leather belt. Her body was still stunning, all curves and swells, and her high heels added an exaggerated sway to her sashay.

She had been every teenage boy's fantasy. The irresistible combination of beauty, grace, sensuality, and the precocious confidence that only God—or a vast family fortune—could bestow.

My lover's tryst with her during our senior year had been more than an act of youthful lust and rebellion. It had been an inexcusable betrayal, one that had driven Emily away forever. I didn't want to reconnect with Marisa, so I did a one-eighty, and for the second time that day, bumped into Tree Macon.

"Jake, my man, you're here. I'll have to cancel the APB I put out on you." He slapped my back and gestured toward the assembled multitude. "Quite a turnout, huh?"

"As crowded as Heaven after a revival meeting."

"Or Hell after a hooker's convention."

Tree's grin faded and his face hardened to black granite. He downed the brown liquid in his glass, crunched an ice cube, and his eyes wandered across the ballroom.

"Tree, are you okay?"

"Oh, yeah. Sorry," he said softly. "Been a bitch of a day. I had to tell my wife that a young woman she knows was found murdered at the quarry. The victim loved men, money, and partying. That makes for a lot of suspects. I got a real strong hunch who the doer is, but no hard evidence to back it up. The case is already beginning to feel like a damn dead-end."

"Maybe CSI will find fingerprints or something."

"You watch too much TV, Jake. This isn't the Big Apple. Here, CSI is a box in the trunk of my cruiser. I did call in the Bureau of Criminal Identification for help. They're a state agency that assists small towns by analyzing DNA and ballistics, loaning forensic techs and equipment, those sorts of things."

"A murder in little old Oberlin of all places. Unbelievable!"

"Happens, but not often."

"Is that why you spoke with McDermott today? What does he have to do with it?"

Tree leaned in and lowered his voice even more. "McDermott's a mean, shit-kicking dumbass, and that's a dangerous combination. He's always on my radar. Like my mama used to say, 'What's in the well eventually comes up in the bucket.'"

We paused as a nearby trio exploded into peals of laughter. Tree draped a heavy arm across my shoulders and guided me to a quiet corner.

"The punk you knew in school, Jake, grew into a greedy, cutthroat businessman. As he did, he seemed to rot from the inside. It's been scary to watch. The more McDermott's bank account grew, the lower he sank as a human being. Or maybe it was the other way around." He chomped the last ice fragment and gazed into his empty glass as if it were a crystal ball. "The dead woman at the quarry worked for him. Rumor has it, he was humping her. That's why I had a heart-to-heart with him today."

"To the best of my knowledge, there's never been a saint named Everett, and the guy we know will never have a feast day, but that doesn't make him a killer."

"True, but guess where we found the dead woman's missing car?"

"No idea."

"Dumped in a gully, not far from McDermott's place. It's all circumstantial, but he lawyered up quick. I plan to spend the week turning his life inside out, then I'm gonna crawl up his ass and pitch a tent till I can nail him." Tree grimaced, set his glass down, and massaged his temples. The spinning, mirrored ceiling globe imparted a subtle twinkle to his shaved head. "Or maybe I'll get lucky and have a stroke before I have to deal with him." He laughed without a trace of humor, then added, "Enough shop-talk. Let's get us a drink."

He strode to the bar and flagged down the bartender.

"Jack Daniel's on the rocks for me. What'll it be, Jake? I'm buying."

After the day I'd had, I felt like I could have chugged an entire Mason jar of Mr. Daniel's fine Tennessee whiskey. I'd just walked into my turbulent past, however, and it was prudent to remain in control until I got the lay of the land and a handle on my own emotions. *Prudence* was a virtue I'd acquired out of necessity over the years after taking my lumps at the School of Hard Knocks.

"Ah … a ginger ale, thanks."

"I hear the Shirley Temples are really tasty and come with tiny paper umbrellas." Tree peered down from his six-foot-six-inch vantage point. "Back in the day, your beverage of choice was anything short of rubbing alcohol. This a priest thing? Your collar's off now, Father. Relax."

"It has more to do with my class prophecy, 'Most likely to get a drunk and disorderly.' " I shrugged. "I used up my quota of *both* after the war, so I take it easy now. I'll grab a drink with dinner."

"Okay. That's probably a good thing, because you were a handful back in school when you were on the sauce. Booze flared up your temper like gasoline on a bonfire. I sure as hell don't want you in my drunk tank tonight." Tree frowned and his eyebrows moved down and in, narrowing his eyes to slits. "Anything else I should know about you?"

"Plenty, but some other time. Let's mingle."

We squeezed through a gauntlet of humanity past the hors d'oeuvres table. Although the Bee Gees recommended "Stayin' Alive," definitely sensible advice, the aroma of fried cholesterol drew folks to the bacon-wrapped shrimp like moths to a flame.

Tree was on a mission, glad-handing and backslapping his way to job security. While he commanded the spotlight, smiling and chatting up the crowd, I lurked in his shadow, watching an eerie 35 mm-filmstrip version of my 1970s life.

We met couples who had been married so many years that they'd begun to look alike, more than a few divorcées, and the occasional trophy wife showcased in designer clothing and sparkling jewelry. If one or two of these wealthy folks belonged to my parish, the church collection basket would runneth over.

The redheads in the room drew my attention. I half expected to see the woman who'd dashed from the confessional. The ladies in the ballroom, however, were decidedly older, stockier, and probably bottle-red.

As Frankie Valli insisted that we were all too darn good to be true, Tree guided me through a haze of perfume, across the raised dance floor, and toward a table.

"Let's park it awhile, Jake."

As we neared, I recognized Emily immediately. My chest tightened and my knees turned to Jell-O.

She was still trim, her features youthful. She wore a simple black dress, a pearl necklace, and despite the dim lighting in the room, sunglasses.

What in the world? My mind reeled through the possibilities. Covering bruises? Bloodshot eyes? Boozing? Drug use? Could marriage to McDermott have completely changed her?

Next to her, a woman in a silver gown growled angrily, pushed away from the table, and stomped off. Emily's scowl said *good riddance.* She twirled a glass of red wine, apparently unaware of our approach.

Tree said, "Showtime, buddy. Let's say hello."

I hadn't seen her since the day I left for boot camp. Time had softened her beauty, somehow enhancing it like a fine cabernet sauvignon. Her hair was cut shorter, framing her face. Although some silver strands peeked through, it remained a stunning golden auburn. She didn't wear much makeup and didn't need to.

"Hey, Emily. Mind if your favorite police chief joins you for dinner?"

She looked up and smiled. "Please do. That would be wonderful."

Tree set his whiskey on the table. "And I apprehended this scoundrel from our past."

"Hi, Em. It's been a long time," I managed to say, the drumming in my chest and ears louder than the backbeat of the DJ's music.

Doubt crossed Emily's face. Had I changed that much?

Tree nudged me toward the table. "Jake recently moved back to town. He couldn't wait to join us all here and catch up."

"Jake?" Her warm congeniality iced over.

I never should have come tonight. A trickle of sweat rolled down the back of my neck. I waited, unsure how she would react. Anger? Sadness?

Instead, she stared at me, then recovered.

"Jake, what a surprise." Emily reached out in my direction. She wore no ring. "I never expected to see you ag ... at the reunion."

I took her trembling hand briefly and released it.

For a moment, there was complete silence. We had once been two halves of a whole, able to complete each other's thoughts. Now, I struggled to find something to say.

Tree picked up his drink and took a swallow. "My lovely wife just walked in the door. Late as usual. Be back in a flash. Save us two seats."

He hurried away, leaving us alone.

Chapter Seven

———•———

Saturday, July 1, 7:50 p.m.

DECADES OF SEPARATION had created a chasm between us, and silence echoed across it. Words failed me.

Emily's expression was impassive, offering no insight into her thoughts. She swirled the wine in her glass, inhaled the bouquet, took a sip, and finally broke the stillness.

"I heard you're a doctor now, Jake. Congratulations." She chuckled. "That's a long way from Mr. Bartlett's last-period detention."

"A lifetime. Literally." An awkward hush descended again. "So, what do you do, Em?"

"Dad and I work at St. Joseph's Hospital. We run the snack shop there."

My heart beat double time as I grasped the implications. We'd be working at the same hospital. There would be no avoiding her, or the lingering ache at the very sight of her, or the jagged memories associated with that time in our lives. I rattled the ice in my glass, wishing I'd laced the ginger ale with bourbon.

"In the snack shop, Em? Wasn't your father an accountant?"

"Dad's blind. He lost his job shortly after he lost his vision. There's not much demand for blind accountants."

Emily turned her head toward the bar. I glanced over but didn't recognize anyone. Her attention shifted to the ballroom entrance. She seemed preoccupied. Or maybe she was meeting someone.

"Sorry to hear that, Em. He wore those Coke-bottle glasses, but I had no idea."

"Dad found work loading X-ray cassettes in the Radiology darkroom at St. Joe's—one of the few jobs where the sightless have an advantage." She rotated her glass slowly, coating the sides with red wine, then took a sniff and another drink. "When the hospital went digital and abandoned cassettes, they offered him a job in the snack shop. He mapped out the building in his mind and memorized every step count until he could function like a sighted person."

I tried to read Emily's expression, but her sunglasses concealed her eyes. For years, I'd wondered how she would react if we met again. I had expected outrage or sorrow or disgust, but her body language suggested complete indifference.

"I know you and your father grew close after your mom died. His blindness must've been hard on you both."

Emily shifted in the chair, directing her gaze toward the DJ.

"Dad struggled to live by himself while I was away at college, and he had to depend on taxicabs and friends for transportation. When the hospital hired him as the resident advisor to the male interns who live in the dormitory, he sold our house and moved into the residence hall. Many of the doctors in training who live there are foreign, far away from home, lonely and scared."

Emily tilted her head, and a crescent moon of hair draped one side of her face. The fluorescent lighting highlighted a few silver stands. Her once flawless skin now showed laugh lines, and I hoped I'd inspired a few. I knew I'd been responsible for many of the faint creases etched by sadness and worry.

"Dad loved it! He became friend, family, and father-figure to generations of interns and residents." Her smile accentuated the delicate array of freckles on her nose and cheeks, and her velvet voice made every word sound like a prayer. "Now St. Joe's is his home and his whole world. He has everything he needs. Room, cafeteria, friends, income. Most importantly, he has his independence again and a sense of purpose." She emptied her glass.

"More wine, Em?"

She shook her head. An earring caught the light and sparkled.

"No, thanks. One glass and I'm half-drunk. Some things never change." Her lips curved into a mischievous grin. "Why certainly, sir, you're aware of my foibles," she said in a coquettish twang reminiscent of Scarlet O'Hara, as if channeling the teen who'd reveled in drama club. "Surely, you wouldn't take unfair advantage of a lady, Dr. Austin."

It felt so natural, so comfortable, to be with her again. She leaned closer and the scent of her perfume ignited flashes of memory that whirled through my mind like sparks caught in the wind. An image of Emily at a picnic in Findley Park appeared, her lips poised for a kiss. I willed it away.

"How about you, Em? Are you still writing poetry?"

"Of course. I've published dozens of poems over the years. You know me. I'm not going to let a few hundred rejections slow me down."

She laughed, a sound I hadn't heard in years, and I was back in high school. The picnic image flickered again and faded.

"I teach poetry therapy at St. Joe's. Writing out thoughts and fears encourages patients and families to unbury their feelings. Sometimes expressing emotions can shim up a fragile, tipping world, Jake. It's a kind of New-Age psychiatry, I guess, but like art and music therapy, it can be as powerful as any psychiatric medication."

She removed her sunglasses and bumped the wine glass, nearly knocking it over as she set them on the table.

"And of course, I help Dad run the snack shop."

Emily's soft blue eyes drifted aimlessly over my shoulder.

"The women's residence hall is my home now, as mentor and advisor to the lady trainees. The hospital provides a safe, compact environment for Dad and me. I count my steps, picture the place in my mind. It's, well … comfortable."

My heart tumbled in my chest. Without thinking, I placed my hand on hers. Her head snapped in my direction.

"My God, Em, you're blind? I'm so sorry. I didn't know. How—"

"Christ, you didn't know? Then you're the only person here who didn't." Her blue eyes flared like gas-jets. "Did you think my shades were for the glaring sunlight in here? Or some poetic fashion statement?"

I'd been so confused by her distracted indifference that the obvious answer had never crossed my mind.

She drew a slow breath. "You really have been out of touch, Jake. I began slowly losing my sight after high school. It's hereditary."

"Can't anything be done? Let me make some calls. I know an excellent ophthalmologist who—"

"You're late to the party! I've already been mauled by an army of specialists. Thanks, but no thanks. False hope is more toxic than no hope."

A phlegmy cough rattled behind us, deep and damp.

"Well, if it ain't my favorite ex-wife."

We spun around. Everett McDermott peered down from hooded eyes over a hawkish beak of a nose. A soul patch of hair crawled from his lower lip down his chin like a dirty-white caterpillar. With his cocky attitude and self-assured bearing, he still seemed like the human equivalent of a bantam rooster, though his face was more drawn now. Hollow cheeks and sunken eyes gave him the appearance of someone who'd gone ten rounds with life and lost on a TKO.

"Hey, Emily. Good to see ya. You're lookin' real fine tonight."

McDermott's eyes fixed on her for a moment, then focused on me. "And just like the old days, here's my Barbie doll all cozied up with her GI Joke."

He cackled in that humorless way he'd perfected since grade school. One bony hand encircled a cocktail glass, his large pinky ring sparkling with diamonds. Tobacco-stained fingers on his other hand caressed an unfiltered cigarette, its smoke curling upward.

"How you been, Austin?" A venomous sneer slithered across his lips. "I hear you gave up making love *and* war. Hell of a loss for the military—and horny broads everywhere." He took a deep drag, filled his lungs with smoke, bent toward me, and exhaled in my face.

The idea of Emily being married to this man lit my pilot light. McDermott's smartass remark, the smoke facial, and our long history of animosity filled my mind with combustible thoughts. I exploded to my feet, my chair crashing against the wall.

McDermott jerked back, spilling his drink on his suit.

"Hey, watch it, this here's Armani!" he snapped, his voice sharp as broken glass, his eyes dark. "You never did have a sense of humor."

"I never found you funny." I closed the distance between us and poked a finger into his chest, rustling the gold chains around his neck. "But with the way you dress and act at your age, McDermott, you really are a joke."

Veins throbbed in McDermott's neck, and his cheeks blazed crimson. He shoved his face forward like a red-hot poker. His breath smelled of booze and decay. Colorless lips parted, revealing yellowed teeth.

"Why don't we step outside, *Father*, and see whose side God is really on."

Emily's look of confusion hit me as hard as a right hook. I faltered. McDermott did not.

"What, you think you pee holy water?" McDermott said,

then turned to study Emily's face. "Guess we got us a big ol' empty bag here without a cat. Ain't no secrets in a small town, Father Teresa. Everyone's business is everyone's business."

"Jake, please, sit down!" Emily swung her head back and forth, as if desperately trying to see us.

"Yeah, why don't you *both* sit down?" Tree Macon wedged his massive body between us. "Don't make me use my angry voice, boys. This isn't junior high. Let's not spoil the evening for the ladies." Tree scowled down at me and said, "Pity you haven't worked on that temper of yours over the years, Jake." Then he pointed across the room like a referee directing fighters to their corners. "And I've seen way too much of your sorry behind today, McDermott. Go park it far away from me, or you'll be calling your dirt-bag lawyer again."

McDermott coughed, loosening something moist and deep in his chest. He gave Tree a half-assed salute and nearly set his hair on fire with the tip of his cigarette.

"And there's no smoking in here," Tree added.

McDermott shrugged, dropped his cancer-stick into my drink, and swaggered away.

Tree took a gulp of his whiskey. "I do believe that boy's class prophecy was 'Will never play well with others.' No wonder he got his Lexus keyed twice last year. The man's an ignore-anus."

"A what?"

"It's a medical term, Doctor Austin: ignore … anus. From the Latin, meaning stupid … asshole."

Good old Tree. Always in the right place at the right time. With a joke and a chuckle, he'd dispelled the tension in the room.

The big man pulled out a chair for his wife. "Sonya, I'm sure you know Emily Beale, Oberlin's own Emily Dickinson. And this *gentleman*—the other handsome guy at our table—is Jake Austin."

Sonya Macon had large, burnt-almond eyes and skin the color of cinnamon. She greeted us with an accent as pleasant as a soft Caribbean breeze.

"Behave yourself tonight, Sonya," Tree continued. "Jake's the new priest at Sacred Heart Church."

Emily's smile evaporated, her expression darkened, and she turned toward me. "I'll take that drink now ... *Father*."

Good idea, I thought. *Think I'll have a double.*

Chapter Eight

———•———

Saturday, July 1, 8:10 p.m.

TREE SAT TO Emily's right. I handed her another merlot, and following proper boy-girl-boy protocol, sat at the table to her left—and grinned. Never had I dared to dream that once again I would be in the company of my two best friends. What a blessing. I took a moment to engrave the image into my memory, then gazed across the room at the new school mascot, the phoenix. Maybe it *was* possible for me to rise up from the charred remains of my arrogant youth.

A member of the wait staff rang a bell and announced that dinner would soon be served. A young man slid out the two unoccupied chairs next to me.

"Mind if we join you? Seats are going fast."

"Sure," Tree said, extending a hand. "And you are …?"

"Richard Carlson. My fiancée's the alum." He sat. "She'll be here in a minute."

"Who's your fiancée?"

We didn't need to wait for an answer.

Marisa Jenkins exited the powder room, returned Richard's

wave, and strolled through the ballroom as if working the red carpet at a Broadway gala. She greeted someone, twirled with the grace of a ballerina, and resumed her promenade. When she spotted Emily and me, her radiant glow dimmed. She surveyed the room for alternative seating, then approached us with all the enthusiasm of a prisoner facing a firing squad.

Richard jumped to his feet. "Darling, I assume you know these folks?" He slid back her chair. Marisa sat next to me.

I took a slug of bourbon and wilted.

Really, Lord? Sandwiching me between former lovers? Are you testing me or just taunting me?

"Hey, Marisa," Tree said, looking almost as uncomfortable as I felt. "This is my wife, Sonya. And you remember Emily and Jake."

Emily's head whipped in Marisa's direction, but she said nothing. They had been close friends before my fling with Marisa. Time clearly had not healed these wounds.

Marisa stared directly at Emily before acknowledging the rest of us. "Hello, Tree. Jake. Nice to meet you, Sonya." Finally, she added, "Emily."

This had the makings of a painfully long evening.

Recovering her poise, Marisa commandeered the conversation as she always had in school. She spoke with a cultured combination of authority and ennui. As she made an exaggerated fuss over Sonya's bracelet, Marisa fingered her diamond necklace and enormous engagement ring like a model in a Tiffany's commercial.

Our high school fight song suddenly marched into the room from the loud speakers, and the conversation ceased as if it were the National Anthem. When it ended, Marisa segued into Tree's football prowess, taking the opportunity to remind us that she had been head cheerleader. Without warning, she whirled toward me, placed a hand on the crook of my elbow, and squeezed it gently.

"Can you believe it's been thirty years? Who'd have thought

back then that we'd all be together again at the dawn of this new century? And I must say, Jake, you look wonderful. We need to catch up. Tell me everything."

Emily turned in our direction, her lips a bloodless razor-slash.

"Not much to tell," I said, trying unsuccessfully to reclaim my arm. I shifted the spotlight. "What about you, Marisa? Where are you now, and what do you do?"

Elaborately decorated fingernails swept flaxen hair from her face. Heavy eye makeup gave her the flat gaze of a predator.

"I'm a publicist and live in LA." She inclined her head toward her fiancé. "Richard's one of my clients. He's a fine actor."

"Currently between gigs," he said with a touch of bitterness. "And *we* live in LA, when *you're* not at some damn board meeting in Ohio, darling." Richard shifted his attention from his manicured nails to me. "Ever since Marisa's father died, she's been living on a plane. She occasionally spends time with me, when she's not here running Jenkins Industries."

Richard was rugged and bronzed, with a strong, dimpled chin that rivaled Kirk Douglas'. Diamond cufflinks peeked from his tailored suit, and his demeanor screamed private schools and exclusive men's clubs. His leather, bolo necktie, adorned with a large silver and turquoise eagle, however, conjured up the image of a country boy who'd just moseyed in over the Beverly Hills to round up women and stake a claim on Rodeo Drive.

"Really, Richard!" She glared at him. "Business is business. LA is my home now … *darling*." I thought for a second that she might retaliate by calling him Ricky or Richie instead of Richard or darling. I had begun to think of him as a Dick.

Marisa's tongue caressed her generous lips. Her perfume was intoxicating and no doubt expensive, probably laced with pheromones. As she enumerated the virtues of the City of Angels, two thousand miles seemed like a safe distance from Oberlin—until she leaned in and her low-cut dress exposed sun-dappled breasts. A moment passed before I realized that she'd begun expounding on her work. I raised my eyes to hers.

"A publicist wears many hats. Bottom line, I polish the stars. Make them bright and shiny." Marisa patted her fiancé's hand. "That's it in a nutshell. Right, darling?"

Richard flashed a picket-row of bleached-white teeth and downed his drink. He was half Marisa's age, and undoubtedly her soon-to-be trophy husband.

"How about you, Jake?" Marisa gently kneaded my forearm. "What do you do?"

"Physician" was not the message I wanted to send this woman, and I wasn't about to recount my past for her. I glanced at Tree and Sonya, hoping for a diversion, but they were debating local politics with Emily.

"I'm a priest," I said quietly.

"You?" She laughed. "You're joking."

"Not even a little."

Marisa bit her lower lip. "Oh. That must be … interesting." She withdrew her hand from my arm and wrapped it around her cocktail glass. Her eyes wandered away. Richard chuckled softly.

An awkward silence blanketed our half of the table until the discussion of candidates ended, and the others rejoined the conversation. Marisa took charge.

"So, tell me about the Macon family."

Tree put both hands in the air as if she had pointed a gun at him.

"I confess. I robbed the cradle. Sonya graduated six years after us." He draped an arm across the back of Sonya's chair and gave her shoulder a tender squeeze. "Been married twenty-one years. We live on Vine Street, near Plum Creek. Picket fence, dandelions, three kids, the whole nine yards."

"And what do you do, Sonya?"

"I teach English and world literature at the high school."

Tree smiled at his wife and said, "But she becomes a teenager again during summer vacation, reading every romance novel she can get her hands on."

"It has nothing to do with being a teenager, Tremont. I *enjoy* them. They're a refreshing change after nine months of teaching Faulkner and Tolstoy.*"* The rhythm of Sonya's Caribbean lilt was hypnotizing, each word an exotic spice. She rolled her almond eyes. "My husband, the literary critic. His idea of *world literature* extends no further than World Cup soccer scores."

Listening to their banter was like hearing a tuba and piccolo perform a strange but charming duet, and I was mesmerized by the concert.

"You're smiling, Jake, because you know it's the truth," Sonya added.

I nodded. Alluring beauty, intelligence, self-confidence, and wit. My friend had married well.

"There's nothing wrong with a good romance novel," Emily said with a grin and a slight blush, "and they're even sexier in Braille." She turned toward Sonya. "I hear some members of your book club actually write romances."

"True. Nancy Burke had published her first novel and had nearly completed her second when she died."

"I know her husband, Oran, very well," Emily replied. "He was so proud of her."

Tree said, "Another member also published a book. Joanetta Carter."

"That's strange. Are you sure?" Sonya asked. "How do you know?"

"I saw her framed acceptance letter from Harlequin Press when I examined her apartment as part of an investigation."

"That is so bizarre," Sonya said softly. "Joanetta was the novice of our group, and she showed no interest in writing. She never shared her work or said a word about being published at our book club meetings." Her eyes moistened. "And now the poor woman's gone, murdered at the quarry."

"Enough said." Tree patted her hand. "I'm off duty tonight, my dear. Did you bring those pictures?"

Sonya passed around photographs of their three daughters, sprinkling in a few amusing anecdotes.

Marisa offered photos of her home in LA, summer house in Kennebunkport, yacht, and Richard's new Bentley with wood-grain interior. Tree rolled his eyes so hard that his pupils disappeared, and I was certain the hands were spinning off his bullshit meter.

When the salads arrived, Sonya asked me to say grace. As I finished, shouting erupted behind us.

The woman in the silver gown, who earlier had stomped away from Emily, wagged a finger in Everett McDermott's face. He flushed the same blood-red color as her nails and lips. The music muffled most of their conversation, but between songs, he screamed, "The hell you didn't! Get on your damn broomstick and fly your ass back to New York!"

"That's enough," she growled, her face inches from his. "Time to powder my nose." She gave him the finger and fled into the women's restroom.

"Probably powdering it with cocaine I paid for, you stupid—"

The music resumed, drowning out the end of McDermott's tirade.

We returned to our salads. No one spoke until Tree said, "Well, that was delightful. Welcome back to Oberlin, Jake."

"I don't think I recognize the *lady*," I replied.

"That's Barb Dorfman. And the unladylike salute she gave McDermott was three fingers and a thumb short of a wave."

Richard slammed his fist down on the table. "The bastard deserves more than that. He was rude to Marisa tonight. I should have decked him."

Marisa gave Richard a frosty glare. "Oh, it's my own fault. My company hired his collection agency, and we had some … issues. I know better than to deal directly with McDermott. I should have let my lawyers handle it."

"You and Barb have something in common, Jake," Tree said. "She's not a member of the McDermott Fan Club either."

Marisa's lips twisted as if she'd tasted something foul. "Barb Dorfman and McDermott are cut from the same grimy cloth. Their fan clubs could meet in a broom closet. Barb's club only needs one chair—for the self-proclaimed wizardess of Wall Street herself." She lowered her voice. "Financial planner, my tush. Barb's a con artist and a thief. She used her talk-radio show to lure unsuspecting rubes to her office and bilk them. She fled Ohio when things got dicey. The bitch achieved gender equality by becoming a prick."

"Barb cost a lot of people in town money, including me," Emily added. "My friend, Oran, told me that he and Nancy lost all their savings. I'm surprised she had the nerve to come to our reunion—and I told her so when she asked to join me for dinner." Her expression darkened. "I'm not surprised that Everett's still angry. He believes Barb invested our money with a company she knew was going belly-up, just to get her fee—kickback, really. That's not the kind of thing my ex forgets."

"Barb is aptly named—as in fishhook." Marisa snarled. "Once she digs into you, it costs a pound of flesh to tear her out. My company lost a bundle too."

"Barb Dorfman? So *she's* the new-age vegan," Sonya Macon said, setting down her fork. "My friend on the reunion committee complained that Barb sent them a letter specifying which ingredients were not permissible in her meal tonight. She made their lives hell."

Our dinners arrived, the usual banquet chicken disguised in a white sauce. The conversation drifted to lighter topics. After dessert, Cathy Meeker, the alumni association president, stepped up to the microphone. She welcomed us and asked for a moment of silence for classmates and teachers who had passed away.

The task suited her. She'd been an accomplished gossip in school. Strangely, the perkiness of the one-time majorette bubbled through as she recited the names of the dead. After an accounting of funds and a pitch for donations, she announced that there would be a surprise guest speaker after a ten-minute intermission.

Sonya went to the restroom. Tree began a second round of politicking, squeezing out chitchat like beef through a meat grinder. Marisa, with Richard in tow, also made the rounds, showing off their photos with a self-importance that would have impressed Jay Gatsby.

I reloaded Emily's drink at the bar. "Another merlot for *madame.*" I paused. "Three glasses? Are you sure you'll be okay, Em?"

"I'm blind, Jake, not blind-drunk. Besides, I don't drive. That's why God invented taxicabs." Her voice was light and reedy. "So, speaking of God ... the priesthood? You? Really?"

Chapter Nine

---◆---

Saturday, July 1, 9:15 p.m.

I KNEW THAT this conversation was inevitable, but didn't want to have it here amid reunion banter and blaring golden oldies. I slid my chair closer to Emily.

"The priesthood." I sighed. "The truth?"

"You owe me no less."

"Okay, you're right." I closed my eyes and opened the door to a prison filled with caged memories. "Em, the war was … there are no words. We raise our children to be decent and caring, take them to church, then hand them rifles and tell them that it's all right to kill other people. The problem is, when you flush that commandment, the other nine go down the toilet too. If murder's okay, then stealing, adultery, and rape don't even show up on the radar—and life becomes a spiritual cesspool."

I opened my eyes. "If you turn the other cheek in war, you get your face blown off. So you shut down your conscience and do your job. And deep inside that moral darkness, you find lurking … the capacity for evil. It's the sordid flipside of the coin of freewill." I remembered the eyes of the man I'd killed, the expression on his face, and tiptoed cautiously through the minefield of my past. "Em, people did things there that are unthinkable in our world, sometimes from fear and despair, sometimes from rage or to avenge friends—me included."

"Jake, I can't imagine. You?" She hugged herself as if cold. "Though, after Marisa, I wasn't sure anymore what …." She fell silent.

The grief I'd caused still boiled beneath her tranquil surface and her words stung, but no more than I deserved.

"Em, I'll regret what I did to you for the rest of my life."

She nodded, slowly regaining her composure, but the pain clearly lingered. "Tell me. What happened overseas? What'd you do over there?"

"I did what war requires. No … worse … what it permits. But sometimes doing your duty can cost you your humanity."

Howling and hooting erupted from a nearby table. I stopped talking until the uproar died down.

"In a guerilla war, the enemy doesn't wear uniforms or care about military rules. When an old man leaning against his hut can suddenly shoot you in the back, or the next door you touch may be booby-trapped, your nerves fray. You become a hair-trigger … and innocent people suffer. That's no excuse, just how it is."

I was on the wrong side of the confessional screen, and baring my soul made the burden no lighter.

Emily didn't respond. She looked fragile, like a sand sculpture ready to crumble in the wind. My hand reached for hers, but I managed to guide it to my drink instead and toss down a mouthful of bourbon.

"Our world made no sense, Em. We used to say, 'It don't mean nothing.' That was our mantra. It applied to everything. To suffering, to love, to life itself."

Emily removed her sunglasses, revealing the sorrow in her eyes. A tear rolled down her cheek and across a pale scar at the corner of her mouth. It hadn't been there when I last saw her, and I wondered if it was McDermott's handiwork.

"People say there are no atheists in foxholes. That's bull. We saw no righteousness in what we were doing, no moral high ground we could claim. To us, God appeared to be AWOL. My best friend used to say, 'Jesus took one look at a napalm-fried village and hightailed it back up to heaven.' "

I couldn't dance around Emily's question about the priesthood forever and took a deep breath. When I released it, words spilled out.

"Either you believe God has some greater plan and all the suffering and hardship have some meaning, or you plummet into the abyss. A lot of guys plunged in headfirst. When I finally accepted that I was part of the evil, I hit rock bottom." I turned my face from her. "God wasn't AWOL. He hadn't forsaken me. He was a conscientious objector. I reached into the blackness within me, and God took my hand."

I fingered the small crucifix under my shirt that my mother had given to me on my First Communion.

"Maybe I was simply searching for forgiveness or some serenity. I don't know. Maybe God had been waiting patiently for me all along."

Emily found my hand. I didn't pull away.

"I tried to atone for what'd happened overseas, Em, by becoming a physician, but I needed to do more. A chaplain friend told me about the Camillian Order's vows of service to both God and the sick. I joined the priesthood in order to rejoin the human race. I was ordained last year."

"I was so scared for you, Jake. Every night on the news they showed …." She squeezed my hand. "I'm glad you made it home in one piece."

"Sometimes I wonder if I'll ever be whole again. Or home. Part of me is still over there, waiting for my DEROS."

"Your what?"

"The answer to a soldier's prayer. It stands for 'Date of Expected Return from Overseas.' "

Emily's crystal wine glass sang a plaintive song as she ran a finger around the rim, then took a sip. "But why *this* church, Jake? Why here in Oberlin?"

The DJ queued up the Rolling Stones' "You Can't Always Get What You Want"—the answer to her question.

"I never expected to be assigned here, Em. The Church is like the military, both moving their pawns around the giant chessboard. When the priest in town got sick, the Diocese needed a replacement, and St. Joseph's Hospital needed doctors. So here I am—two for the price of one. They figured a local boy could get up to speed quickly. Besides, I work for room and board."

An impish twinkle lit up her blue eyes. "You folks really need a better union."

I tried to smile but was completely spent.

"And you, Em? You married *McDermott*, of all people. Why him?"

She spun her glass gently and inhaled the bouquet, growing thoughtful and distant.

"Everett was ... a mistake. He visited me at college, treated me like a lady, took me to concerts, fine restaurants, the theater. He filled a void, I guess."

I had little doubt that *I'd* caused the void.

"My vision was beginning to fail." She crossed her legs and bounced one to an anxious beat. "I was frightened, Jake, and Everett can be ... quite considerate and charming, when he's after something. I believed he cared."

She tapped her wine glass with a fingernail. It rang out *pling, pling*, as clear as vesper bells.

"There's a compassionate side to Everett that few people know. Kids are important to him. He contributes a great deal of money to help neglected and abused children. He's a major donor to local adoption agencies and a shelter in Cleveland. You have to understand, Everett was abused as a child."

"I had no idea. But giving money isn't the same as caring. Those are just tax deductions for him."

"You're wrong, Jake. He volunteers with the Boys and Girls Club. In the short time we were together, he mentored six boys as a big brother. I witnessed his commitment." Her speech had slowed, the words slightly garbled. "When his second wife got custody of his son in the divorce, it crushed him. He spent thousands fighting for better visitation rights. He takes the boy camping and fishing regularly, attends all his ballgames." Sadness seeped through her mask. "But it turns out his son is the only one he truly cares about."

She downed more wine.

"When I discovered Everett's softer side buried beneath his hard exterior and learned of his difficult childhood, I saw him as a diamond in the rough. I thought I could change him, polish the gem within—so I ignored his shortcomings." She toyed with her sunglasses, nibbling on an earpiece. "Idealism, however, can blind you to reality."

Her laugh was bitter.

"After we married, I learned that Everett is all about image and control. When I couldn't have children, I grew ... less attractive to him. He started drinking heavily. Then I lost my vision and was afraid to be alone. So I denied the obvious."

I gazed at Emily and felt a tremendous sense of loss, knowing what an incredible mother she would have been—and what a joy and privilege it would have been to be her husband.

Pling, pling, pling. Her glass chimed three.

"Everett had an affair. A couple, actually. When I'd had enough, I divorced him. End of story." She sighed. "I was pretty damn naïve about men in those days. Dad tried to warn me about dating bad boys, about both of you, but I guess I've always been ... blinded by love."

The alcohol was acting like a solvent, ungluing her lips and her inhibitions. She drained the last of her wine and continued, her speech slurred.

"Funny, though. As my vision faded, my other senses flourished. A heightened sense of sound infused my poetry with a new richness. It was an unexpected blessing, like spending time with Dad in the snack shop."

I could restrain myself no longer. I placed my hand under her chin, lifted it up, and touched the scar at the corner of her lip. "Did McDermott abuse you, Em?"

She hesitated. "Only once ... physically." She let silence underline her words. Her eyes wandered over my shoulder. I felt helpless.

"So, you have no vision at all?"

"Oh, I sense movement, see flickers of light." She slipped her sunglasses back on. "No details though. You resemble a hazy moonlit shadow swaying in the breeze."

"Then let me tell you, Em. Honestly, I'm the best-looking guy here. And as your magic mirror, let me add that you're definitely ... the fairest of them all."

Her smile was immediate and warm as the morning sun, banishing the chill of our unexpected encounter. I basked in its glow until the DJ said, "Okay people, the next dance is just for high school sweethearts."

Uncertainty creased her brow. "Should we ... *Father*?"

"Probably not." I could almost hear the small-town rumormongers. But knowing that this would likely be our last dance, I took her hand and said, "Let's do it anyway."

The music started, and I held Emily in my arms for the first time in decades. The crowd and conversations around us faded, and we were strangely alone on the dance floor. She pulled me close, held me tight, and I lost myself in the scent of her hair. Only when Sonny Geraci began to croon "Precious and Few" did I return to the ballroom. Emily buried her head in my chest and wept. It had been our song.

As the final notes faded, I realized that now, thirty years after we'd first danced to this song, the moments we could spend together had become even fewer and more precious. I guided her back to our table, dabbed away makeup-streaked tears from her eyes with a clean napkin, and blinked moisture from mine. The room became unnaturally quiet.

Cathy Meeker, the alumni president, stepped to the microphone. While the gathering reloaded their drinks at the bar, she spoke of improvements at the school and thanked the reunion committee for planning the event. Finally, she tapped the mic until the room settled down.

"We have a delightful surprise in store tonight. I'm sure most of you have seen the movie, *Devil's Passage*, featuring two of the country's hottest stars, Sean Penn and Katie Holmes. The film has garnered rave reviews and three Academy Award nominations. Those of you from out of town, however, may not know that the movie is based on a novel written by one of our classmates, a man who has quietly perfected his craft right here in Oberlin."

When the wave of murmurs faded, she resumed her introduction.

"Here to tell us how a book becomes a movie, and I hope, share some fabulous personal stories about Hollywood," she paused for effect, "is our home-grown version of John Grisham. It's my pleasure to introduce your classmate, Mr. Oran Burke."

Chapter Ten

———◆———

Saturday, July 1, 9:45 p.m.

ORAN BURKE ROSE to polite applause and approached the podium. He appeared even frailer than he had in high school, his face pale, skin translucent as tissue paper. His gait was so labored and unsteady that he'd have failed a field sobriety test. The doctor side of my brain postulated underlying substance abuse as an explanation, a fairly common malady in artsy people. But he was not my patient and not my problem. I slouched back in the chair, stretched out my legs, and sedated my inner physician with a mouthful of bourbon.

Cathy Meeker bent down and whispered something into Oran's ear. Although she was short, he was shorter, almost elfin, with narrow shoulders and a stooped posture. In his green dress shirt, strawberry-colored bowtie, and pale-yellow vest, Oran looked like a walking fruit salad.

When he adjusted the microphone, it emitted a high-pitched squeal. He jerked away, dropping his written notes. Scattered snickers crackled in the audience, but Oran seemed oblivious.

Cathy retrieved his papers and returned them. As the lights dimmed, he clutched the lectern with one hand.

"Thank you, Cathy. You always did have a flair for hyperbole." Oran chuckled and paused, apparently waiting for others to join in. "John Grisham is much more prolific than I, and he writes legal thrillers. My genre is historical fiction, mysteries to be specific." He turned his attention to the assembly. His thick, round glasses magnified his eyes, giving him a startled appearance. "Prior to *Devil's Passage*, I'd had only modest recognition, so I'm honored to be compared to the esteemed Mr. Grisham. That's quite heady company."

I watched a sea of candlelit faces bob silently like ships in the night, their expressions distant and vacant. He was losing them already. I hoped he'd written his speech with this rowdy bunch of partiers in mind, rather than for a roomful of academics.

Oran shuffled through his notes. "When you asked me to address our class tonight, I was astonished. Bewildered really. So few of you actually knew me in high school."

A voice from the back of the room called out, "I remember you, Oran." Everett McDermott grinned and raised his cocktail. "But I forgot my duct tape tonight."

Oran glanced in McDermott's direction. "And I remember you, Everett," he replied, a quaver in his voice.

Emily leaned over. "What's that about, Jake?"

"Everett duct-taped Oran's genitals after a shower in gym class and pushed him naked into the hallway. As St. Matthew said, 'By his deeds ye shall know him.' "

Oran steadied himself and continued, "We digress. You wish to hear about my novel and the movie." He fumbled with a bottle of water and took a swallow. "Well, the wonderful thing about writing murder mysteries is the abundance of material. Just read the paper or watch the nightly news. Even Stephen King couldn't make up some of that malice and mayhem. There's one way to be born, but a million ways to leave this world—and I've used most of them in my stories."

He responded to the ensuing silence with another sip.

"Anyway, I only spent one day on the set, so I can't tell you much about the movie. It's loosely based on my novel. The screenwriters, however, twisted my characters beyond recognition and completely changed the ending. My protests went unheeded. As you might imagine, I was furious."

"I'm sure that scared the hell out of them," McDermott said, a bit too loudly. Someone at his table hooted with glee and punched him in the arm as others cackled.

"Apparently," Emily said softly, "some of us never entirely outgrow high school."

I was about to agree with her about the lack of maturity in the room, but thought about my behavior on the airplane with Tanya and wondered if I was just pretending to have grown up.

"Adolescence is a scab we keep picking at," I replied. "It never quite heals."

Behind us, Barb Dorfman groaned loudly. She stood, weaved between tables, and staggered into the ladies' room. Violent retching echoed from inside. Oran stopped speaking, looked down, and studied his notes.

With the crowd's attention fixed on the noises coming from the women's restroom, I glimpsed movement at the podium.

Oran's head began a slow writhing motion, as if a serpent controlled his neck muscles. He didn't act surprised or in pain. I'd seen similar involuntary muscle spasms associated with unconscious tics, but also neurologic diseases, prescription drug reactions, and drug abuse. After a few eerie seconds, the movement ceased.

Barb Dorfman reemerged from the ladies' room, her silver gown disheveled and streaked with vomit, her face pale and sweat-soaked. Wiping her mouth with a paper towel, she tottered back to her table, grabbed her purse, and stumbled out the exit.

As she left the ballroom, McDermott muttered, "Yup, this talk makes me wanna puke too."

No one laughed this time. Someone shouted, "Put a lid on it, Everett."

Tree said, "Let's hope *stupid* isn't contagious, Dr. Jake, or there'll be a damn epidemic here."

I returned Tree's wry smile, squeezed a lemon wedge into my ice water, and picked up the glass. A piece of paper stuck to the bottom. I flipped it over. Although moisture blurred the ink, the message was legible: ENJOY YOUR EVENING, BITCH! GOD KNOWS IT COULD BE YOUR LAST.

I read it again, barely able to breathe. The note was closest to Emily, but who would threaten her? And why leave a written message for a blind woman? That made no sense. The "God knows" part suggested it might be intended for me. Was someone calling me his "bitch?" I scanned the room, hoping to catch eyes staring in our direction, but people were focused on McDermott's group of miscreants.

I walked over to Tree on shaky legs and showed him the message.

"I found this on the table next to Emily."

Tree's eyes narrowed as he read it, and his eyebrows knitted into a black V. He carefully grasped the paper by one corner, slipped it into his sport-coat pocket, and said, "Sit down, Jake. I'll handle this."

Oran cleared his throat. "Ah yes, well, the novel. I must say that publication is an arduous task. Writing a book can be onerous, finding an agent problematic, and dealing with contracts and editors is a nightmare. For example ...."

As Oran droned on, the gathering grew restless, shuffling chairs and coughing. Finally, a classmate at McDermott's table bellowed, "Come on, Oran. Get to the good stuff, the gossip. Tell us about Katie Holmes. Did you cop a feel?"

A few hoots and giggles drifted from the assembly. Emily cringed.

Oran's head jerked back as if he'd been slapped. He folded his notes and put them into his vest pocket. He was perspiring profusely, and as he turned toward his hecklers, he slid his eyeglasses back up the bridge of his nose, using his middle finger.

"You want Hollywood scandals? Want to hear the inside scoop? Is that it?" Oran's lips curled. "Are actors as charming in person as they are on the screen? All right, I'll tell you. The day I visited the set, Sean Penn was busy filming an action sequence and barely had time to say hello. But Katie Holmes had read my novel and sought *me* out for an autograph. She spent twenty minutes asking how her character should behave. Katie's a hometown girl from Toledo and very fond of the Midwest. She's bright, engaging, and a total sweetheart. Is *that* what you want to hear?"

Silence filled the ballroom.

"Now, let me tell you what you *need* to hear." Oran slowly surveyed the audience. "I wasn't part of the in-crowd in school, didn't hang out with the hippies, jocks, or greasers. Most of you never knew me and didn't care a whit about me." He grabbed the microphone and hobbled to the front row of tables. "I couldn't wait for graduation. Couldn't wait to leave all of you far behind, with your childish cliques and your cruel caste system."

Oran swayed and grabbed the back of a vacant chair to steady himself.

"College gave me a clean slate. For the first time, people … accepted me. A few girls actually enjoyed my company." He removed his eyeglasses. "One fine woman even married me."

A tear rolled down Oran's cheek. "She's gone now. Nancy died before the success of my book and the movie. She never got to share in my fifteen minutes of fame. But I'm grateful every day for the memories and for her love."

He wiped his eyes, replaced his glasses, and shuffled back to the lectern.

"After college, I marched to the drummer that only my dear wife and I could hear. I published short stories and two novels that never sold well and didn't pay the rent. Then I wrote this quirky mystery set in Oberlin during the Civil War. I actually gave up and threw it in the wastebasket. Nancy rescued it and encouraged me to finish, while she worked nine to five."

Oran took another sip of water, the bottle shaking in his hand. A few drops splashed onto his shirt.

"Nancy believed in me more than I did. She believed in my novel—this minor piece of historical fiction, which caught an editor's eye and became a book that morphed into this trendy movie nominated for an Oscar."

More sweat poured down, but this time he used his index finger to slide his glasses back up his nose.

"When I walked among you tonight, few of you stopped to talk to me or hear my stories—because I wasn't one of the cool kids. And *that*, I guess, never changes." He tapped the microphone. "Yet, here I am, speaking to you tonight. So I wonder … am I now cool?"

Soft murmurs from the crowd, a rustling of fabric.

"From what I observed this evening, it strikes me that *you* haven't changed much. Most of you behave like trained mutts, mindlessly following, eager to please—a bunch of old, lame greyhounds chasing the bunny of popularity around the endless track of envy."

Oran's head tilted to the left and resumed its slow, writhing, snake-dance motion, giving him the appearance of a cobra eyeing its prey. When the movement stopped, he continued, "Most of you will never speak to me again after tonight, and that's fine. You taught me in school that I don't need your precious validation. Once, I let it hurt me. Now, I simply feel sad … sad for all of you."

Oran drained most of the water and set the bottle down.

"Look at the person next to you. That person might be gone tomorrow. Life is like that. Capricious. Serendipitous. The people you hold dear are here today, and then … then life becomes shriveled and meaningless. Unfortunately, I know. That's the lesson I learned when I lost my Nancy."

A trembling finger rescued his sliding eyeglasses again.

"Take a moment tonight to speak with someone you ignored in school. He or she may have some interesting tales to tell. You might find that they're not at all who you thought they were. You might even enjoy their company."

In the stunned silence, he clicked off the microphone and walked unsteadily from the podium toward the exit door. Then Oran collapsed in a heap on the floor.

Chapter Eleven

———•———

Saturday, July 1, 10:15 p.m.

WHILE TREE MACON summoned EMS, I examined Oran Burke. His eyeglasses were broken, and blood trickled down from a laceration over his eyebrow. I lifted his eyelids and his pupils appeared of equal size and reactive to light. He was unconscious, with shallow respirations and a thready, galloping pulse that didn't require CPR—yet. I wasn't sure what had happened. If he'd had an arrhythmia, things could get worse fast. I looked around, saw no defibrillator on the walls of the ballroom, and sent a waiter to find out if the inn had one, just in case.

Tree flipped his phone closed and knelt by my side. "How bad is it, Jake?"

"I'm not sure. Could be a stroke, an aneurysm, irregular heartbeat, or heart attack. I'm hoping it's only orthostatic hypotension. Oran stood at the lectern for a long time, and blood might have pooled in his legs, causing him to faint. We'll know in a minute."

I immobilized Oran's neck, carefully rolled him onto his

back, and raised his legs, allowing gravity to return blood from his calf veins to his heart, and then to his brain. I held my breath and waited.

Within seconds, Oran blinked his eyes open and groaned. The crowd of classmates surrounding us responded with sighs of relief. I did too. Taking a clean handkerchief from my pocket, I applied pressure to the cut on his forehead to stem the bleeding.

Oran gazed blankly at the ceiling. "Wha … what happened? Where am I?"

"You're at the reunion. You passed out."

"Reunion?" His eyes brightened a bit. "Who … are you?"

"Jake. Jake Austin. I'm a physician. Are you in pain?"

"My head's throbbing, and my wrist hurts like hell."

"I don't think this is serious, Oran, but you should go to an emergency room and get checked out." I glanced at Tree. He nodded. "An ambulance is on its way."

Oran tried to sit.

"Don't." I placed a gentle hand on his chest. "Lie quietly."

"Help me up."

"Please. EMS will be here any minute. It's important that—"

"Help me up, damn it!" Oran wrenched himself into a sitting position. "No more hospitals. I'm not going to any ER."

There was no point in debating. As I helped Oran slowly to his feet, the circle of onlookers around us expanded. The little man swayed and clutched my shirtsleeve with one hand for balance, his other arm dangling at his side, the wrist puffy.

I pointed at the swelling before reapplying pressure to his laceration. "You may have fractured your forearm, Oran. At least get an X-ray. And this cut needs stitches."

"No. Absolutely not."

"Please Oran, go to the hospital," Emily pleaded, as Sonya Macon guided her over from our table. "Do it for me, please."

He stared at her and hesitated, his expression softening. "All right, Emily. For you, I'll go." He gestured toward his broken eyeglasses on the floor. "Could someone get those for me?"

Tree picked them up and put them in Oran's vest pocket.

"I haven't met any of the other doctors at St. Joseph's yet," I said, "but I could make some calls, find out who's—"

"No way. Not *that* butcher shop! I hate that damn place. They killed my wife!" He released me, took Emily's hand, and said to her, "I'll go to the hospital on two conditions. No St. Joe's, and no ambulance."

Emily chewed the inside of her cheek for a moment.

"I have an idea," she said. "Jake could drive you to the emergency room here in town, and then take me home. I need a ride anyway. Is that okay with you, Jake?"

"Sure, Em. Be happy to." The hemorrhage from his laceration had slowed. I dabbed it one more time and tossed my handkerchief into a nearby wastebasket. My fingers were smeared with blood, something no doctor likes to see in the age of AIDS and hepatitis. I wet a paper napkin in a glass of water and wiped them as clean as I could. "Okay Oran, let's go. Hang on to me."

He gripped my arm again and shuffled toward the exit. Sonya guided Emily behind us. As we passed McDermott, the corners of his mouth twitched into a smirk and he fired a parting shot.

"You need to go easy on that mineral water, Oran. It packs quite a punch." McDermott raised his highball and tossed down half of it.

Oran stopped and turned his head slowly. His gray hair was matted with blood and a drop trickled down his cheek and dripped onto his shoe.

"And you, McDermott, need to go straight to Hell."

Emily stepped forward. "Damn it, Everett, go home. You're drunk. Again," she added and continued walking. "Let's get out of here, Jake."

I paused for only a moment to watch Tree Macon carefully grasp Oran's water bottle in a folded napkin and remove it from the lectern.

Chapter Twelve

Saturday, July 1, 10:30 p.m.

As in most small towns, Oberlin's hospital was not located far away. On the short ride, Oran asked, "Why do they treat me like that? I'm so tired of being shunned for being different. It's 2002, not 1602, for God's sake! Why do people do that?"

Neither Emily nor I had any answers.

The emergency department's waiting room was empty. Apparently, we had arrived before weekend boozers started tumbling down the stairs or wreaking havoc on the highways. A doctor examined Oran immediately and sent him for blood work, a CT scan of the brain, and X-rays of his wrist.

Knowing his evaluation would take time, I drove Emily through the pitch-black night to the women's residence hall at St. Joseph's Hospital. Lost in our own thoughts, neither of us had much to say, so I turned on the radio and tuned it to a soft-rock station.

When I merged onto the interstate and stepped on the gas, the old Toyota's engine roared.

"Sounds like you finally got that muscle car you always wanted, Jake. Corvette? Mustang? Vintage GTO?" She chuckled. "Or maybe you should fix the hole in your muffler." She paused for effect. "Cripes, Jake, what a heap! There's a huge tear in this upholstery, and I nearly passed out from the exhaust fumes."

Even blind, nothing got past Emily. She was still the complete package—witty, beautiful, and sharp as a tack. What a fool I had been to let her go.

When we arrived, I parked the car, offered Emily my arm, and guided her to the life-sized statue of the hospital's namesake in the lobby. There, she shrugged off my assistance, snapped her collapsible red and white cane to full extension, and marched at a brisk pace through the halls. I was on her turf, and she didn't need or want my help. Her lips moved silently as she counted out steps. Occasionally, she reached out for some familiar landmark and changed direction.

We walked in silence toward the women's dormitory entrance.

"This is it, Jake. My home." She reached out and found my hand. "Gentlemen are not permitted inside—at least in theory." She giggled. "Of course, the resident advisor who lives here is blind, and a little tipsy." She inclined her head to the side and switched to her Mae West impression. "Hey, big boy, why don't you come up and … have a cup of coffee?"

I hesitated, not because I didn't want to go, but because I did.

"Sorry, Em. I should go back and pick up Oran."

"Some other time then." She lowered her voice. "Is there anyone else here in the hall?"

I looked around. "No."

Her hands moved up my arm and my heart shifted into overdrive.

"Then let me get a peek at you." Her fingers explored my face. "Your sideburns are a lot shorter, hair too." She leaned in, the scent of her perfume resurrecting buried memories. "But not *too ugly* for an old guy." She smiled. "When you drive Oran home tonight, tell him I'm thinking of him. Goodnight, Jake."

And with that, she was gone.

A storm of emotions raged inside me. I felt like a teenager after his first date. If the Lord was testing me, He had definitely gotten my attention. And if I wanted to pass His test, it was time to get my act together. Between Tanya this morning and Emily this evening, I was well on my way to a failing grade.

As I trudged back to the parking lot, tired and alone, a night bird sang a sad alto solo, backed by a chorus of crickets. The air hung thick and moist, and my shirt stuck to my back. I desperately needed a shower and a good night's sleep.

The drive back to Oberlin's small hospital seemed to take forever. When I arrived, I was surprised to find that Oran had been admitted.

Visiting hours were over. The receptionist gave me Oran's room number and recommended that I return in the morning. I thanked her, walked toward the exit, then slipped into a stairwell and climbed up one flight. As I approached Oran's room, a physician stepped into the hall. He was overweight, his physique resembling the Pillsbury Doughboy's. The embroidery on his white coat read: "Dr. Taylor, Neurology."

"Excuse me, Doctor. I'm Oran Burke's friend and was with him when he collapsed. Jake Austin." I extended my hand.

He ignored it and checked his watch. "Sorry, you'll have to come back tomorrow. Mr. Burke needs his rest."

"I understand, but I'm a physician and was wondering why he was admitted." Playing the doctor card, I hoped for some professional courtesy. "Did his X-rays show a fracture or a brain hemorrhage?"

Taylor appeared annoyed.

"No, nothing like that. No bleed, nothing broken. Walk with me," he said, rolling down the hallway as briskly as his bulk permitted. "I'm simply keeping him here for a couple days to tune up some underlying medical issues. With patient confidentiality laws, that's all I can say." The elevator opened and he stepped in. "Sorry, it's late. Gotta go."

I was about to mention Oran's involuntary neck spasms and suggest toxicology screening when the elevator door closed. I went back to Oran's room and peeked in. He was snoring loudly, probably sedated.

Admitted, yet no fracture? A neurologist, but no brain injury? One more strange event in a very long and bizarre day. By the time I returned to the rectory, I was so exhausted that I skipped my evening prayers and fell asleep the moment my head touched the pillow.

Chapter Thirteen

———•———

Sunday, July 2, 7:00 a.m.

Kenny Babcock downs his drink, slaps the glass on the bar, and says, "Your turn to pay, Jake. C'mon, y'all."

The hooch is as hot as a wok, jungle heat pouring in through its thatched roof. A half-nude mama-san wriggles on Kenny's lap. She nuzzles his neck, saying all she needs to say without words.

"I swear, Jake, you Yankees are tighter than a gnat's asshole with money." Kenny laughs and takes a draw on his joint, holds the smoke for a moment, then releases it through a wide grin. "Don't sweat it, son. I'm only funnin' with ya. I'll pay for this."

He reaches into his pocket and removes a wad of cash. Blood gushes from the bills, cascading down one leg of his fatigues into a crimson puddle on the dirt floor.

* * *

The pounding in my chest drummed me back to consciousness. The bedside clock cast an eerie green glow in the dim dawn light. I had no idea where I was until I glimpsed my duffle bag and suitcase.

Throwing the covers back, I sat on the edge of the bed and shook the dream from my head. It clung like cobwebs. Kenny visited me often in my sleep. The bleeding money, however, was a new twist on an old, unpleasant theme. An icy chill followed a trickle of perspiration from my neck down my spine. I sat for a long time, the K.B. tattoo on my forearm staring back at me.

Finally I knelt down, recited the Morning Prayer from my Breviary, and began my usual calisthenics. I crunched thirty sit-ups, willed myself through twenty pushups, and finished with fifty jumping-jacks, rattling the framed photograph of the pope on the wall. His Holiness didn't complain, but the noise apparently disturbed Colleen Brady.

"You all right up there, Father?" she hollered up the stairs.

I opened the bedroom door and was greeted by the glorious aroma of freshly brewed coffee.

"I'm fine, Colleen. Just doing my exercises."

"Oh. Sounds as if you're wrestlin' with the Devil himself."

I chuckled. "Be down in forty minutes. Is that okay?"

She replied with a loud grunt.

Outside my window, dawn stained the eastern sky red-orange, backlighting the maple tree. I loved this time of year, before the harsh reality of winter buried Ohio. When I switched on the radio, the weatherman predicted that a brief passing squall-line would usher in another sultry summer day.

The sun spotlighted the mound of clothes I'd dropped on the carpet last night. I untied the cord that held up the navy-blue surgical scrubs I wore as pajama bottoms and let it join the pile. Not wanting to unleash Colleen's Irish temper, I did my imitation of a point guard and launched my dirty clothing into a laundry basket in the closet next to my black cassocks.

Black and blue. That's how I felt sometimes, sharing life with my two extended families—church and hospital. This life I'd chosen. This life that had chosen me. Better to be too busy than to have too much time to think.

After a shower, I squeezed the last dollop from a toothpaste tube, adding a burst of peppermint to my morning and another item to my shopping list. As I shaved away salt and pepper stubble, I glanced down at the jagged reminder of shrapnel on my chest and the tattoo on my arm before studying my reflection.

My father's silver-blue eyes gazed back at me. Each year I looked more like the man I'd spent a lifetime trying to forget. I knew I should have found a way—somehow—to forgive him by now, but when I turned the other cheek, it was only to shave the left side of my face.

Over the years, I'd become adept at reading expressions. At the hospital, I often saw pain, fear, and people trapped in their own flesh; at the church, guilt, regret, and folks imprisoned by their poor choices. The nocturnal visit from my dead friend had etched a haunted expression on my face, and too many bourbons at the reunion had left my eyes red-veined and baggy—like my mother's had been when my old man beat her, or when she drank herself into oblivion after he'd abandoned us.

Another damn stroll down Memory Lane. Lord, I detested mirrors.

While I dressed, thoughts of Emily and our evening together lifted my spirits. Oran's collapse and the threatening note on our table, however, darkened my mood again.

I reached for my Bible on the nightstand, but picked up the manila envelope containing my portable memories instead. I opened it and removed a photograph of my mother holding my father's hand at a picnic. His hand was all that remained of him. I'd torn the rest of his image away and thrown it out years ago. I kissed her picture and emptied the envelope.

On the plane, Tanya had asked about Vietnam. The snapshot taken in Cu Chi was *my* vacation photo. In it, I had one arm around Kenny Babcock's shoulder, the other around Hoa Nho's tiny waist as she leaned against me. I could almost feel her warmth and smell the aroma of the joss sticks she used to burn. Their eyes stared back at me, bright with promise— promise denied.

I turned a piece of amber over in my hand and held it up to the window. The small black insect inside appeared to be imprisoned in sunlight—solid sunlight, like the touch of Hoa Nho's skin. Her name meant *Little Flower*, and she'd been the single bloom in my scorched-earth existence in 'Nam. Her Zen Buddhist insights had always stretched my Western worldview. The day she gave me the amber as a gift, she explained that she and I were no different from this insect—only we were trapped in the sticky flow of history, stuck in the Napalm sap of 'Nam. Even as a priest who believed in God's guiding hand, I wasn't entirely sure she'd been wrong.

I blinked before tears could form and exchanged the amber for a silver band with a heart design, the "promise ring" I'd given to Emily our junior year—before our relationship and my life had unraveled. Another broken promise, another friendship failed.

Emily and I had been a matched set since fourth grade, a couple for nine years. Longer than many marriages. An eternity when you're young. The first poem she'd written for me had yellowed over time, but her youthful joy and optimism still radiated from the page:

May you shake spring, scream summer,
amaze autumn, whisper winter,
soar life's updrafts
on love's wings,
dream music,
and sing
always.

I.L.Y.
Em

It had been ages since I had sung for the sheer joy of it, let alone soared. My days were filled with duty, my nights with dark dreams.

The last item in the envelope was Emily's farewell to me, typed and unsigned. I'd found it in my locker senior year, two weeks before marching off to boot camp.

TWENTY-ONE GUNS

Seven set their sights
on Heaven; each fire's three rounds
of blanks at God's eye,
brass jackets arcing to earth
like His electrified tears.

I looked from Emily's ring to Hoa Nho's photo, then at my Breviary. What a strange journey my life had been.

Returning my youth to the envelope, I threw it on the dresser, then wondered if Colleen's penchant for snooping through my mail extended to my room. I picked up my portable memories and hid them in the back of a drawer under my T-shirts.

I wasn't sure why I kept these things. They were unnecessary. Memories don't live in an envelope, or even in the heart or the head. They live in the senses. Some days, I could hear Kenny's laughter in a crowded room, taste Mom's love in homemade apple pie, and feel Hoa Nho's touch in a warm breeze.

As I finished getting dressed, I heard a peculiar popping sound outside my window and peered out. God was having a bit of fun, showering Oberlin in one of those bizarre summer rains. No lightning, no thunder. Just huge scattered raindrops spattering the roof and driveway like grapes fired from a slingshot.

Cool air, laced with the scent of renewal, floated through the open window. It was only a preview of autumn. The swelter would be back by midday. I closed the window and went downstairs.

"Is this wicked weather going to continue, do you think, Father?" Colleen handed me a cup of coffee. "If it doesn't let up soon, there'll be no one to listen to your homily and precious little in the collection basket. And if the skies open, sure I'll be mopping out the cellar for a month."

She lobbed a scowl at me. I volleyed with a smile, sipped my coffee, and changed the subject.

"You're not going to church this morning, Colleen?"

"I attend on Saturday evenings, so I can prepare Sunday supper. I'll have your meal ready after Mass, Father, so I'd be grateful if you got here before the eggs harden to rubber and the meat gets tough as a tinker's boot."

"Of course, Colleen."

I checked my watch, walked to the front door, and opened it.

She followed me. "Do you want an umbrella, Father?"

"No need." I pointed outside. "See, the storm's already over."

"Well, mind you don't step in any puddles on the way. Those shoes of yours have seen better days."

My grin blossomed into a laugh. What was I to do with this woman? She was one of a kind.

"I'll be careful, Colleen."

She mumbled something in Gaelic as I hopped a puddle and strolled to the church. Today was the premiere of the Father Austin Show. I wanted to arrive early to tweak my sermon and prepare mentally for my debut.

As I crossed the parking lot, the lightness of my step surprised me.

Chapter Fourteen

———•———

Sunday, July 2, 9:45 a.m.

AFTER I FINISHED fine-tuning my sermon, I dressed in my vestments and listened to the commotion of early arrivals entering the church. I peeked from the sacristy. Light from the stained-glass windows draped the nave in festive rainbow ribbons. Parishioners filed in, many there merely to size up the new priest. First impressions were important in keeping the pews filled, and I needed to be at my best today.

Returning to the sacristy, I put on my alb and stole. Although I should have been focused on my homily, my mind kept drifting. I'd driven Emily home last night, but she was still with me. The wail of an ambulance siren carried me back to the memory of Oran's collapse at the reunion, Emily's tears as we slow-danced, her fragrance, and her hands exploring my face.

A tug on my sleeve.

"Father? Are you okay?" My altar girl frowned up at me from under her Orphan Annie curls. "Time to start."

"Thanks, Kristin. I'll be right there."

I slipped on my chasuble like a poncho and said a short

prayer as the organist gave the entrance hymn a bluesy edge. How appropriate. The previous dean of Oberlin College had been a noted jazz musician, and its conservatory of music was the oldest in the country. If I had to choose one word to describe the town, it would be *music*. Some cities screamed, others laughed, and a handful wept. Oberlin sang.

The organ solo led me to the altar. The church was nearly full. Several nuns occupied the front pew where my mother used to sit when I had been an altar boy. And now at long last, we finally had altar girls. The Church took incredibly small steps, but at least they were in the right direction. Maybe someday women priests? I hoped so.

Inhaling the aroma of incense, I cleared my mind of troubled thoughts. My time with the Lord was always the highpoint of my day, as necessary for me as breathing. Each time I stood at the altar, I marveled that my strange journey through life had somehow led me to this gratifying vocation and amazing inner peace. As I raised the body and blood of Christ in my hands, I could feel His arm around my shoulder. I had been blessed. The Almighty definitely worked in mysterious ways.

The Mass went smoothly. Kristin proved to be a competent acolyte, serving with ease and aplomb. The church was too hot and muggy for a long sermon, so I gave my new parishioners what they wanted—a short, uplifting homily, with the emphasis on short.

As the final hymn faded, I heard a muffled ruckus from the "cry room," the glass-enclosed area reserved for babies and young children in the back of the church. It muted noise, and I called it the "mother's chapel" out of respect for the many sacrifices women made for the comfort of others. Through the glass, I watched the young redheaded woman trying to calm her toddler. In the confessional, she had asked me to meet her after Mass. Indeed, it was time for a serious discussion.

I instructed the faithful to "Go in peace," thanked Kristin for her assistance, and marched down a side aisle toward the cry room. I should have greeted my parishioners at the church door, but public relations could wait until next Sunday. From what this woman had told me, something was horribly wrong. She feared for her child's safety and wanted my help. She'd also implied that my past was somehow related to her problems.

As I approached, the woman made eye contact and placed the child on her lap. She was gaunt, her face drawn, eyes sunken.

I'd nearly reached her when a hand seized my arm from behind. I whirled around.

Tree Macon's face was grim, his police uniform out of place in the church.

"Jake, we need to talk," he said softly. A few curious worshippers lingered nearby. He guided me to a secluded corner. "Do you own a handgun?"

"What? No. Why?"

"A souvenir from the war, maybe?"

"No, Tree, I don't own a weapon." Although my entire adult life since the war, including my nightmares, was my souvenir from overseas. "What in the world are you talking about?"

"Someone shot Everett McDermott around two a.m. His housekeeper found him this morning." He fixed me with a long, hard stare. "He's in a coma in ICU. Bullet's too deep in his brain to operate."

"What!" I remembered McDermott's Armani suit, gold chains, and diamond pinky ring. "A burglary?"

"Doubt it. He still had his Rolex and wallet."

"Why then? Who'd do such a thing?"

"The real question," Tree replied, "is who *didn't* want the guy dead. Half the town hated his guts, and the other half hadn't met him yet."

Tree's eyes fixed on mine. I didn't like his expression. Sweat soaked my vestments.

"Do you have any suspects?"

"That's the trouble, Jake. I got too damn many, and too many motives. Not to mention two ex-wives."

"Come on, you can't possibly think Emily did it. She's *blind*. I dropped her off at St. Joseph's in Lorain after we took Oran to the ER here in town."

"You're right. I don't suspect Emily. Be damn near impossible for her to pull it off. McDermott lives out in the country, and nobody took a cab to his place last night from St. Joe's or anywhere else."

"What? You checked up on Em?"

"I'm not ruling anybody out. I also called her to make sure she was okay because of that threat you found on our table. She's fine."

"My God, Tree. Is she in danger?"

"Don't know how that note fits in. I'm pretty sure it was meant for Emily, not you. I'm worried about her, but I got no motive and can't think of anyone who'd want to hurt her." Tree shrugged his massive shoulders. "Far as the shooting goes, my first thought was McDermott's *other* ex-wife. The deadbeat owed her back alimony. I'm gonna drop by her home today and have a heart-to-heart."

The big man wiped perspiration from his forehead. "Problem is, confirming alibis for two in the morning is hard to do. Far as I'm concerned, everyone who knew McDermott is a suspect at this point." There was steel in his voice. His eyes boomeranged back to me. "*Everyone*, Jake."

"What!" A few nearby stragglers stopped talking and turned toward us. I lowered my voice. "Me?"

"Where'd you go after chauffeuring Emily?"

"I stopped at the hospital to see Oran, then collapsed into bed before midnight."

"Can anyone confirm that?"

"No, I'm the only one at the rectory in the evenings. Our housekeeper's part-time and the pastor is in the hospital. That's why the Church sent me here, to fill in for him. You can't possibly suspect me, Tree. You've got to be kidding."

"Seem like I'm joking to you? C'mon, you always had an

edge, hitting wide receivers so hard they'd cough up blood and the ball, then hobble off the field. The whole county knew you were a headhunter. And as I recollect, you got suspended twice for cleaning McDermott's clock on the playground. I sure didn't want to be around you back in the day when you were boozing. There's been bad blood between you and McDermott for years, then he marries and abuses your girl. Hell, you're a combat vet and the day you return to town, you get in a pissing contest with him at the reunion. A few hours later, the guy's shot. What am I *supposed* to think?"

I recalled the pale scar at the corner of Emily's lip, and thick summer air lodged in my chest. "Tell me about the abuse, Tree."

He hesitated. We locked eyes. Finally he said, "From what Emily told me, more psychological than physical, but who knows? Uniforms responded to domestic disturbance calls at their house twice before the divorce." Tree inhaled deeply. "She said McDermott ridiculed her and tried to isolate her from friends and family. Called on the phone all the time to check up on her. After one argument, she woke up from a nap and found him sitting on the bed loading his gun. Not a very subtle message. McDermott always was a mean drunk. So were you. And you hit the bourbon pretty hard last night."

"Come on, you *know* me. I'm not some street punk, I'm a priest."

"You're still a man, one with a temper." He glared. "You've been away for years, Jake. How well do I really know you anymore?"

Tree closed the gap between us and whispered, "I disliked that bastard too. McDermott's a bigot and a bully, but I got a job to do." He mopped more sweat from his brow. "Don't leave town without talking to me."

"Leave town? Between the church and the hospital, I'll be lucky to find time to sleep."

Tree's radio squawked. He ignored it. "So, how's Oran?"

"He was admitted for … observation. Nothing's broken."

"Glad to hear it."

"I saw you pocket Oran's water bottle after he collapsed. Do you think someone drugged him?"

"I'm paid to be paranoid. You saw how unsteady Oran was. Analysis will take a couple days." Tree paused, gazed at the marble floor, and swallowed hard. "It gets worse. EMS transported Barb Dorfman to the hospital this morning with suspected food poisoning. D.O.A. Her motel room was covered with bloody puke, as if she'd swallowed broken glass. I'm waiting on cause of death, but I don't like the way things feel. Far as I know, nobody else got sick last night. If she was poisoned like the woman at the quarry, then …."

Tree abruptly stopped talking and looked back at me. His eyes were baggy, his shoulders slumped, and his shirt rumpled and stained.

"I'm too damn old for this, Jake," he said. "This shit's all over the news, and folks in town are scared. Every nut-job and self-proclaimed psychic is calling our tip hotline, running my uniforms ragged. And the media's on my back, starting to talk about a possible serial killer."

Barb dead, McDermott shot, Oran in the hospital, and Emily threatened … all from the reunion.

"Sounds like someone's targeting our class, Tree."

"Or the whole darn school. The murdered woman at the quarry also graduated from Oberlin High about seven years ago. Doesn't take Sherlock Holmes to deduce we got some kind of vendetta going on. Elementary, my dear Austin." Tree tried to smile but failed. His radio squawked again. "Gotta go."

Wailing erupted from the cry room. The red-haired woman watched us, her child squirming on her lap. In light of the overnight carnage, her words in the confessional took on a dangerous new edge. *Terrible things are happening. No cops. Cops will make it worse.*

I wanted to tell Tree about her, but the confessional was sacrosanct. I was bound by the Seal of Confession never to reveal her sins. If I spoke up, the blowback from the Church would be enormous. But could I stay silent if an innocent child or Emily was in danger?

In truth, this woman had never actually confessed any sins to me. It was a small loophole, but I dove through it.

"Tree, maybe you should talk to that young woman back there." When I pointed in her direction, she stood and scooped up her son, panic in her eyes.

"What woman?"

"That tall, thin redhead in the yellow dress with the little boy." My finger followed her like a gun sight as she scampered toward the exit.

"Why? She involved?"

"I'm not sure. She told me that lives were at stake, and that I might get hurt."

Tree brought his radio transmitter to his lips, then stopped. "Know her name?"

"No."

"Okay, I'm on it." He started to leave, but turned back. "Listen, Jake. Between the church and hospital, there'll be a lot of people who trust you and might drop their guard. Call me if you see or hear anything. I'm up to my ass in bodies and could use some help."

"You got it, buddy. I have your back, just like the old days. Count on it."

Tree nodded, watched the red-haired women vanish through the main entrance, then stomped out the side door of Sacred Heart Church into the oppressive Ohio heat.

Chapter Fifteen

———◆———

Sunday, July 2, 12:15 p.m.

WITH ONE CLASSMATE dead, two hospitalized, and Emily in danger, Tree was under enormous pressure. And given my past, he had every right to doubt me—yet he'd been my best friend in school and his suspicion hurt.

I'm not ruling anybody out. You've been away for years, Jake. How well do I really know you anymore?

I hung up my vestments, locked the sacristy, and walked from the church. Most of the rain puddles had retreated before the harsh glare of the sun, but I managed to step in one anyway as I pondered Emily's vulnerability. Water seeped in through my well-worn shoes, soaking my socks.

Ten yards from the rectory, I glimpsed motion and stopped. The living-room window curtain twitched, then twitched again. I'd had enough surprises for one day. Turning the doorknob cautiously, I crept inside.

Colleen stood there, arms folded across her bosom, her lips pursed. She glared at me.

"Well now, is it yourself, Father, back at last?"

One of my teachers, Sister Mary Nancy—better known as Sister Very Nasty—had always looked at me that way, seconds before reinforcing her displeasure with the smack of a ruler.

"I'll not be playing ducks and drakes with your digestion, Father. You'll have an ulcer before you know it."

"Sorry I'm late."

She glanced down at my wet shoes, her expression unchanged.

"I see you failed to heed my warning." She frowned. "And if you don't keep up your strength, Father, you'll be no use to man or beast." She placed her hands on her hips. "Well, no harm done, I suppose. I can have something ready in the twinkle of an eye. I'd appreciate it in the future if you'd mind your waywardness at mealtimes."

My *waywardness*? Where did she get this stuff?

Like Sister Very Nasty, Colleen apparently required an explanation for my tardiness because she impatiently tapped her toe and refused to move out of my way.

I certainly wasn't going to tell her about my classmates and feed her addiction to rumor and scandal, so I skipped to my brief encounter in the church parking lot.

"I can't ignore my parishioners. Mr. Diaz needed consoling. He's lonely and misses his dear wife terribly."

"Raymundo Diaz? Well, by all accounts he never missed her with his fist when he got home late from the pub. His aim was true, despite the drink taken."

She snorted in disgust and headed for the kitchen. I followed.

"That sounds like gossip, and you shouldn't contribute to it."

"Gossip, is it? And that poor woman lying there in her coffin with the remains of a black eye plain to be seen."

"I have no reason to doubt Mr. Diaz. Judge not, Colleen, lest ye be judged."

"God bless you, Father, but you're an awfully trusting man. I swear, if Lucifer himself knocked at your door, you'd ask him in for a warm at the fire." She handed me a cup of coffee. "Off you go now. Sit at the table till I'm done."

I slipped off my Roman collar, unbuttoned my clerical shirt at the neck, and eased onto a dining room chair. As I sipped my coffee, contemplating the red-haired woman's fear of the police, Colleen emerged from the kitchen carrying a tray laden with food. She lifted a plate using the corner of her apron and placed it in front of me. It overflowed with enough scrambled eggs, sausage, and fried potatoes to feed an entire congregation, or a small third-world country.

"That should keep you going. Have a care, it's hot," she said with satisfaction. "I heard about your reunion, Father, that poor man collapsing and all."

I suspected little happened in town that Colleen didn't hear about.

She foraged in her apron pocket and pulled out a copy of *Devil's Passage.*

"Thought you might be wanting this." She slid it across the table with one finger, as if it were toxic waste. Her book report was succinct. "Not to my liking. Couldn't trouble myself to finish it. So there you are, it's all yours."

"Thanks, Colleen. I'd love to read it." I motioned at the mound of food on my plate. "Please join me. I can't possibly eat all this."

"Indeed, I will not. That would be altogether inappropriate. Fancy me hobnobbing with the parish priest. No thank you. I know my place. Besides, I've far too much to do."

She retreated into the kitchen.

"Well then, please grab a cup of tea and join me," I called after her. "Even God rested on Sunday, Colleen."

She reappeared in the doorway and wagged a finger in my direction. "God didn't spend His days taking care of helpless clergymen, neither."

I shook my head, devoured twice as much as I wanted, and

was wondering whether to choke down the rest when the telephone rang.

Colleen rushed in from the kitchen, but I snatched up the receiver first.

"Austin here."

Colleen produced a cloth from her voluminous apron pocket and began dusting the credenza.

"Hello, doctor? This is Harvey Winer, the administrator at St Joseph's Hospital. All of your privileges have been approved. You're now officially a staff member."

My Irish Mata Hari cocked her head and buffed with renewed vigor.

Winer continued, "You're scheduled to work in Urgent Care tomorrow. Please stop by my office first to sign your contract. Say seven o'clock? I'll have your ID badge and white coats."

"No problem. I'll be there. Bye." I hung up. "Sorry, I have to run, Colleen."

She stopped cleaning and pointed at my plate. "But your food, Father …."

"Duty calls." I snatched Oran's book from the table. "Can I borrow your car keys again?"

"Ha! 'Tis not my car. That rust-bucket belongs to the church, and I wish you luck with it. Held together by Faith, Hope, and Charity, far as I can tell. And the parish is pinching pennies, so don't get your heart set on a new one." She laughed. "So Father, *your* car keys are hanging on a hook by the back door."

"Thanks for lunch, Colleen. Not quite so much next time, okay?"

Leaving her staring mournfully at the remnants of my meal, I grabbed the keys and made my escape. The only "duty" that called was shopping. I squeezed into the driver's seat, crunched the old Toyota into first gear, and drove east on Lorain, then south on Main Street. The car's air conditioner blew searing heat the entire way, and my damp shirt chilled me when I entered the refrigerated cool of Walmart.

I tossed toothpaste, razor blades, and deodorant into a shopping cart. My usual craving for junk food was a lot easier to resist stuffed with Colleen's eggs and sausage. In the audiobook section, I noticed *Devil's Passage* on CD, thought of Emily, and added it to my cart. After checkout, I had twenty dollars left in my wallet.

Back in the parking lot, I observed the Toyota in the sunlight. It was pockmarked with dents, Bondo patches, and peeling paint. Time and ultraviolet rays had faded its plum color to a patchy, pale orchid, and the "Choose Life" bumper sticker was washed out and nearly unreadable. The tires were balding and I was, in fact, riding on a prayer. Worse, I smelled gas.

After stowing my purchases, I moved the car to an adjacent space, examined the concrete where the Toyota had been parked, and found a small pool of clear liquid with the distinct aroma of gasoline.

Great. A leaking fuel tank, broken air conditioner, and bald tires. With parish funds low, I would have to ask the bishop for the cost of repairs.

As I chugged off to visit Oran Burke at the hospital, the driver ahead of me launched a cigarette butt out his window. It sparked on the asphalt, and I swerved around it, not quite ready to meet my Maker.

Forget repairs. Maybe His Excellency would spring for a moped, or even a bicycle. Anything would be better than this damn Molotov cocktail on wheels.

Chapter Sixteen

———◆———

Sunday, July 2, 2:00 p.m.

ICOLLECTED A visitor's pass at Oberlin Community Hospital, mounted the stairs, and found Oran Burke reading in bed. His room was devoid of flowers and get-well cards, and smelled of disinfectant. A dressing covered the laceration above his eyebrow. His injured wrist was bandaged and the nose-piece of his broken eyeglasses taped together. His skin was parchment-pale, and he looked as if he'd aged a decade overnight. I cleared my throat and he turned toward me.

"Jake?"

"Hey, Oran. How're you feeling?"

"Better than last night, thanks." Bloodshot eyes blinked steadily, like flashing traffic lights. His head tilted to the side, and for a moment I expected to see the writhing neck movement I'd witnessed the evening before. Instead he said, "So, you're really a priest? And a physician?"

"I really am."

"No, you're an enigma. Have a seat." He pointed at a chair.

"Answer a question for me. Does being a man of science challenge your belief in the existence of God?"

I'd been asked this before and answered without hesitation.

"Not at all. Science gives us knowledge, religion gives us meaning. God is like gravity or the force that holds atoms together. You may not be able to see it, but you know it must be there." I fingered the small crucifix under my clerical shirt. "It doesn't matter whether the universe is guided directly by the Almighty's hand or by forces and laws of His creation. God is the cause of all causes. *Faith* is accepting that mysteries are simply truths we don't yet understand."

"So, you agree with Einstein. Science is merely a way to discover the mind of God."

"Exactly."

Oran appeared withered and frail. Could someone at our reunion really have poisoned or drugged his bottled water? Hard to believe. Why would anyone want to hurt this harmless bookworm?

"You look tired, Oran. Maybe I should go."

"No, don't leave. I had trouble sleeping last night, that's all. I guess they found me sleepwalking." Oran set his book on the tray table, poured some water, and took a sip. "Thanks for your help yesterday."

"No problem." The EKG monitor on the wall showed a continuous parade of regular green blips. The bedside clipboard indicated normal vital signs. "You're being well cared for medically. Can the priest half of me do anything for you?"

Oran hesitated. "My wife was a devout Catholic and very active at Sacred Heart." His eyes wandered to the window and lingered there. "You could pray for Nancy. I'd appreciate that."

"Absolutely. I'll say Mass for her."

"As for me, I'm a devout agnostic and well beyond salvation."

A nurse entered and checked Oran's pulse, blood pressure, and temperature. She scribbled her findings and left the room.

"I heard someone shot McDermott." Oran pointed at the

television. "I can't say I'm surprised. Everyone despised that piece of shit. And I can't say I'm saddened, given our history. Sorry, Father Jake, forgiveness is not one of my virtues."

"It's worse than that. The town was already on edge about the murder at the quarry. You know, the woman in the book club with Sonya Macon and your wife. Now, with what's happened to you and McDermott, folks are downright terrified."

"Me? Why me?"

"Tree Macon's testing the water bottle you drank from last night, to see if it was tampered with."

The nurse returned with a medication cart. Oran glanced suspiciously at his water cup and swallowed his pills dry.

After she'd gone, I said, "There's more. Barb Dorfman died early this morning under suspicious circumstances."

"What the hell's going on?" Oran frowned. "And how do you know all this?"

"Tree told me."

"Are you the police chaplain or something?"

"No, apparently I'm a *suspect*. McDermott and I have … a history."

"Now I've heard everything. Please inform our illustrious police chief that he should focus his attention on Marisa Jenkins. She argued with that lowlife about money. Behind every vast fortune is an appalling crime. And Marisa's fiancé nearly hit McDermott last night."

"Richard, violent? I doubt he'd be willing to break a manicured fingernail."

"The police should also examine McDermott's *associates* at his collection agency. They're all thugs, losers, and felons."

Enough talk of violence and intrigue. I pointed at the tray table. "What're you reading, Oran?"

"*The Town That Started the Civil War*, about antebellum Oberlin. It's research for the sequel to *Devil's Passage*." He gestured at the book that Colleen had given me. "How about you?"

"Oh, I wanted to get your autograph before you became too famous to speak with me."

I handed him the book.

Oran snatched a pen off the nightstand, wrote haltingly on the title page in an angular, uneven scrawl, then read, "For Jake, the sole literate athlete in existence."

He feigned a forward pass and handed the book back.

"Thanks. I'll put it in my trophy case, along with the deflated game balls and my lucky jockstrap."

"May I ask another question, Jake?"

"Sure."

"I'm a history buff, fascinated by the behavior of the deeply religious. Like the fundamentalist preachers in the South who never spoke out against the lynching of blacks. How'd they bridge the divide between Christianity and a culture of bigotry?"

I could only shake my head.

"Or the clergy in Nazi Germany who remained mute during the Holocaust. How do you explain that, Jake? Was it fear that silenced them, magical thinking, or did they justify the genocide in their minds?" His face flushed and he threw his pen down, bouncing it off the tray table onto the floor. "Where was their *righteousness* back then? If I had been there, I'd have found some way to combat that evil, no matter what the consequences. How can you believe in a *just god* while people are being slaughtered around you? Where was God during those atrocities? Explain *that* to me."

"A rabbi friend of mine once told me that he believes God was in the Nazi concentration camps, suffering with His people. That's not unlike what Jesus did, living among the poor and downtrodden, dying on the cross between them. Both versions ring true to me."

He pondered that for a moment, then said, "*God* is such a small word, the short answer to such a long and complicated question." He paused. "I don't mean to pry, Jake, but may I ask something personal?"

I assumed the worst and waited as the tornado of my past spun toward me.

"Were you a priest in Vietnam?"

"I was nowhere near ready for the priesthood back then. No, I was a medic." I considered how much of my soul I wanted to reveal. "*Pro Deo et Patria.* That's the Chaplain's Motto. *For God and Country.*" I sighed. My turn to gaze out the window. "Cain was killing Abel by the thousands. Even as a teenager, I couldn't believe that God was on anybody's side. Most chaplains were career military, content to bless the ammo dumps and the troops. To me, they seemed like hypocrites. No, I preferred being a medic."

"It takes enormous courage to do what you did."

"Courage? Most of us were just trying to survive. Every day we became more like jungle animals, living by instinct, dodging death, hoping for a million-dollar wound."

"What's that?"

"An injury serious enough to get you shipped home without being permanently disabling. A guy in my squad was so desperate, he shot himself in the thigh—and blew a hole in his femoral artery. He went home in a body bag."

"Still, I don't think there's a higher calling than caring for heroes, Jake."

"Heroes? I learned more than I ever wanted to know about courage and cowardice in Vietnam. I met lots of brave people there." Kenny Babcock's face flashed in my memory. "But none braver than the Tunnel Rats."

Oran's eyes brightened. He sat up and threw his legs over the side of the bed.

"Tell me about them. I want to write about their exploits."

"The tunnels gave the Vietnamese home-field advantage. Long before we arrived, they used that underground maze of guerrilla bases to fight invaders from China, Japan, France—"

"Were you a Tunnel Rat, Jake?"

"Me? God, no. I'm claustrophobic."

I remembered that day, fury driving me through that dark labyrinth, the walls closing in, dirt crumbling around me, the smell of gunpowder and decay, the taste of terror and despair mixed with the lust for blood and vengeance.

My breath caught in my throat, and it took a moment to recover.

"No, I'm way too big, Oran. Tunnel Rats were small men, like you, capable of maneuvering in narrow spaces. Those little guys had tremendous courage. They fought the VC in pitch-black passageways, then set charges and blew up the tunnels. Most were half-deaf from underground explosions and gunfire."

"That sounds like real-life *Mission Impossible* to me."

"But without the glamour. They crawled into the blackness armed with a flashlight, a handgun, and grenades. Not only did the Cong wait in ambush, but some tunnels were booby-trapped, and all were filled with snakes, spiders, and bats. Hell, forget claustrophobia and my size, Oran. I never had the guts for that job."

I pictured Kenny again in my mind. "My best friend was a Tunnel Rat. A good ol' boy from Alabama, all stock cars, hunting dogs, and grits. A born spelunker. Kenny used to say he crawled directly from the birth canal into the caves near his home. We called him *Mongoose* because he had reflexes quicker than an Asian pit viper. He was the toughest, craziest SOB I ever met."

"Was?"

"Both of us were *short-timers*, a few weeks from being shipped home. Kenny had just crawled out of a tunnel in Cu Chi." I closed my eyes and plunged into the nightmare that often wrenched me from sleep. My chest tightened. "We were having a smoke when he holstered his weapon and said, 'Been thinking about my Southern Belle. Thinking maybe I'll make an honest woman of her.' I said I'd inject him with a whopping dose of penicillin as a wedding gift—for his bride. Kenny was trying to pee, laughing so hard he sprayed every which way."

I tried to smile at the memory, but couldn't.

"A bush suddenly jumped to the side, and a VC soldier sprang up from a hole in the ground. I pointed my sidearm at his belly and told him in Vietnamese to drop his pistol. He had no chance and knew it." In my mind, I saw the Cong's fear and surprise mutate into a vicious sneer. "I should have killed him but ... I'd never shot anyone. I hesitated."

My pulse pounded in my ears. "I expected him to drop his weapon. Instead, he let out a caustic sound, contemptuous and bitter, like acid chewing through metal—the sound of someone with nothing left to lose. Then he shot my friend in the chest and dove back down the hole. I grabbed Kenny as he fell, but the bullet had hit him in the heart. He was dead by the time I laid him on the ground."

Guilt bowed my head. Something inside of me shattered every time I remembered the expression on Kenny's face.

"I jumped down the hole, caught up with the bastard, and shot him in the throat."

I skipped the part about crawling after him through the tunnels, the gun battle, shrapnel tearing into my chest, getting lost in the maze afterward and being unable to find my way back out, feeling certain I'd crawled into my own grave—and the flies and gnats on Kenny's body when I finally reemerged from that hellhole.

Oran appeared pained, but he didn't break the silence.

"I spit on the Cong's corpse, but as I turned to leave, I heard gurgling and saw him reach into his pocket. I put my revolver against his temple and blew him away. His hand flopped to his side holding ... a photo of a baby girl, cradled in his arms."

I opened my mouth to finish the thought, but nothing came out.

Oran handed me a box of tissues, and I wiped away a tear.

"Heroes? The jungle was littered with them. Cowardice? Now *that's* something I understand." I found Oran's eyes and held them. "Sometimes a coward is simply a hero with a wife and kids. Sometimes he's a guy ... who lets his friends down."

I touched the inked initials on my forearm and closed my eyes. Kenny Babcock and Hoa Nho stared back at me.

I hadn't spoken these words since my feet touched American soil, and I wasn't sure why I'd opened this dark door to a stranger.

But deep down, I knew the answer. Telling this to Tree or Emily would have been too painful. Confessing to someone I didn't know well was easier. My indecision, my panic, had cost Kenny his life, and my rage had robbed a child of her father.

I wanted to run from the room to escape Oran's questions, but my body went limp.

"Hesitating to kill another human being doesn't make you a coward." Oran patted my shoulder. "I'm sorry I pried. Most of my life I've been a spectator, not a participant. Sometimes, I wonder about things."

"Don't worry about it." I stood and took a step toward the door. "Can I do anything for you before I go?"

"No, I'm leaving this butcher shop today, with or without my doctor's permission. I've been here too long as it is. I'm sleeping in my own bed tonight. I loathe hospitals. Truth be told, I'm not too fond of doctors either. No offense." He paused. "My dear wife, Nancy, went into St. Joseph's for a routine procedure and came out in a coffin."

"I'm so sorry, Oran. I didn't know." Since I'd driven him to the hospital, I asked, "Want me to drive you back to the Oberlin Inn to get your car after you're released?"

"No, thanks. It was a beautiful night and I walked to the reunion."

"How about a lift home?"

"Not necessary. I need some fresh air, and my house isn't far from the hospital."

"Suit yourself. Call me if I can help in any way." I wrote my cellphone number on a paper napkin. "Thanks for the autograph. Get well soon."

I nearly sprinted away from Oran's probing and my rampaging ghosts. As I walked past the elevator, the door opened and Dr. Taylor greeted me.

"Ah, Dr. Austin, right? Sorry if I was curt last evening. I had a tough night on call. How's Mr. Burke today?"

"He's okay, except for a tremor in his hands and some difficulty sleeping."

"So I heard. His nurse called me around three this morning and said they'd found him sleepwalking in the basement, of all things. He'd torn open his stitches and bloodied himself without waking up. Damnedest thing."

"Let me warn you. Oran's determined to go home today."

"Thanks for the heads up." Taylor stepped from the elevator and held the door for me. "Be my guest."

"No, thanks, I prefer the stairs." And wide-open spaces. Even stairwells were narrow and forbidding on my bad days.

We said goodbye and I scampered out of the building into blinding sunlight. Inserting my clerical collar, I headed from Oberlin's tiny hospital to St. Joseph's sprawling complex in Lorain.

Chapter Seventeen

———◆———

Sunday, July 2, 3:00 p.m.

Aʟᴛʜᴏᴜɢʜ Sᴛ. Jᴏsᴇᴘʜ's was a Roman Catholic facility with its own chaplain, I felt obligated to personally attend to hospitalized parishioners from Sacred Heart Church. I draped my stole over my arm and stowed the ritual book for the Anointing of the Sick, Holy Oil, and my gold-plated pyx containing the Blessed Eucharist in my pockets. Then, like a traveling tent-preacher working backwater towns, I carried my portable church from floor to floor in search of troubled souls. I heard confessions, offered Communion, but mostly held hands, listened, and provided what solace I could.

My last stop was the small VIP wing, six private rooms clustered around a nursing station. The door to Room 203 was open and I peeked in.

Father LaFontaine sat semi-upright in his electric bed, watching a baseball game. He was adrift in a sea of roiled bed sheets. His Cleveland Indians cap was too large and flopped to one side. In contrast to Oran Burke's room, LaFontaine's looked and smelled like a florist's shop. When he noticed me, he reached for the remote and switched off the television.

"Yes? Come in."

LaFontaine's face was skeletal, his cheekbones nearly poking through the overlying skin. He groaned as he turned toward me and removed his baseball cap. Only scattered tufts of gray hair remained. His eyes were sunken and the whites stained a dark egg-yolk yellow. His complexion was lemon-colored and so translucent that the veins beneath took on an eerie green tint. Jaundice.

I stepped into the room. "Father, I'm Jake Austin."

The hint of a smile tugged at the corners of his pale lips. "Ah, the cavalry has arrived at last. Please call me Henri. Colleen told me all about you."

No surprise there. She'd already listened in on my phone conversations, opened my mail, and demonstrated a penchant for gossip.

"I'll bet she has."

"Oh, don't mind Colleen. She's all bark, no bite. I couldn't get by without her. She's my 'Girl Friday,' the guardian angel of Sacred Heart Church."

Angel was not the word I would have chosen.

"Then she probably told you that the bishop assigned me to hold the fort until you recover."

LaFontaine inclined his head to one side. "That would make Bishop Lucci either an optimist or misinformed." He gestured toward a chair. "Please sit. May I call you Jake?"

"Sure."

"Colleen says you're also a physician."

"That's correct."

"Then you'll understand. I have pancreatic cancer. I've done my homework and know I'm dying. But because I'm a priest, the doctors here dance around my questions and coddle me like some holy relic." Pain creased his face when he shifted position in bed. "Please review my chart and tell me the truth. How much time do I have?"

"I don't know, Father. You should speak with—"

"I've lost so much weight the last few months," he said, pointing to his Indians cap, "even this hat no longer fits. With the cancer and chemo eating at me, Jake, it's like I'm rotting from the inside." His breathing was fast and labored. "C'mon, you're a doctor. All I want is a second opinion. Tell me the truth. Please."

I nodded and walked to the nursing station. Because I was dressed in clerical attire and the head nurse had never seen me before, she was reluctant to help. I pulled my state medical license from my wallet and handed it to her. She studied it, wrote down my license number, and finally relinquished Father LaFontaine's chart. I spent fifteen minutes examining his test results and several pages of nearly illegible doctors' scrawl. Things were not as bad as I had feared; they were worse.

When I re-entered his room, the game was back on.

"Who's winning?"

"Cleveland eight, New York one, in the ninth. Sometimes the good guys win—though my allegiance is less clear when the Indians play the Angels." LaFontaine conjured up an impish grin and hit the mute button. "I pray for the souls of Yankee fans, but fear only God himself can save them."

I chuckled. "I've rooted for the Indians my whole life, but I'm beginning to think our Lord is not a Tribe fan."

"When Cleveland won it all in 1948, Jake, I was a kid. If it's going to happen again in my lifetime, it'll have to be this season. I won't be around next year." He waved me over. "So, what's the verdict? Give it to me straight. I'm good with God."

Some days, I wished I'd skipped medical school and gone directly to the seminary. At least the afterlife offered hope to the hopeless.

"Sorry, Henri, the news is grim. Your surgeon couldn't remove the entire tumor, and now it's blocking your bile ducts, causing your jaundice. The cancer's spread to your liver, bones, and lungs. The prognosis is poor."

"How long?"

I hated this question. The answer was, at best, a wild guess.

"A few weeks. Two months at most."

LaFontaine's response surprised me.

"Sounds like an eternity. I can't take this belly pain much longer. My doctors act like God will strike them down if they give me too much morphine and I meet St. Peter at the Pearly Gates a week early."

Current laws and the malpractice climate forced most physicians to straddle the fine line between over-medicating and under-medicating—and some patients suffered as a result. It could be difficult to do what you believed was right with a bull's-eye painted on your back.

LaFontaine grimaced, then looked up. "Please, Jake. It's the bottom of the ninth and you're up. Can you help me?"

I flopped onto the chair. "I'll speak with your oncologist about getting Hospice involved, adding a morphine pump so you can medicate yourself, and doing a celiac block."

"A what block? No more operations, Jake. I'm done."

"It's not surgery. We just inject medicine through a needle to kill the nerves that transmit pain sensation from your abdomen to your brain. If the pain never reaches your mind, you can't feel it. Make sense? It's not a cure, Father, but it should help."

"Kill nerves?" LaFontaine's brow furrowed. "Will it paralyze me?"

"No. We use the CT scanner to guide the needle to the spot where only pain-conducting nerves are located."

"I don't know. Sure sounds like surgery to me. I don't have much fight left." LaFontaine lowered the head of his bed and released a muffled cry. "Guess I don't have much choice. I can't go on like this. Okay, Jake, set it up."

After several phone calls, I returned from the nursing station.

"Your doctor said the morphine pump and Hospice are no problem, Henri. The celiac block, however, is a tricky procedure and should be done by the interventional radiologist. St. Joe's only has one."

"And …?"

I had telephoned the interventional radiologist at his home and explained the situation. He was on vacation and leaving town in the morning for a medical conference. He refused to come to the hospital, so I'd threatened him with a turf battle over control of the scanner, telling him that I would do the procedure today without him.

The CT scanner was the Radiology Department's baby and firmly under their control. By protocol, I was supposed to request their permission to use it.

I was an internist with specialty training in pain management, and I let the interventional radiologist know that I'd received hospital privileges for X-ray-guided needle injections. I didn't lie to him, but I did fail to mention that my hospital privileges didn't officially start until tomorrow. He was furious, but grudgingly agreed to come in. No doubt, the Radiology Department would be up in arms. The thought of catching hell on Monday for doing what I could to minimize Henri's suffering, however, felt darn good today.

"The radiologist will be here in an hour or so to do the procedure."

"Thank you, Jake. I need to ask another favor."

"Of course, anything."

"Hear my confession and give me Communion."

"Certainly."

A nurse came in and checked his vital signs. When she left, he said, "I'm not going to make it back to Sacred Heart, am I?"

I shook my head.

"Then I have one other request."

"Name it."

LaFontaine's gaze drifted down. "Promise to destroy my briefcase in the closet at the rectory. Don't open it."

What in the world? Dear Lord.

"Henri, I don't think—"

"There's nothing illegal or dangerous inside. Those things …
are personal. No one's business but mine. Trust me on this."

"I don't know … I can't—"

"This is my dying wish, Father Austin. Honor it, please."
LaFontaine's eyes, moist and pleading, found mine. "I can't ask
Colleen. I'm *begging* you, Jake."

I searched for a kind way to say, "Not a chance in Hell." But
I too had secrets I preferred to keep private.

Finally, under the weight of his stare, I buckled and agreed,
then slipped my purple stole over my shoulders and ministered
to the spiritual needs of Father Henri LaFontaine.

Chapter Eighteen

---•---

Sunday, July 2, 4:45 p.m.

WITH MY THOUGHTS churning over Father LaFontaine's bizarre request to destroy his briefcase, I craved coffee and a moment of quiet reflection. I ambled to the hospital cafeteria, but it didn't open until five o'clock.

Outside the entrance, the latest addition of the *Lorain Morning Journal* peeked through the glass front of the newspaper vending machine. Tree Macon's photograph gazed back at me, his expression grim. Next to it were pictures of Barb Dorfman, McDermott, and Joanetta Carter, the woman found dead at the quarry. The headline read OBERLIN SCHOOLS UNDER SIEGE! POLICE BAFFLED. I wondered if Oran Burke had been the fourth intended victim. As I skimmed the first two paragraphs, the black ink summary was pitifully inadequate to describe the blood-red carnage of the past two days.

I needed caffeine, not conjecture, so I walked down the hall and entered the snack shop. I'd hoped that Emily would be working this afternoon, but her father manned the counter.

He sat by the cash register drinking a can of Coke, waiting for his next customer. He was hunched over, balding, and now blind. The past three decades had not been kind to Irv Beale. I stopped inside the doorway, uncertain what to say to him after all these years.

Two teenagers charged in, jostling me away from the entrance without even an *excuse me*. The tall, skinny one in a Cleveland Cavaliers T-shirt laughed and shoved the stocky teen wearing a Browns jersey, resulting in a short burst of profanity. Brownie glanced at me, then at Irv, grabbed a handful of Milky Way bars, and nodded to Cav. Then the two rummaged through the front counter offerings, shoving chocolates and snack food into their pockets.

Halloween in July?

Irv heard the commotion and turned, his rheumy eyes directed over Brownie's shoulder. "May I help you?"

"Just a pack of gum," Cavalier said. He threw some change on the counter, his grin widening, as he grabbed more loot and the two sidled toward the door.

Heat flared in my cheeks and my fists clenched. I was sick and tired of watching the Ten Commandments downgraded to options, and wondered what the heck parents were teaching their kids these days.

I'd struggled for years to exorcise the angry young man who relished the violence of the football field and the vengeful soldier who'd shot a man at close range, but I knew that they both still lurked somewhere inside me, and I could feel them stir.

With recent headlines about priests abusing children, I needed to be cautious. If this situation detonated, the fallout from the Church and the press could be career-ending. Prudence dictated avoiding confrontations with young people.

Brownie slapped Cav on the back and whispered, "See, like taking candy from a baby."

Irv's mouth opened, but no sound came out. His helplessness set a time bomb ticking in my head.

To hell with caution. Sometimes prudence and punks need a swift kick in the ass.

I emptied my pockets of all religious items, placed them on a nearby table, and held my ground in front of the exit.

"Where do you think *you're* going, boys?" The words flew out white-hot and razor sharp. *Tick. Tick.* I pointed to the red-lettered sign on the wall: THE MIDNIGHT CAFE. RUN BY THE SOCIETY FOR THE BLIND. I took a step forward. "Are you stealing from a blind man? Or can't you read?"

The two exchanged glances.

"Maybe *you* oughta pay the blind dude for us, Preacher," Cav said, "and put a twenty in *our* collection plate—like for health insurance, old man."

Old man, huh. Though, when I was a teenager, people in their forties looked eighty to me too.

"Think about what you're doing, son."

Brownie gave me the finger.

"Clearly, you both need at least twenty." I sighed, removed my clerical collar, and paused for effect. *Tick.* "Twenty more points might raise your IQs to triple digits."

Their blank expressions transformed to anger.

"Fuck off, grandpa!"

I imagined Emily working the counter instead of her father, and the demons of my youth rose to their feet.

"I should slap you both into next Tuesday. You took it, now pay up."

Irv grabbed the telephone. "Get me the Security Office!"

Brownie headed for the door. "Outta my way!"

"No one's going anywhere till—"

Before I could finish, Brownie launched a right hook.

Tick … BOOM!

This was no contest. Trained in hand-to-hand combat and madder than hell, I could have easily blocked his fist and leveled him with an uppercut. Instead, I stepped to the side, grabbed the teen's wrist, and used the power of his punch to spin him around, twisting his arm behind his back into a hammerlock hold—just like Uncle Sam had taught me. I could almost hear my old drill sergeant's nasty snicker as Brownie squealed and dropped to his knees. I released his wrist and yanked the boy's jersey halfway up, pinning his arms above his head.

Cav came toward me.

"I wouldn't, son."

For a moment, it appeared that he might charge at me, but his bravado cratered. He inched toward the exit.

"Not another step."

Brownie yanked his shirt back down and staggered to his feet. Both teenagers eyeballed me, but the fire was gone. Clearly, they'd had enough. I, however, was still seething.

I took a slow breath and reined in my demons. *Blessed are the merciful.*

"Think how hard your life would be if *you* were blind."

They suddenly found the tile floor fascinating and studied it intently.

"There's always the cops, boys. That how you want to play this?"

Cav shook his head. I encouraged them with a shove, and they shuffled to the cash register.

"Now, pay the man. And apologize."

Brownie fumbled for his wallet and placed six one-dollar bills on the counter.

"Sorry," Cav muttered.

"I don't think the gentleman heard you." I grabbed the wallet and laid a ten-dollar bill on the pile of singles. "And say it like you mean it."

They added two stuttering apologies that held the ring of sincerity. Without a doubt, they were very sorry they'd been caught.

"Now, get out." I tossed the wallet back to Brownie. "And don't let me catch you back in here. Ever."

The teens slithered out the door.

"Never mind. Problem solved," Irv said, hanging up the phone. He made his way over. "Thanks. You new here?"

"Yeah." I collected my ritual book, holy oil, and stole, my pulse beginning to slow.

Irv scooped up the cash and chuckled. "Failed anger management, huh?"

"I prefer to think of it as righteous indignation." As my adrenaline levels faded, my knees became wobbly, and I slumped against the counter. "And also penance. As a kid I … wasn't much different from those two."

"This a George Washington?" Irv said, holding up a bill.

"Nope, it's a Hamilton. The boys also left you six Georges as a tip."

"I'm Irv. I run this fine establishment." He extended his hand and I took it. Paper-thin skin covered bones as slender and fragile as glass rods.

"Been a long time, Mr. Beale. It's Jake. Jake Austin."

"Jacob Austin. Wow, déjà vu all over again. Emily said you'd returned to town." Irv frowned. "Come to think of it, you *were* a lot like those hooligans. Can't say I was much of a fan."

"Looking back, I can't say I blame you."

"What can I get you? On the house."

"Coffee to go, thanks." I waited a beat. "Is Emily around?"

Irv finished pouring. "Try the hospital courtyard. She's often there reading."

"Thanks, Mr. Beale." I took the Styrofoam cup, splashed in some cream, and headed for the door. "Nice seeing you again."

"Jake, two things. It's *Irv* now. And coffee's always on the house here for you."

Chapter Nineteen

———◆———

Sunday, July 2, 5:15 p.m.

THE COURTYARD WAS an expansive, well-manicured flower garden, a pleasant and unexpected surprise in the heart of an inner city. The beauty and solitude reminded me of a monastery, and the baritone hum of nearby traffic resembled a strange, urban Gregorian chant.

Emily sat on a concrete bench shaded by an ancient birch tree, wearing shorts and a sleeveless, floral blouse. Above her, the leaves fluttered like a thousand emerald butterflies. I listened to the soft refrain of nearby sprinklers, watched her fingers dance across a page of Braille—and my heart hurt. Another friend failed. She had once been my soul mate, but my adolescent lust and arrogance had cost me our relationship.

As a teenager, I'd thought that a game-saving interception or tackle and a letter sweater entitled me to strut through life with this beautiful and intelligent woman on my arm. What a fool I'd been. Maybe in some inexplicable way, my self-destructive youth had been part of God's plan to guide me toward the priesthood. Who could say? Knowing that I'd lost

Emily forever certainly had made entering the seminary and accepting the austerity of my vows much easier.

Yet, here she was again, within arm's reach.

I cleared my throat. "Hi, Em."

She turned toward me, wearing her sunglasses and a quizzical smile.

"Father Austin, I presume."

She bookmarked her place and patted the bench. As I sat next to her, her glow dimmed. She found my hand and squeezed it.

"Poor Everett. Can you believe it? Someone shot him." Her chin dropped to her chest. "He's unconscious in ICU. I stopped by to check on him this morning, but he can't have visitors yet."

I wondered if her compassion for and loyalty to a drunken, abusive scumbag like McDermott qualified her for sainthood but said, "I'm so sorry, Em."

Who was I to judge? What the hell did I know about relationships?

"And Barb Dorfman dead? My god, Jake! Tree called me this morning to make sure *I* was okay. Why would he be worried about me? Just because I was married to Everett? I don't understand. Is someone targeting our high school class?"

She remained quiet for a while. I deliberated whether to tell her about the threatening note, but didn't want to terrify her. After all, I wasn't sure she was the intended recipient.

Emily raised her head and asked, "How's Oran?"

"He was admitted to Oberlin Hospital last night for observation. Except for a sprained wrist and a few stitches, he was fine when I saw him this afternoon. He's a feisty little guy." I opted not to mention Tree Macon's concern that someone had tampered with Oran's water bottle. "He's determined to leave the hospital today."

"That's no surprise. Determination is Oran's middle name."

"He's such a strange man and always looks so, I don't know … ill at ease."

"Oran's the proverbial fish out of water." Emily set her book on the bench. The bangles on her wrist chimed softly, like distant church bells. "He's a nineteenth-century man trapped in the twenty-first. Honorable. Selfless. Chivalrous. He should've been born two hundred years ago."

"You know him well, then?"

A sunbeam fought its way through the birch leaves, igniting ruby and gold highlights in her hair.

"Yes, as well as anyone does. We've been in the same writing group for years. We evaluate and critique each other's work, provide support, that sort of thing."

"When I saw him, he was working on the sequel to *Devil's Passage*."

Emily arched her eyebrows. "I'm surprised ... but that's fantastic."

"Surprised?"

"Oran hasn't written much since his wife died. He and Nancy were—what did Kurt Vonnegut call it?—a duprass. A community of two people, a couple whose lives revolved around each other." Her earring found the sunlight and twinkled. "When he lost her, Oran floated into space like a moon without a planet. He completely shut down."

"He certainly had good reason to be depressed, Em."

"It wasn't just depression. He changed into a different person. He went from Mr. Stable to Mr. Labile. Then the lawsuit crushed him."

"Lawsuit?"

"Oran sued his wife's doctor and St. Joseph's for malpractice. The case dragged on for years. He lost."

"Who was the doctor?"

"Phineas Byrd."

"Chief of Medicine? Now *I'm* surprised. He has a national reputation as one of the best."

"Even excellent doctors sometimes make horrible mistakes. But I'm biased. I've only heard Oran's side of the story and don't know the details."

She pushed an errant strand of hair behind one ear.

"Losing that lawsuit sent him over the edge. He became volatile, quick-tempered." Emily made a *tsk* sound with her tongue. "He even confronted Dr. Byrd and got in a shoving match with him." She frowned. "It's hard to believe how Oran's changed since Nancy's death. It's also affected his health."

I recalled Oran's writhing neck movements and his tremors. "In what way?"

"He gets spasms in his arm muscles and drops things. I've felt his hands shake. I'm told he's very unsteady."

Emily removed her sunglasses and nibbled on the earpiece. She'd done this at the reunion whenever we talked about something unpleasant. Her blue eyes remained alarmingly still as her composure crumbled.

"I worry Oran's in pain. He denies it and dismisses my concerns. It's like he doesn't care anymore, Jake." She grew silent.

I decided not to say that Oran's depression may have led to drug or alcohol abuse. Emily was already anxious, and I didn't want my conjecture to add to her burden. Instead, I sipped my coffee and allowed my eyes to wander from her face to the secluded courtyard.

Nearby, a russet-colored squirrel peeked around a statue of Saint Francis of Assisi and chattered at us. The patron saint of animals provided the squirrel with an oasis of shade in an expanse of searing sunlight. His upturned ceramic palm had filled with rainwater from the morning downpour. A sparrow bobbed there, partaking of his offering. Birds had speckled Saint Francis in white droppings, but he didn't seem to mind.

Flowerbeds around the statue exploded in a riot of azure, yellow, and magenta, filling the garden with a heavenly fragrance. The roses buzzed with the excitement of honeybees.

Although the Catholic Church had banished him as a heretic, Martin Luther had definitely been right about one thing. God indeed had written the Gospel not merely in the Bible, but also in the trees, the flowers, and the clouds.

"This garden looks so unbelievably gorgeous, Em."

Looks? What a poor choice of words. Apparently, I'd been absent the day God gave out sensitivity. She appeared not to notice my faux pas.

"I love the scent of the lilacs, the velvet breeze, the rustle of leaves, and the birdsong." I could hear the voice of Emily's inner poet even in her casual conversation. "This is my private Eden."

I almost said *I can see why*, but bit my tongue. "So, what're you reading, Em?"

"A romance novel."

"More sensual in Braille, Em?" I chuckled when she blushed. "Those were your exact words at the reunion, as I remember."

"They're *fun*, Jake. Like a mini-vacation. Sometimes I just need to … get away." She replaced her sunglasses and tapped them with her finger. "Reading good writing is like having my vision back. I can see the whole world again in my mind."

We sat quietly for a while, caressed by warm summer winds and the delicate perfume of flowers, somehow comfortable in the silence. Finally, she ran a finger across her watch.

"It's nearly suppertime. Would you like to join Dad and me in the cafeteria? They're serving pot roast tonight, which is usually good."

"'Usually good.' Now there's a ringing endorsement. Between school, the Army, and the seminary, I've eaten more institutional meals than I care to count. Why don't we go to a real restaurant to celebrate my homecoming and our renewed friendship?"

"That sounds wonderful. Can I invite Dad?"

"Sure," I replied with more enthusiasm than I felt.

She handled her cellphone deftly. Seconds later, Irv Beale declined the invitation, claiming a ravenous desire for pot roast. Emily suggested the Red Clay Restaurant, and soon we were rumbling toward Vermilion in the Toyota. It rattled, groaned, and farted toxic exhaust.

"Sweet wheels, Jake. If you keep it long enough, it may become a classic. Does this thing have air conditioning?"

"Only in theory."

She shook her head and cranked the window down. A bank of cotton-candy clouds in the western sky had taken the edge off the swelter, and the breeze helped.

I pondered what Emily had said about Oran's transformation. It worried me.

She turned in my direction. "Cat got your tongue?"

"Sorry, I was thinking about Oran." I hesitated, not sure if I wanted to stir this pot. "Is there any chance he might be suicidal?"

"Suicide? Oran? I can't imagine. Why?"

"It's just that ... he fits the profile in some ways." I drummed my fingers on the steering wheel. "The highest risk groups for suicide are older men with failing health, gun owners, and people with depression after the loss of a loved one."

Emily stiffened. "That certainly describes Oran—well, until recently. The gun part too."

"He owns a weapon?"

"A display case full, actually. He's a history buff, Jake, and a collector. Oran tells me he has all kinds of weapons—antique revolvers and rifles, crossbows, blowguns, and an ornate Confederate sword."

She removed her sunglasses and fidgeted with them again. Another mile slid under the car before she spoke.

"I can't believe he would kill himself, Jake. Oran doesn't have children, but he's very close to his niece and wouldn't put her through that."

"You said something changed recently?"

Any radical transformation in personality was a red flag.

"A few months ago, his gloom evaporated and the old lovable Oran returned. He was still having trouble physically and not writing much, but he started joking around again. I think the invitation to speak at our reunion did the trick. It allowed him to show off his success."

This worried me even more. People on the verge of suicide sometimes relaxed and grew cheerful *after* they made the decision to kill themselves.

I tucked the thought away.

"Maybe his doctor prescribed anti-depressants, Em."

"I doubt that's it. Oran said the pills made him feel like a zombie and he threw them away. He'd had enough of doctors. I really believe the reunion gave him a chance to strut his stuff."

I wheeled the Toyota into the restaurant lot and parked near the entrance.

"You're probably right, Em." I sure as hell hoped so. It was after seven in the evening and my stomach rumbled. "Let's have some dinner."

Chapter Twenty

Sunday, July 2, 7:15 p.m.

WE WERE SEATED at a waterside table on the veranda of the Red Clay Restaurant. A boisterous crowd filled the air with banter and merriment. Below us, the Vermilion River meandered slowly toward Lake Erie, wind gusts carving Vs in the brick-colored water.

The endless parade of sail and powerboats fascinated me, and I wished that Emily could see it. The aromas from the kitchen, however, captured her attention. I read her the entire menu twice before she finally selected the sesame-crusted wasabi tuna over orzo. I ordered the seafood pasta in a cream sauce. The meal would max out my already crippled credit card, and soon I'd be borrowing from Saint Peter to pay Saint Paul, but I didn't care.

Our waitress delivered luscious salads and steaming-hot bread wrapped in a navy-blue cloth. We played the what-ever-happened-to game, and Emily updated me on long-forgotten classmates. Then, with a glass of chardonnay in hand, she talked about the joys and trials of mentoring foreign-born interns, their cultural hurdles, lack of local family support, and the complexities of learning medicine in a second language.

When dinner arrived, I said a blessing and offered to cut her food. Emily refused. She ran a finger around the edge of her plate and I confirmed the position of each item. Then I sat transfixed as she wielded knife and fork by touch and memory alone. The woman was still fiercely independent.

A faint flickering of lightning on the western horizon caught my attention. I never heard the thunder, but apparently Emily did.

"Is it going to rain again, Jake?"

"I don't think so. Not for a while, anyway."

"Good, I hate rain. Crowded rooms and traffic noise too. They make it hard to hear. My ears are the only eyes I have."

"What else do you *hate*?"

"Icy sidewalks, of course. Cooking's difficult for me, that's why I eat in the cafeteria a lot. And I want to strangle people who are rude because my disability *inconveniences* them. But mostly, I can't stand being reliant on others for little things, like when there's toothpaste on my face, my blouse is buttoned wrong, or worse, partly unbuttoned. My coffee maker leaked last month, and I felt completely helpless. And it's impossible to multitask anymore, because I have to listen and think before I do anything."

"How do you do it, Em, deal with …."

"The blindness? It's all about keeping a sense of humor and perspective. Otherwise I'd be a raving lunatic."

I smiled. "And what do you *love*, Em?"

"Besides spending more time with Dad? Sleeping. Definitely sleeping." She sighed. "Because my dreams are vivid and in full color."

A quartet at the nearby yacht club filled the evening with velvet blues, and we stopped to listen as fading sunlight transformed the river into liquid gold. Our waitress lit the table candle and its flame danced to the music.

Slowly, the conversation grew more personal, and all our years apart fell away. I realized how much I missed her friendship.

Emily removed her sunglasses. She was still beautiful. The faint lines at the corners of her eyes were her one concession to time. She raised her wine glass like a wish and leaned her head back.

"Do you ever wonder what might have happened if you'd gone to Canada instead of Vietnam?"

"Every day, Em."

"Who knows? We might be living together in Toronto."

And there it was, the truth I'd never permitted myself to contemplate, let alone utter. Her words uncorked forgotten emotions that bubbled to the surface like fine champagne. It felt intoxicating and exhilarating. I gazed at her lips, remembering a passionate embrace at our junior prom. I wanted to hold her in my arms and kiss her.

Not only *intoxicating* and *exhilarating*, but also stupid, pointless, and masochistic. The barbs of first love were buried deep, but why spend time with her again rekindling desires that could never be fulfilled? Was I deceiving Emily, the Church, or myself? I'd been a priest for only a short time and was still wet behind the ears with the oil of ordination. I wondered if all new priests struggled on their lonely, spiritual journey through this secular world, or if my commitment to the Lord was simply flawed and fragile.

Her hand found mine and squeezed it. "Jake? Talk to me."

And I did. Once the flood gates of truth were opened, there was no stopping either of us. For twenty minutes, we spoke in the easy rhythm of our lost youth, sharing dreams and desires, struggles and triumphs, wishes and wants.

I felt happier than I had in years. Strange, though. When I'd first been assigned to town, I wanted nothing more than to flee the dark memories lurking in the shadows. Now, with Tree and Emily back in my life, Oberlin was beginning to feel like home again. Maybe, if I could fill the pews at the church and make myself indispensable at the hospital, Bishop Lucci would ask me to stay.

The lingering question of why Emily hadn't written back to me when I was young and scared and trapped in a bloody overseas war, however, kept circling the back of my mind like a homing pigeon. For a moment, it landed on my tongue and I nearly released it from its decade's long cage, then slammed my lips shut. No matter how I phrased the question, it would sound like an accusation and most likely destroy our lovely evening together and probably our renewed friendship. That was the last thing I wanted. Perhaps, after our budding relationship blossomed, it would be safe to ask her. Not tonight.

For her part, she was generous enough not to mention my transgression—my affair with Marisa in high school. But I'd owed her an apology for years. Finally, I gathered my courage and said, "I'm glad we found each other again, Em. I know you can never forgive my betrayal with—"

She held up a hand. "Don't, Jake. I already have. That was a long time ago."

As her forgiveness washed over me, I felt newly baptized and absolved of my sins.

The quartet fired up a jazz number, and I slid my chair next to hers. We savored the last of our wine as the sax player made Charlie Parker proud, and the gilded sky slowly changed to silver and finally to amethyst.

Our waitress brought the check, snapping me back to reality. I handed her my credit card. Emily objected.

"No, Jake. Dutch treat." She pulled a twenty and two fives from her purse. Her disability was no match for her organization. "Will thirty dollars be enough?"

I started to protest, then conceded. After all, this wasn't a date—merely two friends having dinner. And I'd learned long ago not to provoke this woman. A lioness lurked within.

Halfway back to Lorain, Emily said, "It's so bizarre to think that someone we know might be a murderer."

I was mellow from the wine and pleasant conversation, and had hoped not to discuss death again tonight.

"Terrifying and surreal, Em."

"One of Tree's patrolmen came by today and questioned me about the reunion." She turned toward me. "He asked if I'd ever been threatened, or if I had any enemies. I'm scared, Jake."

Worry veiled her face, and she appeared close to tears. I thought about the ominous note on our table, but feared that mentioning it would distress her even more. My head said that it couldn't have been intended for this gentle, blind woman, but my gut wasn't as certain.

"What'd you tell the police?"

"There's nothing to tell, Jake. Who'd want to hurt me?" She sniffled, then said, "I did mention the phone calls."

"What calls?"

"Two strange hang-ups on my answering machine the night of the reunion."

"Strange? In what way?"

"They came a few minutes apart. A male voice only said, 'Emily,' then there was raspy breathing and he hung up. Probably nothing, but after all that's happened …." She faced forward again. "The officer's questions made no sense. He asked if I knew Joanetta Carter, the dead woman at the quarry. When I said I didn't, he wanted to know if I disliked Barb Dorfman. I admitted I did and he hounded me about Barb for ten minutes. Finally, he asked about large donations Everett made to charities the day he was shot, including a check to the Society for the Blind. How would I know? We've been divorced for years, and I hadn't seen him in months." Her expression darkened. "Jake, you don't think the police suspect me?"

"I'm certain they don't." As for the donation, I didn't have a clue. Emily had spoken about McDermott's generosity to orphaned children, but I couldn't imagine him donating money in her honor unless he was trying to get back in her good graces. He hadn't acted the least bit interested in her at the reunion. I added, "Maybe Everett was being thoughtful, showing his respect for you."

The comment was so ludicrous that anyone who knew McDermott would have scoffed—anyone except Emily. She nodded. Maybe she still saw him as a diamond in the rough.

With far more questions than answers, we retreated into silence. I turned on a soft-rock station. After a few minutes, Emily said, "The Northern Ohio Youth Orchestra is giving a concert at Oberlin College on Thursday night. I'd like to hear them. Want to go?"

"It's a da—" I recovered immediately. "It's a … definite possibility. I work till five. We could have dinner first."

"Great. And Jake …. Dutch treat."

"Of course."

The instrumental Muzak version of "Precious and Few," complete with a full string section, floated from the radio. I lowered the volume, but not fast enough. The warmth of her embrace as we slow-danced to the song yesterday came roaring back.

Lead us not into temptation.

I wavered for a moment, then said, "I heard that Sonny Geraci and Climax are reuniting for a concert this September in Cleveland. Would you be interested?"

"Do you think you'll still be in town then?"

"God only knows. Well, God and Bishop Lucci."

"If you're still here, Jake, then yes. I'd love to go."

I parked the car in the hospital garage and removed my purchase from the backseat, wishing I'd gift-wrapped it. I opened the passenger door.

"This is for you. It's the audio version of *Devil's Passage.*"

She faltered briefly before taking it. Was giving her a present inappropriate? Had I crossed some sort of line?

"Thank you."

"Something wrong, Em?"

"No, nothing's wrong. It's just that … Oran already gave me a CD. I helped him write and revise the book, remember? But this was very considerate of you. Thanks for thinking of me. Our library can always use another audiobook."

We entered the hospital, and I walked with her to the women's residence hall. She fumbled with her keys, pausing for a moment. "Do you want to come up for coffee?"

I hesitated, maybe a little too long. "No, sorry, I can't. I have to get going."

"Well, I have something for you too. Do you have a moment?"

"Sure."

She opened the door and disappeared. I stood there for a few minutes with the awkward anticipation of a teen waiting for his date. When she returned, she handed me a folded sheet of paper.

"I've been working on this poem for a while, but this morning's storm, with those huge scattered raindrops, gave me the twist I needed." She smiled up at me. "Isn't it funny how sometimes things just fall into place? Let me know what you think."

"Thanks. I'm glad you're still writing poetry, Em. And thanks for tonight."

"Take care." She touched my arm. "I'll see you on Thursday for the concert."

I watched her leave, unfolded the paper, and read:

SQUALL

You sense sharp edges
in the air, the aroma
of rot and renewal, a chill
in the restive wind, yet

this summer rainstorm is all bluster.
Silence explodes, not in thunder,
but the popping of plump raindrops,
like ripe tomatoes smacking pavement

with the sting of hurled insults,
the drops so far apart
the memory lingers on the sidewalk
in a mosaic of wet and dry.

Then, with a distant flash,
a low rumble
more groan than growl,
it's gone—

like anger
after a spat
over nothing important,
the concrete already drying.

Was this a poem about a cloudburst, or old wounds healing?
A confusing surge of hope and helplessness washed over me.

She had said, "Let me know what you think."

I couldn't tell her what I thought or what I really felt. I wasn't sure. She was forbidden fruit—and I had a mouth-watering desire for the taste of apples.

Sleep did not come easily that night.

Chapter Twenty-One

Monday, July 3, 5:00 a.m.

Kenny Babcock leans his rifle against a tree, lights a doobie, takes a hit. He releases the smoke and a stream of urine into the jungle. A bell clangs in the distance, followed by an explosion. The bell peals again as gunfire erupts. A bush becomes a VC soldier, his laugh bitter. He draws his weapon, fires, and Kenny dissolves into a puddle of blood, seeping into the undergrowth.

Clang. Clang. The bell tolls over and over again.

* * *

The grandfather clock in the living room chimed me to consciousness, the fifth stroke echoing in the darkness.

I sat up in bed, dizzy and drenched in cold sweat. *Sweet Jesus.* How many times would that dream force me to relive that moment?

There would be no more sleep for me this morning. Morpheus had left the building. I rolled out of bed, recited psalms from my Breviary, showered, and dressed. After a bowl of cereal, I drove to my appointment at St. Joseph's Hospital. As I maneuvered through the maze of hallways, the PA speakers came alive with a female voice.

"It's seven o'clock. Time for the morning prayer." A momentary silence. "Our Father, Who art in Heaven, hallowed be Thy name. Thy kingdom come, Thy will be done …."

All movement of people and gurneys in the corridor ceased as if someone had pushed the pause button on a movie. Non-Catholics and first-time visitors probably found this ritual peculiar. I considered it reassuring. Grounding. A reminder that those of us in the medical profession were merely assistants of the true Great Healer.

When the prayer ended, I made the Sign of the Cross and continued down the hall. A new assignment always filled my belly with butterflies, and they fluttered wildly as I entered the hospital administrator's office.

Harvey Winer wore an impeccably tailored blue suit, matching silk tie, and a yarmulke that partially covered his bald spot. His large earlobes drooped like melted candle wax.

He greeted me warmly and handed me a white lab coat with "Dr. Austin" embroidered over the pocket. After we'd signed the hospital employment contract and legal papers, he snapped my photograph. Within minutes, he produced a red staff ID badge with my image on it and clipped it to my coat.

"There, now you're official." He opened the office door. "This should be interesting. I've shepherded more physicians and priests through these halls than I can count, but never anyone who was both. You may need occupational bifocals, Dr. Austin. Or two heads."

"Same head, just two hats. And please call me Jake."

"I'm Harvey." Winer gestured to his right. "The wards are this way."

Wards? That politically incorrect term had vanished decades ago, but as we navigated the corridors, the word seemed appropriate. I'd trained in hospitals similar to St. Joe's. They were filled with refurbished equipment, like hand-me-down organs transplanted into a decrepit body. Even the institutional gray walls were the color of an old person's skin. It was the last hope of the indigent in the county. The facility should have been renamed: *St. No-Where-Else-To-Go.*

Although he was near retirement age, Winer marched through the hospital with the vigor of a teenager, greeting everyone he met by name.

"Pharmacy's to the right, Jake. Doctor's lounge to your left. It's stocked with fresh doughnuts each morning." He grinned. "Get there early if you want one. Surgeons are competitive creatures, and they gobble them up fast."

Like a tornado, Winer spun through the hospital, gesturing and joking. He found humor in nearly everything. His manicured, frost-white beard and rosy complexion brought the phrase "a right jolly old elf" to mind.

We stopped at the intersection of two hallways.

"That's our auditorium," Winer said. "Grand Rounds are held there on the first Monday of each month. Today, in fact. We present difficult and interesting teaching cases to the interns and residents. And Liver Rounds is the last Friday of the month in the faculty lounge."

"Liver Rounds?"

"An essential hospital function. Everyone gets together over cocktails to brag about their accomplishments as they pickle their livers." He lowered his voice and assumed a self-deprecating expression. "And to complain about the administration." Winer waved an index finger in the air. "The most important get-together, however, is poker night at my place on the second Saturday. Do you play?"

"I haven't in years."

"Perfect. Then come, and bring plenty of money. Maybe you can *borrow* from the collection plate, Father. Think of it as a charitable contribution to the retirement fund for underpaid hospital administrators."

We took an elevator to the second floor. As we exited, a young man in surgical scrubs sprinted past us, carrying a bag of blood. We stepped back to avoid collision.

"These are the medical wards, Jake." We heard raised voices to our left and turned. Winer whispered, "Fantastic. We're in time for the show. Watch this."

A door burst open, and a tall string bean of a man powered into the hall like the prow of a ship, parting nurses and orderlies. Four white-coated interns trailed in his wake. He sported a Van Dyke beard below a handlebar mustache, which he twirled almost continuously. He lectured his entourage in a loud, theatrical voice. When one of his charges waved at a cute nurse, he stopped mid-stride and his voice became a growl.

"Stay focused, Chan. Eyes on the prize. This isn't anatomy class … or date night. Do it again and I'll double your night call."

"That's the illustrious Dr. Phineas Byrd," Winer said. "Chief of Internal Medicine and president of the Medical Staff."

And according to Emily, the physician Oran Burke had sued for malpractice over his wife's death.

Winer whispered, "Dr. Byrd's brilliance is exceeded only by his arrogance and ferocity. He demands perfection. Mistakes are not tolerated. They call him, 'The Vulture,' and I think he's circling."

Without warning, Byrd whirled and swooped toward one of his minions. "No excuses, Palikar. While you're on my service, you'll memorize every lab value and know all the details of your patients' lives, down to whether they prefer their groceries in paper or plastic. I'll see you in my office after rounds. Now, get out of my sight."

Byrd and his interns darted into a patient's room, leaving a stunned Dr. Palikar alone in the hallway.

"The Vulture will pick their bones clean by noon. Our young doctors may look as bright and shiny as their recently minted MD degrees, Jake, but they're just fresh meat to him. Not good to draw Dr. Byrd as your first rotation out of medical school."

And it wasn't good for patients either, I thought, when hospitals harvested their yearly crop of interns each July 1st and Rookie Roulette began—a bit like Russian Roulette, with the chambers loaded with inexperienced trainees staffing an unfamiliar facility. Patients were especially at risk on the July 4th holiday, when faculty and upper-level residents fled the hospital for time off with their families, leaving the rookies with minimal backup, and the patients vulnerable.

Winer offered me a piece of paper.

"Here's your schedule, Jake. You'll be working Urgent Care this month. You want the good news first, or the bad?"

"The good. Always the good."

"I've arranged it so that you never have to work Sundays, Christmas, Easter, or Holy Days. You're also off duty this Fourth of July."

Thank God for that.

"The bad news is that the staff doctor scheduled to work overnight this evening is ill. I can't find a replacement, so you're on call tonight until Tuesday morning."

Winer handed me a pager and I clipped it to my belt.

"Thanks a bunch, Harvey. Nothing like leaving the new staff doc to backstop a bunch of green interns who can't find the john without a map. Heck, I don't know where the bathrooms are. This should make for a long night and very little sleep."

Winer shrugged. He dodged two women delivering breakfast trays and led me to the nursing station for introductions. We paused when a roly-poly man, as wide as he was tall, ambled into the corridor. He came to a stop and his interns formed a circle around him as he quoted a series of medical articles.

"Read the November issue of *Radiology* by Haaga, et. al. on Menghini needle biopsies. Page four-oh-five. And the May issue of the *British Journal* proves beyond any doubt that …."

Pens fluttered on paper. The young doctors' eyes glowed like newly lit candles, their ears open shells, ready to collect every pearl of wisdom their mentor offered.

"That's MD Taylor, MD—our renowned chairman of Neurology. He's a skillful doctor and a born teacher." Winer chuckled softly. "Even his initials tell you he was destined to be a physician."

"We've met." Outside of Oran Burke's hospital room. "He's caring for a friend of mine."

Dr. Byrd returned, churning past the nursing station with his interns streaming behind him. The tall, thin, impeccable Byrd offered a strange contrast with the round and rumpled Dr. Taylor.

The loud speaker on the wall came to life. "Grand Rounds will begin in the auditorium in ten minutes."

"Taylor's presenting. Join us." Winer clapped me on the back. "And Jake, welcome to St Joe's."

Chapter Twenty-Two

———•———

Monday, July 3, 8:00 a.m.

M Y LONG WHITE coat and red staff badge had transformed me from Father Jake into Dr. Austin. I took a seat next to Harvey Winer in the back row of the auditorium. Interns and residents streamed in, switched their beepers to vibrate, and collapsed into soft seats. Their short, white coats and blue nametags indicated their low rung on the hospital totem pole. Many looked disheveled, having just finished twenty-four-hour shifts. Some dozed off.

A young man stepped up to the microphone. He was as lean as a greyhound, probably from missed meals, long hours, and the physical demands of caring for sick patients. *Intern* and *resident* were simply modern terms for indentured servant.

He tapped the mic and said, "I'm Neil Katkey, second-year resident. I'll be presenting with Dr. Taylor this morning."

An image of St. Joseph's Hospital appeared on the projection screen.

Katkey shuffled some papers. "Our patient, EC, is an eleven-year-old Hispanic female with a chief complaint of progressive lower extremity weakness and tingling paresthesias, which began two days ago. Upon examination, she was unsteady, with a wide-based, tentative gait. Initial history and physical exam were otherwise unremarkable. We admitted her to Pediatrics and consulted Dr. Taylor in Neurology."

He pushed a button, and the results of extensive blood work replaced the photograph of the hospital.

"As you can see, her labs were unremarkable except for a slightly elevated white blood cell count. Imaging was also inconclusive." He flashed through a series of X-rays and MRIs.

Dr. Taylor approached and the room lights came on. He carried himself with the same air of self-importance that he had displayed when I'd first met him at Oran Burke's hospital room. His involvement suggested that Oran's collapse at the reunion might have been due to an underlying neurologic disorder, but patient privacy laws would keep him from being forthright with me about the cause.

Taylor touched his young resident on the arm and said, "Let's stop for a moment, Dr. Katkey, and field some questions." He turned to the audience and pointed to his right. "Yes, you there."

A dark-skinned man in a turban stood. "Should we not be considering genetic and infectious causes?" he asked, his accent thick. "Are any relatives affected?"

"Her family history is unremarkable," Taylor replied, "and none of her close contacts are ill. CSF was normal, and we found no evidence of active systemic infection. Next. Yes, over here."

A series of questions followed, some thoughtful, others just wild guesses. The answer to each was the same. Negative. When no more hands waved, the room lights dimmed again, and Neil Katkey resumed his slide show. A few more interns slumped into dreamland. Vibrating pagers occasionally droned like cicadas on a summer night.

When Katkey finished his presentation, Dr. Taylor took command.

"Since admission, EC's arms have become weak, her speech slurred, and she's more disoriented. Her legs are now completely paralyzed." He motioned to his left, the room brightened, and a nurse entered the stage, pushing a young girl in a wheelchair. A frazzled woman trailed after them. When she saw Taylor, she rushed to him and clutched his coat sleeve.

"Please, doctor, you save my baby! You heal my Esperanza, no?"

Taylor whispered in her ear and guided her to a chair. He then performed a neurological examination on the girl, highlighting teaching points and demonstrating profound paralysis in her legs and early weakness in her arms.

He stepped forward. "All right, diagnosis?"

The man in the turban rose again. "I am thinking botulism poisoning, perhaps?"

"You're right, Dr. Ahmadi, botulism can produce a similar picture," Taylor replied. "We investigated that and ruled it out. Other ideas?"

Harvey Winer tapped me on the shoulder and whispered, "You're frowning, Jake. Not buying it? Feel free to play *Let's Make a Diagnosis* along with the studio audience."

"It's too soon for a diagnosis. They haven't asked enough questions yet."

After a few suggestions, a dark-haired woman in a red and gold sari stood.

"Given the ascending nature of her symptoms, must we not consider Guillain-Barré?"

"Excellent, Dr. Patel. Guillain-Barré Syndrome is the most likely possibility." The crowded room had become warm, and Taylor patted his brow with a handkerchief. "We've discussed using a ventilator if her respiratory muscles weaken further, and we'll move EC to—"

"You no call her EC!" The girl's mother leaped to her feet. "Her name Esperanza. Esperanza Cisneros." She steepled her shaking hands in prayer position and raised them to her lips. "She my baby!"

"Quite right, Mrs. Cisneros. Esperanza it is." Taylor shifted his gaze to the audience. "As I was saying, we'll move Esperanza to ICU today." He lowered his voice. "Given the ominous progression of symptoms, her prognosis is, needless to say, extremely guarded."

He thanked the mother and daughter for their participation, and the nurse began escorting them from the stage.

Winer leaned over. "Still frowning, Jake? Any thoughts?"

"A couple." I cleared my throat. "Dr. Taylor, may I ask a few questions?"

"Certainly." Taylor squinted and peered toward the rear of the auditorium. "Ah, Dr. Austin. We meet again." He motioned for the nurse to remain. "Ask away."

I rose to my feet. "Does Esperanza live out in the country, near a woods?"

The girl's mother shook her head.

"Does she have dogs or other outdoor pets?"

Another headshake.

"Has she traveled out of the city recently?"

Esperanza's mother looked up and said, "We just come from Virginia. A cabin in mountains."

"Has Esperanza been examined for ticks?"

Taylor sagged against the lectern. "Oh my God!"

The focus of the room rocketed in my direction, then boomeranged back to the stage.

"Well, Katkey, did you check for ticks?" Taylor asked so loudly that his microphone screeched feedback.

The young man's face flushed, and he fumbled with the hospital chart. "The pediatric intern did the admission physical, sir," he stuttered. "I only did a neurologic exam. I wasn't thinking about … never—"

"Somebody give me a damn comb!" Taylor demanded. He nearly tumbled from the edge of the stage as he grabbed one from a woman in the first row.

He combed slowly and meticulously, section by section,

through Esperanza's long, black hair. The auditorium became as silent as a morgue.

Taylor froze. "Get me tweezers and a specimen jar!" Several short white coats flew out the door. Whispers hissed through the audience like a lit fuse and many of the staff rose, craning for a better view. Taylor produced a small camera from his lab coat, snapped three quick photos, and returned it to his pocket without taking his eyes off the girl's head.

"Tweezers," Taylor said, reaching out. A young woman raced down the aisle and slapped them into the palm of his hand. "Esperanza, please hold very still."

In slow motion, he reached behind her right ear. The child flinched slightly but remained silent. He carefully removed an engorged tick and placed it in a specimen jar. Esperanza looked up at him, fear in her eyes. Taylor heaved a loud sigh and turned his attention to the auditorium.

"Damn fine call, Dr. Austin. Damn fine." Taylor used the sleeve of his coat to wipe sweat from his forehead. "I've read about tick paralysis, but never had a case."

"I trained in the Carolinas. Lots of ticks there." I shrugged. "It's easier to diagnose if you've seen one."

Taylor pointed in my direction and said, "And he's modest too. May I speak with you afterward, Dr. Austin?"

I nodded.

"Okay, everyone, be seated." Taylor straightened his white coat and gathered his composure. "This is why we hold Grand Rounds—to bring the collective mind of the hospital to bear on difficult cases. And to teach. You've just witnessed a *facinoma*—a disease both rare and fascinating."

He knelt by the wheelchair and whispered in the girl's ear. She smiled weakly.

Taylor approached her mother. "What this all means, Mrs. Cisneros, is that your daughter's going to be fine. She'll be dancing in a week. I'll explain things—"

He never got to finish. Esperanza's mother bear-hugged Taylor, squeezing him like a plump cantaloupe.

"You save my baby? Thank the Lord!" Tears poured down her cheeks. She released Taylor and pointed heavenward. "Jesus saved my baby. Thank you, Jesus!"

Harvey Winer uttered a hearty laugh and whispered, "If they only knew how close to the truth that is, *Father*. You make one heck of a first impression. Guess I won't have to introduce you to anyone. You'll be a legend by lunchtime." His beeper chirped. "Thank you, Jesus, indeed," he added, chuckling as he left to answer his page.

When the nurse wheeled Esperanza offstage, Dr. Taylor stepped forward.

"Before we go further, think about how close this child came to disaster. Consider what can happen if you do a half-assed physical exam and are not on your toes every day." Taylor pointed at his young charges. "We are medical detectives." He paused for effect, raised the plastic comb in the air, and grinned. "Sometimes you literally have to *comb* for evidence."

The horrible pun drew a chorus of groans, much to Taylor's delight.

"The good news is that once you've removed the source of the toxin," he pointed at the specimen jar, "the patient usually begins to improve within hours." He wiped more perspiration from his face. "Now for some old-fashioned medical education. See one, do one, teach one. Ticks cause Lyme disease, Rocky Mountain spotted fever, and on rare occasions, paralysis, especially in children." Taylor held up the specimen jar. "Read the January issue of the *New England Journal of Medicine* by Felz et. al. on tick paralysis. Now, let's talk dog ticks and deer ticks. *Ixodes scapularis* can …."

As Taylor continued his professorial drone, Harvey Winer entered the auditorium.

"I had two messages, both for you, Jake. Bishop Lucci needs to see you this morning. ASAP. I'll tell Urgent Care you'll be late." He wrinkled his brow. "And I don't know how you managed it, but you've already angered the chief of medicine.

Dr. Byrd wants you in his office tomorrow morning. Something about harassment of the Radiology staff, misrepresenting your hospital privileges, and hijacking control of the CT scanner. Byrd sounded livid. Be careful, Jake. The Vulture is circling you."

Chapter Twenty-Three

Monday, July 3, 9:00 a.m.

I HAD ASSUMED the Radiology Department would go on the attack today, but I'd hoped they would speak directly to me about Father LaFontaine's treatment before complaining to Dr. Byrd. I felt badly about coercing a colleague into working during his vacation, but the private lives of all medical professionals are often infringed upon. Relieving LaFontaine's pain was worth any punishment Byrd might dole out.

When Dr. Taylor finished his lecture on tick-borne diseases, I rose from my seat and joined him on the auditorium stage.

"Ah, Dr. Austin." We exchanged handshakes. "I'm Marcus Taylor."

"Yes, I remember. Please call me Jake."

"Thanks for your help with Esperanza. I'm embarrassed I didn't make the diagnosis. But you know the old adage: 'When you hear hoof beats, think horses, not zebras.' I focused on the more common diseases and missed the rare cause of her symptoms." Taylor produced a handkerchief and mopped his brow. "I heard the hoofs pounding, expected ponies, and a damn zebra ran right past me."

"I'm just glad I could help."

"We all sometimes forget that so-called 'all natural' things like some mushrooms, pretty oleander blossoms, and nasty little bugs," he pointed at the tick, "can be deadly. And today was a stark reminder that I sometimes depend too much on the residents and forget how inexperienced they are. Guess my *new* adage is: 'Don't even rule out unicorns till the dust settles.'" He shrugged. "Nice call, Jake. I'm in your debt."

What better time to collect than now?

"So, you work at Oberlin Hospital too? How's Oran doing?"

"I have consulting privileges there," Taylor replied. "Mr. Burke is stable. I discharged him yesterday."

"Please help me understand, Marcus. Oran's injuries weren't serious enough to warrant a hospital admission. Especially by a neurologist. What's going on?"

Taylor's eyes darkened.

"If you're asking as his friend, you know I can't discuss his case with you." He picked up the specimen jar and stared at the tick. Filled with blood, it resembled a large bean with legs. Taylor's lower lip curled between his teeth. He glanced both ways across the empty stage and lowered his voice. "But if you're asking me as a physician and colleague, I guess I can tell you that Oran Burke has been my patient for six months." A pause. "He's in the early stages of Huntington's chorea."

My gut tightened.

Huntington's? I hadn't thought about that cruel disease in years. Long-forgotten medical-school lectures drifted back. One aberrant gene, dormant for decades, reactivated in adulthood, causing unrelenting mental and physical deterioration and ruthless progression to complete incapacity and death. Maybe there would be a cure someday, but not in 2002, and not for the foreseeable future.

Huntington's disease accounted for the bizarre writhing neck movements I had witnessed at the reunion and the unsteady gait I'd misinterpreted as substance abuse. It also explained Oran's tremors, his jagged handwriting, and the mood swings that Emily had described. Like Dr. Taylor, I'd heard hoof beats, expected horses, and failed to see the zebra. Huntington's disease. I should have put it all together!

"Does Oran understand what this means?"

"Oh, he knows and comprehends fully," Taylor replied. "Mr. Burke is an exceptionally intelligent man."

Chapter Twenty-Four

———•———

Monday, July 3, 9:15 a.m.

DRIVING ALONG I-90, I changed mental gears from Oran Burke's disease to my appointment with Bishop Lucci. The parish's old Toyota shifted less smoothly, grinding and lurching. July heat had Ohio in a death grip, and the air conditioner merely whirred and rattled, so I rolled down the windows. It didn't help. The idea of a daily thirty-minute commute in this car through sweltering summer heat between the church in Oberlin and the hospital in Lorain was depressing. With Sacred Heart parish currently operating in the red, I hoped His Excellency would be willing to fund the repairs on this rolling junk heap.

Exiting the interstate, I navigated a crosshatch of streets named after dead Ohio-born presidents. McKinley led to Hayes, where the paint and American dream faded from matchbox-sized houses jammed closer together than teeth. On Grant, pawn shops and vacant lots replaced the homes, and the American dream became a nightmare. I passed a gang of kids flying blue Crips colors, locked the car doors, sped along

Garfield to East 9th Street, and parked near the Diocese of Cleveland's administrative building.

The only occupants in the lobby were four life-sized, ceramic saints with angelic faces. As I crossed to the directory of names on the wall, my footsteps echoed from the polished marble. The Church hierarchy apparently extended to office space—the loftier your status, the higher your floor. The bishop's penthouse suite was located at the very top, just below Heaven. A richly appointed, wood-paneled elevator opened, but it was as tiny and suffocating as a coffin inside, so I opted for the stairs, humming "Nearer, My God, To Thee" as I climbed.

The Most Reverend Antonio Lucci's antechamber was a study in opulence. The vaulted ceiling and hardwood floors conveyed a sense of wealth and power. Oriental rugs dampened sound, imparting the aura of a cathedral.

In contrast to Order priests like myself, Lucci was a Diocesan priest and had taken no vow of poverty. The room, however, was far too extravagant and wasteful, given the obvious need in this neighborhood and throughout the world. I was less comfortable in this monument to excess than in the homes of the sick or the chaos of an emergency room.

No one in my Camillian Order had explained why I'd been assigned to the Diocese of Cleveland and placed in the hands of their bishop, only that the directive had come from "the top." I felt like a ballplayer who'd been traded to the Tokyo Swallows, about to enter his first game in a foreign land.

Elegantly framed paintings of pastoral scenes adorned one wall. Portraits of every Cleveland bishop lined another, dating back to Louis Amadeus Rappe in 1847. Lucci's image suggested a well-fed, forbidding man.

A large oil painting on an adjacent wall, however, shouldn't have been there. The image of my boss, the Very Reverend Father Stefano Demarco, appraised the room with a knowing smile. He wore our traditional cassock emblazoned with a red cross.

Somehow, Bishop Lucci and my Superior General were connected. Maybe that explained why I'd been sent to fill in here. Demarco had ridden the Vatican fast track and acquired almost as much influence in Rome as the "Black Pope," the head of the Jesuits, who bore that nickname because he wore his black robes and vast power openly.

I thought I caught the aroma of church politics.

The waiting room receptionist noticed me and pointed to a chair, then busied herself by touching up her makeup and curtly dispatching the occasional telephone caller. An hour after my arrival, she finally raised a small bell from her desk, jiggled it, and broke the silence.

"His Excellency will see you now." She returned her attention to her fingernails.

Carved human figures representing the Stations of the Cross adorned the paired oak doors leading to the bishop's inner sanctum. I muscled one open and entered a cavernous office lined with hundreds of bound volumes. The scent of leather vied with the sweet smell of pipe tobacco. Ornate crown molding and wainscoting added frosting to the rich décor. Except for the cream-colored walls, the room's primary color was scarlet, down to the matting on photographs of the pope, suggesting that the bishop had aspirations to the office of cardinal.

An obese Antonio Lucci sat at a tennis-table-sized desk, raised up on a carpeted platform. Moses on the mountain. His enormous robes overflowed the chair. He wore the violet zucchetto skull cap and purple sash indicative of his rank. A large pectoral cross encrusted with gemstones hung from a gold chain around his neck. Without glancing up, he scribbled furiously with one hand and motioned with the other toward a chair.

Finally, Lucci shoved the paperwork into his outbox, gazed down at me, and shook his head, his wattle and jowls wobbling.

"What in God's good name am I supposed to do with you,

Father Austin?" he began, forgoing any pleasantries. "You don't even *look* like a priest."

"I'm sorry, Your Excellency. I came directly from the hospital and didn't have time to change clothes."

"In my diocese, we are more ... *conventional.*" A shaft of sunlight emerged from behind a cloud, streamed through his window, and illuminated him like a chubby cherub in a Raphael painting. "In the future, you will dress appropriately, including a Roman collar."

He removed tortoise-shell glasses, rubbed his eyes, and picked up a manila folder.

"I must say, your background is both unusual and disturbing. It looks as if you've spent your entire life wandering like a lost sheep. I know I'm a *good shepherd*, but really ...." He grinned, amused by his own wit. "So many false starts, so many U-turns. As aimlessly adrift as a ship without a rudder," he added with a practiced weariness.

"I guess that's true. It took me a while to discover who I am, who I want to be."

Lucci had the build and comportment of a bull, and he snorted as if deciding whether to charge. "God help me, another of the sixties generation *finding* himself."

He returned his glasses to his nose, the thick lenses magnifying the bags under his eyes. He opened the folder and shuffled the papers.

"Let's see ... first, a soldier. Then educated by those liberal Jesuits at Xavier University." Lucci grunted his disapproval. "Followed by medical school and a residency at the VA."

"I served as a medic in the war, so med school was the logical next step, and—"

"Yes, yes." Lucci flipped to the next page and ran a sausage-shaped finger down it several times like a bull pawing the ground. "After that, the Army Medical Corps, honorable discharge, then private practice. And finally the priesthood. Correct?"

"Correct."

"And your hospital income?"

"It all goes to the Camillian Order. I'm allowed a small monthly stipend."

Lucci frowned, and his demeanor grew cooler. He waved my file.

"This is all terribly interesting, but *not* why we're here."

He leaned forward, his great bulk shaking like gelatin as his belly collided with the desk. His eyes widened and the bull charged.

"From trained killer, to healer, to priest?" His voice rose an octave. "Nursing bodies back to health wasn't enough? Now you want to mend souls?"

Blood rushed to my cheeks. "Your Excellency, the soul and body are intertwined, braided into who we are. I believe they both can be healed, that they—"

Lucci slammed a fat fist down, and his monogrammed gold pen jumped up from the desktop and clattered on the floor.

"And I believe in restraint and prudence. Order and priority." Ropey veins throbbed in his neck. "In my diocese, the soul trumps the body, and God's law trumps science."

So that's what this is about.

Lucci took a slow, calming breath, and his color faded from hell-fire red to rosy, as the veins receded.

"The Church has nothing against science or medical advances, Father Austin."

I thought about Galileo's lifetime house arrest, and the Church's current opposition to stem cell research, but remained silent, allowing him to continue.

"In fact, my brother survived cancer and is alive today because of the care he received from the Camillians. Their mission is a noble one, and I respect them. We Diocesan priests, on the other hand, have a simpler calling. Unlike Camillians and Jesuits, we don't have many *hyphenated* priests, as in professor-priest or physician-priest. But your medical practice … concerns me." He spun his chair around and faced the window, his voice cold. "We're here today to determine where your commitment lies, and whether allowing you into my diocese was a mistake. I need to know that the Church is your first priority."

"Of course it is."

"You see no potential conflict, then? That may be a bit naïve, Father. What about birth control and abortion? What *I see* is the potential for your actions to reflect on me. And any malpractice suits against you could spill over into lawsuits against my diocese." Lucci swiveled around and stared at me. "I pray that your ordination wasn't another of your many midlife crises."

Unable to find a comfortable position, I squirmed on the hard, wooden seat like a condemned man in the electric chair. I made my pitch for a stay of execution.

"There is no conflict, Excellency. Science and religion are simply two different ways to explain the same mystery. Joining the priesthood allowed me to help heal both a patient's body and spirit, to care for the *whole* person.

Our eyes locked and his expression hardened to stone.

"You sound more like a shaman than a doctor, mingling magic potions and faith healing."

Lucci was a ticking time bomb, and I needed to defuse him. "Bishop, everyone knows that the doctor-patient relationship is broken. Medicine has become merely a contract, an exchange of knowledge for money. It's sterile and constrained." I leaned forward. "What we need is a biblical kind of *covenant,* not a legal contract filled with loopholes. It must be a solemn unconditional promise, an indissoluble bond forged by mutual trust, one human being caring for another's body, mind, and spirit in a holistic approach. The Episcopalians already have dozens of ordained priests currently practicing medicine who—"

Lucci shook his head, light twinkling on his balding pate.

"I don't care about your personal philosophy or what the *Protestants* are doing. That sounds like *holy-istic* medicine to me, a laying on of hands, just more New Age claptrap. There's plenty of that twaddle on Sunday morning TV. Send a dollar, splash some holy water, and be healed." The bishop waved my folder in the air. "My concern is with you and … *your past*. I don't have time for damage control."

Uh-oh. Incoming. Take cover.

"A barroom brawl? Really? Lord, as if the Church doesn't have enough allegations, lawsuits, and bad press without that kind of behavior."

"When I got back from Vietnam, a hippie called me a baby killer … and spit on me." I hung my head. "I should've walked away."

"And arrested for marijuana possession? And a DUI? I have a clergy shortage, and they send me you." Lucci threw my folder on his desk and crossed his massive arms over his chest. "It's my responsibility to make sure our priests have the moral and ethical fiber to lead our parishes."

"Your Excellency, that was all twenty years ago." Back when I searched for answers in Zig-Zag rolling papers and booze bottles. "I'm an entirely different person now."

"I've heard *that* before! The Church is under a microscope, Father, so I will require random drug testing from you … until I'm comfortable."

"Of course." He'd completely drained my energy and sapped my will. And this was definitely the wrong day to ask him for car repairs. "Whatever you say."

"Let me be clear. I needed a priest, and my good friend, Stefano Demarco, suggested that you were a perfect fit, a local boy who could get up to speed fast and also treat the sick at St. Joseph's Hospital. So I permitted your transfer at his request on a trial basis."

Lucci gazed up at the crystal chandelier. "Stefano and I were seminarians together and earned our doctorates at the

Gregorian in Rome." He laughed. "Actually, I got mine and left the Greg. Stefano stayed and collected three—one apparently in ecclesiastical politics."

The church scuttlebutt was that Lucci had unexpectedly been promoted to Cleveland from an obscure post in the middle of nowhere. He'd grabbed hold of Demarco's coattails and was riding along with the Church's rising star, maybe all the way to Cardinal Archbishop of New York—with me as a potential speed bump on his journey. He didn't want me here but couldn't rebuff Demarco's generous offer and dismiss me, at least not without a good excuse.

All the years I'd spent rebuilding my life, and this man could topple my world on a whim with one phone call to my superior. I felt completely naked and vulnerable.

Lucci returned his attention to me. "Shortages of priests and inner-city doctors aside, Father, please understand my position. The priesthood is demanding enough without playing doctor. If I find you shirking your religious duties in any way, I'll pull the plug on you … in a heartbeat."

An icy smile froze on his plump, red lips. He picked up a sheaf of papers and gestured toward the door with a theatrical wave.

"You may go," he said without looking up.

I staggered to my feet and scampered from Lucci's office like a beaten dog.

Chapter Twenty-Five

---·---

Monday, July 3, 11:45 a.m.

WEARY AND BATTERED after my encounter with Bishop Lucci, I grabbed some comfort food at a McDonald's drive-through on my way back to the hospital, hoping that my next encounter with The Grand Inquisitor wouldn't involve thumbscrews and the rack.

When I arrived at St. Joe's, I threw on my white coat and hurried to the Urgent Care Center. The waiting area was sparsely furnished, the plastic chairs all occupied. The room smelled faintly of body odor. Dog-eared magazines and a few toys littered the well-worn carpet. Wile E. Coyote silently chased the Road Runner across a muted TV mounted to the wall. The air was thick with conversations in Spanish, English, and an Asian dialect. Downtown Lorain was a miniature United Nations. A short, six-block stroll from the hospital could provide a buffet of seven different languages and cuisines.

I entered the main work area and introduced myself to Susan Ochs, the supervising nurse.

"Welcome, Dr. Austin." She gestured to a young woman with

inky black hair and penetrating eyes, wearing a short white coat and blue ID badge. "Meet your intern, Dr. Ocampo."

After we exchanged pleasantries, Dr. Ocampo nodded, grabbed a chart from the rack, and entered a patient examination room.

I turned back to Nurse Ochs. "So, where do I begin?"

"You can begin by filling this," she said, handing me a specimen jar. "Urine drug test, ordered by Dr. Byrd." She raised an eyebrow.

Terrific. Double-teamed on day one by Byrd and Bishop Lucci.

Nurse Ochs waited for a response.

I shrugged. "Penance for the sins of my youth." I began to walk toward the restroom.

"One moment, please. DeQuan will observe." She pointed to a young, dark-skinned orderly. "Per Dr. Byrd's instructions."

Perfect. Nothing more humiliating than peeing in a cup with an audience. DeQuan didn't appear happy either as he followed me into the john.

A few minutes later, I returned to the nursing station and held out the container, but Ochs didn't take it.

"Put it on the cart with the other lab samples." She scowled and her lips stretched into a thin line. "Dr. Byrd's secretary called. He wants you in his office tomorrow morning at eleven. Test results, I assume."

"On July fourth? You're kidding. The chief of medicine works holidays?"

"Byrd? He's always here. No wife or kids. Arrives early, stays late. St. Joe's is his life."

"Well, if Dr. Byrd doesn't require any more of my bodily fluids, I'd better get started. Who's first?"

"I have the perfect patient for you behind door number three. Chronic back pain." Ochs gave me a wry grin. "I hear you're *into* pain, doctor."

It took a second to catch her meaning. "Yes, I have specialty training in pain management."

Mischief flashed in her eyes. "Battling both pain and the devil?"

At least someone was having fun. Clearly, rumors traveled at light speed here.

"Sometimes they're one and the same, Nurse Ochs. Pain is the devil, and the devil's a pain."

"Well, you'll need all your skill with this pain in the tush. She's a frequent flyer. Zooms from ER to ER and lands at our establishment about once a month, complaining of persistent backache. She's a relentless drug seeker with Flugal's Syndrome."

Ochs handed me a thick chart.

"Flugal's? Never heard of it. What's that?"

"It's seen in folks with severe chronic illnesses like cancer, but also in hypochondriacs and drug addicts. Flugal's Syndrome is," she smirked, "when the patient's medical record weighs more than the patient."

I hefted the chart and thumbed through reams of blood work, thousands of dollars' worth of radiology reports, and several normal physical exams.

"Back pain, huh? Has anyone talked with her about rehab?"

"Of course, though you're welcome to try again. And get this—she can't sleep because of the news stories about the recent murders, so she wants Valium too."

"What?"

"That's all the Oberlin patients talk about. And with the continuous media hype, fear is becoming epidemic. The whole county is in a panic."

"Headline-induced insomnia? Now I've heard everything."

"I doubt it—your Urgent Care shift is still young." Ochs opened the exam room door. "You got to love this job."

MY FIRST DAY in Urgent Care was uneventful. The team of Ochs, Ocampo, and Austin labored through the usual series of accidents, sad stories, and unbelievable behavior. Summer colds, fractures, a sinus infection, sprained ankles, a

skateboarding wreck, and two cases of the "dizzy-woozys"—
one, an elderly woman with vertigo due to inner ear problems,
the other a middle-aged biker with more tattoos than teeth
who'd roared up on his Harley with a blood alcohol level higher
than his IQ and three times the legal limit. Over a cup of black
coffee, I gave him a sermon about drinking and driving, and
warned him that I would have to notify the police if he got
back on his bike. He expressed his displeasure in a tirade of
four-letter words, complaining that he had no money for cab
fare. After he finally relented, I used the last of my cash to send
him home in a taxi.

When my Urgent Care shift ended at five o'clock and Dr.
Poporad arrived to relieve me, we had whittled the waiting
room down to three patients. I finished charting, drove to the
rectory, and managed to eat dinner and shower before my on-
call pager vibrated like an angry insect.

My first all-nighter backstopping the interns and residents
started quietly. I fielded a few questions about antibiotic
selection and how to proceed with abnormal lab results, but
I was consulted infrequently. Either the young house staff
working at the hospital was exceptionally competent, having a
slow night, or too cocky to ask for help.

I plopped on the living room couch and watched the Indians
game between calls. Around ten p.m., pre-July 4th gunpowder
combined with post-alcohol stupidity got the party rolling. My
phone and pager finally took a break after the eleven o'clock
news.

I retired to my bedroom, read Evening Prayers from my
Breviary, then opened Oran Burke's novel. In the first chapter, a
slave steals food from the mansion house and slips through the
moonless, Georgia darkness toward Canada and freedom. The
overseer witnesses the escape and the antebellum version of a
fox hunt begins—bloodhounds, horsemen, and a hangman's
noose in hot pursuit. As the slave crashed through swamp
water and brambles, I dozed off.

My beeper rattled me back to consciousness. The bedside clock read 2:05. I bookmarked the novel and drove to St. Joe's to perform a lumbar puncture for a resident who couldn't guide the needle past the arthritic bone spurs in an elderly man's spine.

As is often the case when the moon is full, the carnage commenced in the early morning hours. Soon, the hospital overflowed. I stayed to help an intern incise the first boil of his career, draining pus that resembled guacamole and smelled like crap. By then, the meeting of the Knife and Gun Club was in session, and ambulances unloaded at the ER entrance like Ferris wheel cars.

Exhausted and near the end of my shift, I felt my mind playing tricks. Auburn-haired women sparked thoughts of Emily. To make matters worse, all redheads reminded me of the woman who had fled the confessional, leaving me hip-deep in unanswered questions about her child's welfare, her link to me, and the volcano of violence that had erupted in our town.

Around six in the morning, things finally quieted down. My meeting with Dr. Byrd was only a few hours away, so I opted not to drive back to Oberlin. Disheveled, unshaven, and completely spent, I asked the page operator to wake me at ten and collapsed fully-clothed onto an on-call-room bed.

Chapter Twenty-Six

Tuesday, July 4, 10:00 a.m.

FROM A BAR lined with empty shot glasses, I watch Kenny Babcock leave the hooch, his mama-san clinging to him like a bronze second skin. Hoa Nho sits next to me, slowly tracing the H and N on my tattoo with her finger. She plants a long, deep kiss and whispers, "You pay now, Jake. You pay big now."

Her slap is so sudden, so hard, that my head recoils and my cheek burns. Then her face becomes Emily's face, pennies covering her eyes.

* * *

MY PAGER'S SHRIEK drove ice picks into my eardrums. As the dream faded, a curse formed on my lips, but miraculously a prayer emerged. My watch read 10:04. I had survived my first night on call at St. Joseph's Hospital.

Sitting on the edge of the bed, I felt stiff, dazed, and not quite willing to commit to the vertical position. Finally, I said my morning prayers, shook out the kinks, and headed to the cafeteria. Exiting the stairwell, I nearly collided with a young black orderly wheeling a stainless-steel cart through the hallway. He looked familiar, but I couldn't remember why. His nametag read DeQuan Kwame. Then it came back to me. He had monitored my random urine drug test in Urgent Care.

He pointed at the yellow specimen containers on his cart and whispered, "I hope I did not scare the piss out of you again." His accent was reminiscent of a British colony. "Always a pleasure to see you again, Doctor."

DeQuan clearly enjoyed my discomfort, and probably wouldn't allow my embarrassment to lapse any time soon. He chuckled, gave me an I've-seen-you-with-your-pants-down grin, and before I could respond, rumbled down the hall toward the laboratory.

Gathering what was left of my dignity, I entered the cafeteria. The coffee was free for staff members, but thick as tar and not as tasty. After a sniff and a swig, I tossed the cup into the trash and sauntered to the snack shop.

When he heard the door open, Irv Beale put on his sunglasses and stood. "Can I help you?"

"Good morning, Irv. Any young punks in here need their attitudes rearranged?"

"Ah, Jake. Morning. What'll it be?"

"A Snickers Bar and takeout coffee, please."

"What size?"

"Enormous."

"One large St. Joe's cup-of-joe to go." Irv plucked the top cup from a nested tower of Styrofoam. "Emily got all her poetic mojo from me. But of course, we in the caffeine trade call this a Grande Deluxe so we can charge more."

I opened my wallet. Empty. I'd used the last of my cash yesterday to send the drunk biker home in a cab. "Ah Irv, do you take credit cards?"

"Don't worry about it. I already told you, your money's no good here." He filled the cup and set it on the counter. "You wearing your collar and black habit this morning, Father?"

"Ah, so you've spoken with Emily. No, blue scrubs and a white coat today. I'm on my way to get my wrist slapped by Dr. Byrd for not dotting my i's and crossing my t's."

"Principal's office already, Jake? Well, some things never change." Irv laughed. "Speaking of Byrd, the strangest thing happened. I got blind-sided, so to speak, outside his office a few hours ago."

"What do you mean?"

"I always start my day with a stroll through the administration wing, past research and the lab. Nice and quiet there in the morning, and I don't disturb the patients." Irv grabbed another cup, filled it, and took a sip.

"So, what happened?"

"Hold your horses. I'm getting there." He sniffed his coffee like a fine wine. "I'm walking by the staff offices about seven and hear loud footsteps coming fast—but with this odd, clip-clop rhythm, an uneven tempo, y'know? I turn the corner and *wham*, some guy slams right into me and knocks me on my butt." Irv massaged his back and grimaced. "My lumbago's been acting up ever since. All he says is *shit*. No excuse me or nothing. You'd think he'd at least help me up and say *sorry*."

"Any idea who it was?"

Irv tipped his head to one side. "My vision's not so good, Jake, if you haven't noticed. A real little guy with a low voice, probably a damn intern."

"That describes half the house staff."

"The world's become downright uncivil, I tell you."

Irv looked as if he wanted to spit, but blew across his cup instead.

"Once upon a time, folks would help you cross the street. Nowadays, they knock you on your ass without so much as a howdy-do. You tell Dr. Byrd to teach those upstarts some manners, in addition to medicine."

"Will do, Irv." I finished the last of the candy bar, picked up my coffee, and headed for the door. "Try some ibuprofen for your backache. If you're still having pain, let me know and I'll write a prescription for something stronger."

Irv nodded and raised his cup in salute.

I left the snack shop, turned the corner, and recognized a familiar voice that resembled flute music. Drug company reps roamed hospitals like cockroaches in tenements, so I wasn't surprised to see Tanya. She was pitching her latest wonder cure to Dr. Taylor in the hallway. Her black business suit did little to conceal her stunning figure.

My flirtatious behavior on the airplane embarrassed me. Would I ever outgrow my inner teenage boy? Given the unsettling resurrection of my feelings for Emily, I doubted it. And given all that had happened since my return, part of me wished I'd never boarded the plane.

Tanya handed Taylor a box of samples, then spotted me. Her plastic saleswoman smile evaporated.

There was enough drama in my life without adding Tanya to the mix. I pretended not to notice her, slipped into a stairwell, and climbed to the administrative level.

Dr. Byrd's outer office was vacant. No surprise on a holiday. I checked the time. Eleven on the dot.

A "Do Not Disturb" sign hung from the doorknob of his room. I knocked gently. No reply. I knocked harder. Nothing.

Maybe Byrd had been up all night with a sick patient or decided to make morning rounds. *Fine by me.* I had no desire for a confrontation.

I turned to leave. The appointment calendar on his secretary's desk had JACOB AUSTIN—COERCION in large red letters in the eleven-a.m. time slot.

Byrd was already upset with me. Blowing off this meeting wouldn't help things.

I set my coffee on the desk, picked up the office phone, and asked the operator to page the chief of medicine. Within seconds, beeping echoed from Byrd's inner office.

I knocked again, got no response, and opened the door slowly.

"Hello … Dr. Byrd?"

Phineas Byrd lay face-down on the floor near his desk, his skin the color of fireplace ash. His Vandyke beard and handlebar mustache floated in a pool of vomit. An open fifth of Glenlivet had spilled onto the linoleum, and the room reeked of puke and booze. I charged in, dropped to my knees, and examined him.

Byrd had no pulse and felt cool to the touch. I yanked the stethoscope from around my neck and listened. No heartbeat, no respirations.

I rolled him onto his back, pounded his chest, and cleared vomit from his mouth before giving him two quick breaths. Then I called a Code Blue on the office phone and began the loneliest job in the world—first responder CPR. I continued until the Code Team swarmed through the door a few minutes later and took over.

Stepping out of their way, I collapsed onto Byrd's desk chair. An empty prescription bottle with the label torn off, two insulin vials, and a syringe lay on his desktop, next to a half-glass of Scotch.

The Code Team was a swirl of organized chaos. They inserted multiple intravenous lines, pushed a pharmacy of drugs, and shocked Byrd numerous times with a defibrillator until I smelled seared flesh. They even considered opening his chest right there in his office to perform cardiac massage. In the end, with a chorus of headshakes, Dr. Phineas Byrd—Chief of Medicine, President of the Medical Staff, and nationally renowned internist—was pronounced dead at 12:16 p.m. on Independence Day.

Chapter Twenty-Seven

———•———

Tuesday, July 4, 2:00 p.m.

I LEANED AGAINST the wall in the corridor while CSI techs and the Lorain PD examined Dr. Byrd's office. Exhausted from my night on call and dazed by the horrific scene I'd stumbled upon, I struggled to stay focused as a policewoman interrogated me.

Short and squat, with a bell-shaped body that tested the fabric of her uniform, she was a tugboat of a woman, chugging relentlessly toward answers I didn't have.

"How well did you know Dr. Byrd? Was he diabetic? Depressed? A heavy drinker? Suicidal? Any enemies?" The questions kept coming.

My answers remained the same. "Don't know. I never met him."

I told her about Irv's early-morning collision with a man near Byrd's office. The officer's excitement waned, however, when I explained that Irv was blind and couldn't give a visual description.

She sighed, stopped writing, and stepped toward me.

"Dr. Austin, were *you* having personal problems with Dr. Byrd?"

"No. I just started working here yesterday."

"Then why were you meeting him on a holiday? You're his only appointment of the day. Seems damn unusual, like he had a problem with you. And why does it say 'coercion' after your name on his appointment calendar?"

I explained that I'd pressured the interventional radiologist to treat Father LaFontaine's pain immediately, rather than wait until he returned from his medical meeting in Hawaii. Undoubtedly, Dr. Byrd had considered this a breach of protocol, if not outright intimidation, but I portrayed myself as the compassionate physician in the scenario. My ploy didn't work.

"Lemme get this straight. You threatened another staff member and forced him to come in to work during his vacation?"

"All I said was that I'd do the procedure on Sunday if he wouldn't."

"So, why didn't you just do it?"

"I hadn't officially started working at St. Joe's yet. It was a bluff, Officer. I was desperate and needed the radiologist's expertise."

"Hold on a minute. You were seeing patients before you were employed here?"

"I'd been hired, just hadn't signed the paperwork yet."

"I can see why Dr. Byrd was angry. You're a loose cannon. Maybe he was going to fire you. It's odd that *you* were the one who discovered his body." She visually frisked me from head to toe. "You look pretty scruffy, Doctor, like you're coming off a bad drunk. You always see patients in this condition?"

"Come on, Officer, cut me some slack. I've been working twenty-four hours straight and I'm beat."

"Hold on. Last night? Here in the hospital? Where were you between six and eight this morning?"

"Asleep in an on-call room."

"Was anyone there with you," she winked, "sleeping?"

"Of course not. I wasn't shacked up with anyone."

"So, no alibi. I don't know. Your whole story smells like week-old fish." She eyeballed me as if she'd caught me siphoning gasoline from a cop car. "What is it you're not telling me?"

I opened my mouth, but decided not to volunteer that Byrd and Bishop Lucci had required a random drug test on me yesterday. Things were bad enough. I must have hesitated too long.

"What? Tell me."

I shook my head.

"Maybe we oughta take a trip down to the station house."

With each of her questions, I was sinking deeper into judicial quicksand. I grabbed for the single lifeline available.

"Listen, Officer, the police chief in Oberlin, Tree Macon, knows me. He can vouch for me."

This was a gamble. I'd placed a bet on our friendship, tossed the dice, and hoped that they wouldn't come up snake eyes. I had no idea what Tree might say.

She told me to stay put, stepped away, and made a phone call, then she spoke with the white-haired woman examining Dr. Byrd's body. After an animated conversation, the two approached me. The officer took charge.

"I spoke with Chief Macon. He vouched for you, but let slip about the shooting and murders in Oberlin. You've been in spitting distance of a lot of bloodshed since you came home. Sounds a bit … suspicious, don't you think?"

I didn't like where this was headed.

"They were high school classmates. I saw them at our reunion. That's all."

The officer wrote in her notebook, then exchanged glances with the older woman.

"Did you know Joanetta Carter, Doctor?"

"Did? No. Who's she?"

"I'll ask the questions. You own a gun?"

"No. I already told Tree Macon I don't."

The white-haired woman straightened her lab coat and stepped forward.

"Dr. Austin, I'm Dr. Gerta Braun, the county coroner. Are you an anesthesiologist or doctor of pharmacy?"

"No, I'm an internist."

"So you prescribe a lot of controlled substances as part of your job?"

"Some. I have specialty training in pain management."

The coroner tilted her head. "Then you're familiar with the drug, succinylcholine?"

"Sure."

"Do you ever use it?"

"No. It's used mostly in surgery to paralyze muscles. I leave that to the anesthesiologists."

"Know anything about the drug, curare?"

"Only what I've seen in movies about the Amazon. Why?"

"Two recent murder victims were poisoned, one paralyzed before she was dumped in the quarry." The coroner stepped close enough that I felt her breath on my cheek and smelled onions. "Dr. Byrd was a good friend of mine. Think I might find poison in his system when I perform the autopsy?"

"What? How would I know?"

"Thanks, Gerta. I'll take it from here." The police officer placed a hand on the coroner's arm and gently drew her back. "Lemme see if I got this straight, Dr. Austin. You were in the hospital last night. *Opportunity.* You have access to drugs, including insulin, succinylcholine, and god knows what. *Means.* Dr. Byrd caught you breaking hospital rules and harassing the medical staff before you were even hired, and maybe he was about to fire you. *Motive.* And you've been knee-deep in a bloodbath since you returned to the county. Have I got that right?"

We locked gazes. I'd gone from frightened to mad as hell and wanted to scream that this was all circumstantial evidence and total bullshit. But I understood how things looked through her eyes, so I said nothing.

"I'm releasing you at Chief Macon's request. I have your contact info, Doctor. You're free to go for now, but let's stay in touch." She handed me her card, and for the second time in three days, I heard, "Just don't leave town."

Chapter Twenty-Eight

Tuesday, July 4, 2:45 p.m.

WHEN THE POLICE officer and coroner walked away, I threw my lab coat over my shoulder and wandered down the hallway, my mind as unsettled as Lake Erie in a November gale. I needed to hear a friendly voice, thought of Emily, but called Tree Macon instead.

"Thanks for your help, Tree. I know St. Joe's is out of your jurisdiction."

He hesitated. "No problem." The tone of his voice suggested that it had been a major problem.

"So much has happened the last few days, and now I'm considered a suspect in Dr. Byrd's death. Could we sit and talk? I need to try and make sense of things."

Another pause. "Sure, why not? Sonya's out of town at her mother's, so how about we grab a bite to eat. Say, Presti's Restaurant, around five?"

"I'd love to … but my credit card is on life support."

"Okay, we'll just call you a *police consultant* and make it a working dinner."

"Thanks, Tree. I'll see you there."

On my way to the wards, I passed a statue of St. Luke. Someone had placed a surgical cap on his head, which was appropriate attire for the patron saint of physicians and surgeons ... and butchers. Funny though, most doctors preferred not to be likened to butchers.

Dr. Taylor came out of a patient's room, saw me, and waved me over.

"Esperanza, the girl with the tick bite, is responding beautifully, Jake. With only minimal support and some IV fluids, her body has cleared most of the toxin. She's walking again and should go home soon. It's the closest thing to a miracle I've seen in a long time."

"Thank God for that."

"God had some help." He patted me on the back. "Thank you. I really thought I'd lose her and didn't want to get my hopes up." Taylor chuckled. "I should have known."

"Known what?"

"Esperanza is Spanish for *hope*."

"Hope has incredible healing power. Prayer too. We should all carry both in our black bags. So, how's Oran Burke doing?"

"Fine, for now. He's back home and stable. With his Huntington's disease, it'll take an act of God, not a neurologist, to save him. I don't hold out much hope for Mr. Burke."

I wanted to update Emily, and since Taylor was in a sharing mood, I said, "I heard you're taking care of Everett McDermott. What're his chances?"

"Slim. He's still in a coma, but hanging on." Taylor shrugged. "The bullet did a number on his cerebral cortex. Lots of hemorrhage and edema. All I can do is reduce the swelling and cross my fingers."

I had nothing to offer medically. A good Christian would have prayed for McDermott, but I'd seen the scar on Emily's lip and lumped him in the same category as my old man. My long memory and short temper always provided me with plenty of sins to confess.

We spoke about Dr. Byrd's death and the terrible loss that it represented for the hospital until Taylor checked his watch and rushed off to finish rounds.

As I entered the small VIP wing and approached Father LaFontaine's room, a middle-aged nun scurried out. Her habit couldn't conceal her anguish as tears streamed down her cheeks. She collided with me and staggered momentarily, dropping her Bible. It hit the floor, flopped open, and an airline ticket fell out. I reached down and picked it up. The ticket was for a flight to Seattle in four hours.

I handed the ticket and Bible to her, but she appeared to be in a trance and didn't take them. "Are you all right, Sister?"

She shook her head and mumbled, "Not sure. So lost ... without him." Then she noticed me for the first time and reclaimed her things. "Oh, sorry. I'm okay. Thank you." She hurried toward the elevator.

When I peeked in LaFontaine's room, he also seemed catatonic, fixated on the window, oblivious to a baseball game playing on the muted television.

I knocked on the door frame and entered.

"Hi, Henri. Who's winning?"

"Ah, come in." He stared at the TV as if he'd never seen one, then recovered. "Tied, one to one in the sixth. A nail-biter. The Indians have a chance to sweep the Yankees in the broom-game of the series. That would definitely qualify as a miracle."

"Did that injection by the radiologist help?"

"The pain's better. Still hurts like a son of a bi ... billy goat. At least, now, it's tolerable." He forced a thin smile. "Cancer ain't for wimps."

I'd seen his photographs at the rectory. He had been a powerfully built man in his younger days, and Colleen had described him as a vibrant, energetic leader. To see him now, helpless and wasting away, was heartbreaking. I wondered if I could muster the same unshakeable faith and courage if I was dealt a similar fate. I hoped so, but LaFontaine had set the bar very high.

"Hang in there, Henri. Your pain will continue to improve over the next few days."

With the radiologist back on vacation, I wanted to be sure his injection hadn't caused any complications. I removed my stethoscope, listened to Henri's abdomen, and was relieved to hear normal bowel sounds. Poking with my fingers produced no rebound tenderness. So far, so good.

"Glad you stopped by, Jake. I wanted to thank you—especially for this." He pointed to the morphine pump.

"Happy to help. Put in a good word for me with Bishop Lucci. He's convinced I can't be both a good priest and a good doctor."

"Will do. He and I go way back. He's a stickler for the rules, but a decent man." LaFontaine inspected me with a furrowed brow. I hadn't shaved, and my white coat was filthy. After a moment, he said, "The bishop hates waves, and I suspect you're rocking the heck out of his boat. I'll speak with him."

"I'd appreciate it."

"You just missed Colleen. She brought me a piece of cinnamon-apple pie." LaFontaine grinned. "And all the gossip I can swallow." He shifted in bed, winced, and dosed himself with more morphine. "She told me about your classmates. The shooting. And a woman poisoned? Guess you can't escape violence, even in a small town."

"Oberlin's always had an edge. More than Mayberry, less than the Big Apple. Did you know the victims?"

"No, thank God." LaFontaine took a bite of pie. "*Heavenly.*" He set down his fork. "I do know Oran Burke. Colleen said he fainted at your reunion."

I nodded. "Is he a parishioner?"

"No, but his wife was. Nancy was a wonderful woman, truly one of the faithful. When she couldn't marry Oran at Sacred Heart, it crushed her."

"Why couldn't she? Did he object to raising their children as Catholics?"

"Moot point. No kids. But Oran would have done anything for her. Problem was, Nancy had married an abusive alcoholic as a teenager and divorced him within a year. I helped her file a petition for annulment with the Tribunal of the Diocese and testified on her behalf, arguing that her ex-husband's behavior before and during their marriage precluded any chance for a lasting union. The three Tribunal judges, however, ruled it a valid marriage and refused Nancy's request."

LaFontaine savored another bite of pie before continuing.

"I even traded on my friendship with the bishop by asking for his support. Who knows? A word from His Excellency might have swung the vote. He said he didn't know Nancy and refused to get involved. Lucci lives by the rulebook, and has always taken a hard line against annulments. He's more about the letter of the law than the spirit, and not fond of exceptions of any kind."

"Yeah, he made that crystal clear to me yesterday."

Although LaFontaine raised his eyebrows, he didn't ask for details.

"Despite being denied an annulment, Nancy Burke attended church regularly and volunteered for fundraisers and bingo. Oran usually accompanied her. He sat quietly at her side, but didn't participate. Solidarity, I guess." He frowned. "Nancy understood that Canon Law gave the bishop no flexibility, and she forgave him for not helping. Oran never did."

"The bishop didn't have a vote. It was the Tribunal's decision."

"True. I tried to explain that. Oran, however, focused his resentment on Lucci because of the way he treated Nancy, dismissive and cold, as if listening to their plea wasted His Excellency's valuable time. His callousness hurt Nancy, but enraged Oran."

LaFontaine washed down the last of his pie with some milk.

"Oran calmed down after a few days. On the subjects of Lucci and the annulment, however, he was like lava—cool and rock-solid on the surface, but a river of simmering anger just below. I don't think Oran ever forgave the bishop."

I knew well that Lucci was an easy man to dislike.

LaFontaine set his plate and fork on the tray table.

"After Nancy's funeral, I finished the graveside blessing and the mourners left the cemetery. Oran just stood there. I tried to comfort him, but he was inconsolable. When I finally gave up and headed for my car, he started screaming and swearing, using obscenities that would've made Lucifer blush."

"Oran?"

"He cursed the doctors, Bishop Lucci, the Church, people I'd never heard of, and even God Almighty. Shook his fist at the heavens, yelling, 'You'll pay for this.' Passing cars stopped. People at other gravesites scurried away. I thought I'd have to call the authorities." LaFontaine's eyelids slid lower, either in contemplation or in response to the morphine. "Then, suddenly, Oran went silent, kissed the casket, and walked away. I haven't seen him since."

"Poor Oran. He sounds like a man at rock bottom, completely devastated. When we were in school, he was always so kind and gentle."

Huntington's disease, however, could cause volatile emotions.

"Colleen said he's in the hospital, Jake. How is he?"

"They patched him up and sent him home."

"Will he be okay?"

"Okay? I wish I could say yes, but he's got a tough road ahead."

"Most of us do." LaFontaine tapped his belly and grew wistful. He slipped on the Indians baseball cap, which slid down over his eyes. He pushed it back up. "And Jake, you haven't forgotten my other request, about my briefcase, right?"

I wished that I *could* forget. I should have refused.

"No, Henri, I haven't forgotten."

Chapter Twenty-Nine

———— • ————

Tuesday, July 4, 3:45 p.m.

ON MY WAY to the doctor's lounge, I stopped in the men's room. DeQuan Kwame was washing his hands at the sink.

He smiled and pointed at the urinal. "I assume that you do not require any assistance from me this time, Doctor." His British accent somehow added gravitas to his wisecrack.

God help me, I couldn't even go to the john in peace.

Hospital orderlies usually don't feel comfortable harassing physicians, and I was sure that DeQuan never spoke this way to any other doctors, but given our unique relationship, he owned my discomfort like a debt. Whenever I needed my ego deflated, he would probably be there to oblige. But he was a minor irritant; I had more important things to worry about.

I stepped up to the first urinal and looked at him. "Don't you have stool samples somewhere to collect?"

He chuckled as he left the restroom.

In the doctors' lounge, I changed into my civvies and threw

my filthy white coat in the laundry basket, then stopped by the hospital chapel to savor the sweet silence.

Working Urgent Care yesterday, shepherding the house staff all night, and dealing with Dr. Byrd's death this morning had prevented me from offering Mass. With Father Vargas covering weekday services at Sacred Heart Church, I wasn't obligated to do so, but it was something I wanted to do. The chapel was unoccupied, and I had time before my meeting with Tree Macon, so I celebrated a private Mass, rejoicing in my time with the Lord.

When I'd finished, I genuflected and entered the sacristy, the shared dressing area used by all of the various clergy who ministered in the hospital chapel. I returned the sacred vessels to a cabinet and relocked it, flopped onto the desk chair, and began composing a homily for my upcoming Saturday Mass.

Between fatigue, my jumbled feelings for Emily, and my concern about her safety, I made little progress and returned to the chapel, lighting candles for my mother and the friends I'd lost overseas. Then I knelt in the front pew and prayed for them as well as for the soul of Dr. Phineas Byrd. Soon I became lost in the balm of prayer and meditation. When my knees started to ache, I realized that I'd lost track of time and would soon be late for my dinner meeting with Tree.

I ignored the speed limit until I entered Oberlin, slowing as I drove along East Lorain. I passed a yellow Greek revival cottage with white gingerbread trim. As a boy, my friends called it "Ghost House" because the abolitionist who built it in the mid-1800s reportedly had made fugitive slaves vanish into thin air. In truth, he'd hidden them in a secret room located behind sliding panels.

My old Toyota rumbled past the town square, Oberlin Community Hospital, and Sacred Heart Church, humid summer heat pouring through the open car windows like molten glass. My shirt hung wet and heavy by the time I arrived for dinner.

At five fifteen, only a few cars dotted the restaurant's parking lot. When I entered, my sweaty clothes hit the air conditioning and I shivered. The bar's muted TV screen displayed headshots of recent victims above the caption WHO'S NEXT? A blonde newswoman mirrored the panic that had swept through town, her overly dramatic gestures better suited to a nineteenth-century melodrama. I thought of the unexplained hang-up telephone calls Emily had received and shivered again. If she was the next intended victim, I needed to find a way to protect her.

Gene Presti, the restaurant's proprietor, greeted me. A corpulent man who enjoyed his own cuisine, Presti flashed an innkeeper's grin and led me to a secluded booth where Tree Macon contemplated the inside of an empty beer mug.

"An order of buffalo wings and another Killian's draft for me, Gene. What'll you have, Jake?"

I slid into the booth. After the chaos at the hospital, I was coiled tighter than a toy top. A beer sounded therapeutic. The St. Pauli Girl on the neon sign above the bar enticed all in the room with a tray of frosted steins, her lush, come-hither lips beckoning.

I came hither. "St. Pauli, please."

"Is there some Church rule," Tree asked, "that you have to drink beer named after saints?"

I pointed at the buxom lady on the wall. "Does she look saintly to you?"

"No, but she'd give a guy something to pray for."

Gene Presti smiled, handed out menus, and withdrew.

Tree glanced at his and set it down. "You called this meeting, Jake. What's up?"

"I guess I just need to talk about the last few days and try to make sense of it all."

"No problem. Sometimes kicking back and shooting the bull helps me get a different angle on things. So talk."

"Since coming home, it's as if I've been tossed into a blender.

Oran's collapse, McDermott shooting, Barb Dorfman's death … and now, Dr. Byrd at St. Joe's. I haven't seen this kind of carnage since 'Nam."

"Definitely bad juju." Tree massaged the stubble on his chin. "Plus, I've got a young anorexic woman dead at the quarry who also graduated from Oberlin High, suggesting a vendetta against the *school*. I doubt Byrd's death is related." Tree's eyes were bloodshot and weary. "Problem is, if the leads on these cases were any colder, I'd have to wear fleece-lined gloves. Hell, my number-one suspect in the quarry case was McDermott, and someone shot *him* in the head."

Tree dragged a big hand across his face. "The town's scared shitless, and get this, a concerned parents' group is patrolling the school, some armed with baseball bats. The media's already calling for my head on a platter." He slumped down in the booth. "I feel like the kid in that movie with the sixth sense. Everywhere I look I see dead people."

"Anorexics sometimes die of arrhythmias or heart attacks, Tree, even young ones."

"Not the one at the quarry. Joanetta's feet were tied together and weighed down to hold her under water. Somebody ransacked her apartment, but left her jewelry and credit cards. Her computer was the only thing missing, far as we know. The coroner said she'd been paralyzed with *curare*, of all things. Curare? How'd you even get your hands on that stuff? Her murder screams 'Personal,' with a capital P, and her killer is definitely one rage-filled, crazy bastard."

Curare, first cousin of succinylcholine—both difficult drugs to obtain without medical access. So *that* was why IU jumped to the top of the suspect list when the cops found a syringe on Byrd's desk.

"Now I'm scared, Tree. What if that same rage-filled crazy left that threatening note for Emily?"

"It's possible, I suppose. But that seems more cunning than flat-out nuts."

"I don't know, Tree. Using curare as a weapon sounds pretty calculated to me. Did you find any fingerprints on the note?"

"Just yours and mine."

My jaw dropped, which apparently amused Tree.

"No, I didn't test it specifically for your prints. The computer spit out your name 'cause your fingerprints are in the system from the military ... and an old DUI. But someone was real careful not to touch that piece of paper." Tree twirled his empty mug. "Jake, I'm going with my gut and our friendship here. I don't really consider you a suspect anymore, but I'm worried about Emily. With her way over in Lorain, I could use your help. I'll do what I can, but I've got my hands full. You're in a better position at St. Joe's to keep an eye on her."

I nodded but had no idea how to protect her.

"Whatever happened to Oran's water bottle? I saw you snatch it from the lectern after his speech."

"Nothing. No evidence of tampering. I was just covering all the bases." Tree paused. "Speaking of covering bases, I ran a background check on Marisa's fiancé, Richard. The guy's got anger-management issues. Two assaults in LA, but both charges were dropped. Marisa had legal problems with McDermott, and bitched about Barb Dorfman cheating her. Even if her boyfriend's not involved, God knows she has enough money to hire a hit man. I asked them both to extend their visit to town for a few days. They were none too happy."

"What about the redheaded woman at the church? The one with the child."

"By the time I got outside, she was in the wind. I put out a BOLO—a be-on-the-lookout—but I wouldn't get my hopes up."

"Anything new on McDermott?"

"The usual motives for a bullet to the head—money, jealousy, drugs, revenge, sexual kinks—which pretty much describes McDermott's lifestyle. Plenty of suspects. I got the BCI forensic guys working on that, too. Maybe we'll catch a break."

Our drinks arrived, and the big man took a gulp of beer before continuing.

"Strange, though. McDermott wrote a bunch of checks to charities the day he was shot. Five grand each. I'm not sure what that means. Maybe he got religion and changed his ways."

"McDermott? I believe in miracles but ...."

Tree's cellphone rang and he examined the screen.

"Gotta take this." He headed for the exit, leaving me gazing into the emerald eyes of the St. Pauli Girl.

Chapter Thirty

Tuesday, July 4, 6:00 p.m.

TREE MACON RETURNED and slid back into the booth, shoulders slumped and wearing a scowl.

"That was the coroner, Jake. I asked her to keep me posted on Dr. Byrd's autopsy. She found no evidence of a struggle or violence. He washed down a bunch of sleeping pills with expensive Scotch, then OD'd on insulin. No suicide note. Estimated TOD between six and eight this morning. Byrd was a diabetic and had been on insulin for years. Maybe his death was accidental. With booze and pills on board, could be he got confused and screwed up the dose."

"The chief of medicine? A longtime diabetic? I don't buy it, Tree."

"That's what the coroner said too. She suspects suicide. Byrd's insulin level spiked off the charts and his blood sugar was in the toilet. Tox screen is pending."

Tree took a gulp of Killian's and came away with a foam mustache.

"She also told me Byrd was ticked off at you, so they were

suspicious when *you* found his body? Not my jurisdiction, but I can't blame them for giving you a hard look."

"I had an appointment with him. He arranged it, not me."

I snatched my St. Pauli Girl from the table and took a long draw. With an empty stomach and lack of sleep, it felt like a French kiss. The sultry neon lady over the bar smiled approvingly.

"Wait, Tree. What'd you say the time of death was?"

"Between six and eight."

"Huh. That's interesting."

"What?"

"Irv Beale told me someone crashed into him and knocked him down in the hallway near Byrd's office about that time. Irv's blind, so he can't ID the guy."

"A man?"

"Yup. Irv said he was small, with a low voice."

A waiter set a plate of buffalo wings on the table. Tree ordered a twelve-ounce prime rib, hash browns with sour cream, and a salad with extra blue cheese.

"Low cholesterol diet, Tree?"

"Buzz off, Doc! I hit most the food groups. You got your veggies, protein, dairy, roughage. Been a long day. Let me enjoy my comfort food in peace."

The waiter, looking amused, turned to me. "And you, sir?"

Being under suspicion of Dr. Byrd's murder hadn't exactly piqued my appetite.

"A bowl of French onion soup, please."

"Very good, sir."

I broke off a piece of a roll and nibbled. Tree dipped a finger in his beer foam and licked it like cake frosting.

"Okay, Jake, where were we? Oh yeah, Byrd's suicide."

"I don't buy the suicide idea either. I talked with hospital staff this afternoon. No one thought Byrd was depressed, let alone suicidal. The guy lived for his job. He was king of the hill at St. Joe's and nationally."

"Sometimes kings abdicate." Tree drew a frowning face in the condensation on his frosted mug and spun it toward me. "So, if not suicide, what?"

On the drive to the restaurant, I'd reexamined the events of the past few days and had an epiphany—an unholy epiphany, not the kind I'd always hoped for.

"This may be a bit off the wall, Tree. I think Byrd's death could be related to McDermott's shooting."

"What! How?"

"The common thread is Oran Burke."

My epiphany made me consider the possibility that Oran might have been ensnared by the lure for vengeance. I was no stranger to it. Kenny's death had filled me with blind rage and a lust for revenge that had driven me through the tunnels of Cu Chi to kill a man.

"Oran? I don't see the connection." Tree closed his eyes so long that I wondered if he'd dozed off. Finally, his eyelids popped open. "In my job, reading people is as important as reading clues, and I can't picture Oran as a murderer."

"Think about it, Tree. Emily and Oran are close friends. She said Oran became angry when he found out McDermott abused her. And we know McDermott tormented Oran for years."

"Come on, there are legal remedies available for that. Restraining orders, slander suits. No need to resort to a cold-blooded gunshot to the head." Tree sucked down more beer. "That doesn't sound like the Oran I know."

"Hear me out. Dr. Byrd was Nancy Burke's physician, and she died under his care. Emily told me that Oran held Byrd responsible and sued him for malpractice. When Oran lost the case, he got in a shoving match with Byrd."

Tree appeared uninterested as he devoured a buffalo wing. I pressed on.

"Remember, someone Oran's size ran into Irv Beale near the

physician offices about the same time Byrd died. Irv said the guy had an uneven gait. Oran has a limp."

"That's not *evidence*, Jake. Aside from a push, did Oran actually assault Dr. Byrd? Throw a punch?"

"No, not that I know of." I paused and rubbed my eyes, so tired I could barely think. "Although Oran might have threatened him."

"Threatened? When?"

"Father LaFontaine said Oran went ballistic at Nancy's burial. He stood at the gravesite screaming, 'You'll pay for this.' "

"Did he name Byrd specifically?"

"Not that LaFontaine told me. He said Oran cursed the doctors, among a host of other people." I hoisted my beer mug, surprised to find it almost empty. "Nancy died of a medical complication, so I'm guessing Oran meant Byrd."

"I'm not allowed to guess—but that's a reasonable theory. I'll interview Irv, Emily, and LaFontaine. Maybe drop by Oran's place for a chat."

When the waiter arrived, the conversation died. My Gruyère-encrusted French onion soup was delicious. Tree worked his way through a mound of lettuce buried under a snowdrift of blue cheese dressing. He slathered a roll with a glob of butter, brandishing his knife as if guarding his meal. After he'd emptied his salad bowl and filled his bread plate, he refocused on me.

"With no sign of violence, how does a little guy like Oran inject insulin into a big man like Byrd? There would be evidence of a struggle."

I considered this as I savored my soup.

"Oran's a gun collector, Tree, so he could have shot McDermott. Emily said he has a display case full of weapons. An armed man can force someone bigger to do lots of things— including drink booze laced with sedatives. After Byrd passed out, Oran could have injected the insulin. It doesn't take any skill. Have the Lorain police checked for Oran's fingerprints?"

"I doubt *Mr. Clean* has any on file ...." Tree stopped mid-sentence and grinned. "As a matter of fact, I already have Oran's prints—on the water bottle from the reunion. Be interesting to run them through the computer. Problem is, a doctor's office will be full of prints, including Oran's, if he visited Byrd's office with Nancy in the past."

"Then examine the syringe and insulin vials for Oran's fingerprints—and for Byrd's."

"Good idea." He tapped his temple with an index finger. "If we find Oran's prints, we got him. If there are no prints, not even Byrd's, then someone wore gloves or wiped everything clean."

"Exactly. Meaning murder, not suicide."

"I like the way you think, Jake."

Tree's prime rib arrived. He cut a piece, dunked it in au jus, and gobbled it down. The hash browns were partially buried under the beef. He uncovered them, slathered on sour cream, and dug in.

Although it is always unwise and hazardous to poke a hungry bear, I couldn't resist. "Does Sonya approve of your diet?"

"Hell, no. When the warden's away, the inmates will play." Tree smirked. "Sonya's out of town, and *we're* not gonna tell her, right? Now, you were saying ...."

"Well, this may really sound off the wall."

"More?" Tree inclined his head to one side. "Oh, goody."

"What's the status of Barb Dorfman's death?"

"Coroner says she ate poison mushrooms." Tree produced a small notebook from his pocket and flipped through the pages. "Amanita Virosa—nicknamed Destroying Angels. Barb was a strict vegetarian. Could be she ate lots of mushrooms and got careless."

"I doubt that she jumped off an airplane from New York and went out picking mushrooms."

More page flipping. "Coroner thinks she ate them Saturday

night, maybe at the reunion. That's hard to confirm. Leftovers are long gone and the plates are washed." Tree peered at me over his notepad. "Why are you asking about Barb Dorfman?"

"Emily said that Barb was Oran's financial advisor. She cost him and Nancy most of their savings."

"From what I heard, Barbie cost a bunch of people money, Marisa included. Motive maybe, but a lot of locals hated Dorfman." Tree attacked another chunk of beef. "You thinking Oran added some garnish to Barb's salad?"

"It wouldn't take much. That species is deadly." I finished my beer and thought about another. Instead, I plucked the lemon wedge from the rim of the glass and squeezed it into my ice water. "Heck, Oran writes murder mysteries. He's probably researched every possible way to kill a human being. I'll bet he knows all about Destroying Angel mushrooms."

"That's quite a stretch, Jake. You sound like some dime-store-novel detective. Besides, the timing's all wrong. Oran's wife died several years ago. And Oran could have retaliated against Barb Dorfman before she moved to New York and shot McDermott any time since graduation. If Oran's the killer and revenge is the motive, then why'd he wait all these years to act?"

"Good question." I dropped the lemon rind into my water. "Emily told me Oran's mood changed several months ago, from depressed back to his old jovial self."

"That could be due to a lotta things. Maybe Oran got his head shrunk by some shrink." Tree loaded the last piece of prime rib on his fork and aimed it for his mouth. "Sometimes that happens when a depressed guy finally decides to end it all. Suddenly, out of nowhere, he's happy as a pig in poop and his friends think he's fine … till he blows his brains out."

"I suppose. But if Oran's depression ended because he finally decided to kill himself, why take months to do it?"

I sipped my water, wondering if Oran's Huntington's chorea was behind his change in behavior. He must have known that time was running out. If he really intended to settle scores, it wouldn't be long until he couldn't do it physically. And if his disease was progressing rapidly, he could have become delusional and paranoid to the point where a friend might appear to be an enemy. If that was true and Emily was in danger, I didn't give a damn about patient privacy laws.

Leaning in, I lowered my voice. "This is off the record. I know for a fact that Oran was recently diagnosed with a terminal illness, Huntington's disease. What about the flipside of the suicide coin? Oran figures he's lost everything and his time on earth is running short. He has nothing left to lose, so ...."

Tree's brown eyes grew large and dark. "So why don't I take the bastards down with me?"

"Bingo. You get the kewpie doll."

"I'll find out if any security tapes were rolling near Dr. Byrd's office." Tree's head jerked up. "Hold on a minute. What disease does Oran have?"

"Huntington's."

Tree pulled out his notebook again. "You know the checks McDermott mailed to charities the day he got shot? He wrote one to the Society for the Blind, but I figured he was trying to get back in Emily's good graces." He turned more pages, then stared as if the words were written in Latin. "Well, looky here. One check for five grand went to the Huntington's Disease Society."

This time, my head jerked up. "There's no way McDermott knew about Oran's illness or did anything nice for him. Maybe Oran forced him to write those checks at gunpoint and mailed them himself."

"Circumstantial, but suspicious as hell. Except, you're forgetting one important fact. Even if Oran killed Barb Dorfman and Byrd, he was a patient at the hospital when McDermott got shot. The doors are locked and alarmed at night." Tree leaned forward. "McDermott lives way out in the country. His house isn't within walking distance of town. Even if Oran snuck past the ER reception desk, he didn't have a car.

You drove him to the hospital. So, tell me, how did he get to McDermott's place?"

"He could've grabbed a taxi."

"Come on, man. A taxi to and from an attempted murder? You just wandered off the reservation into whacky town. I'm the one paid to be paranoid." Tree wrote in his notebook, stowed it in his pocket, and pushed his empty plate away. "Motive and means aren't enough. I need *opportunity* too. Either Oran had an accomplice, or we're back to unrelated murders."

"I guess you're right." I finished the last of my soup and thought for a while. "It's a jigsaw puzzle with some of the pieces missing."

"That's usually the way it goes in my job."

Tree drained the last of his beer, took out a business card, and scribbled on it.

"Here's my cellphone number." He picked up the check and smiled. "The department will cover the tab. You're now officially a police informant. Give me a buzz, snitch, if you hear anything interesting or have any other crazy-ass ideas."

We walked out to the parking lot. Tree roared off in a black Crown Vic and my Toyota rumbled and rattled back to Sacred Heart. Our conversation had left me frustrated, exhausted, and in need of a good night's sleep.

Chapter Thirty-One

———•———

Tuesday, July 4, 7:00 p.m.

I DROVE INTO the rectory driveway, noticed a silver van in the adjacent church lot, and wondered if some kids had chosen the spot for a make-out session. I should have gone over to check, but I'd had enough confrontation and drama for one day. I parked near the back door of the rectory and entered through the kitchen, pondering the ominous note I'd found at the reunion and the hang-up telephone calls Emily had received. Tree's words echoed in the stillness.

I'm worried about Emily ... I'll do what I can ... You're in a better position at St. Joe's to keep an eye on her.

I shook my head. How the hell could I protect her?

Adding water and freshly ground beans to the coffee maker, I set the timer for morning, then noticed a red light winking on the answering machine. I pushed the message button and a robotic voice announced that one call had been recorded. Colleen's voice filled the room.

Father, I saw on your schedule that you'll be working

tomorrow evening, so I'll drop in around eleven and prepare a nice bit of lunch for you. Right, then …. What I'm really calling about is that redheaded lass, the painfully thin one. Snooping around again she was, and with an innocent child in tow. "Can I be of assistance," I say, "Father is not home at the moment." Well, didn't she turn as red as her hair. Dashed off like Lucifer had poked her with his pitchfork. So, I took note of her motorcar. Can't be too careful these days, saints preserve us. A silver van with out-of-state plates it was, but I didn't get the license number. By the way, you left the back door unlatched. I do believe you're inclined to meet trouble halfway, Father. And another thing—

As usual, Colleen had rambled on until the message cut her off abruptly.

I suspected that the long arm of the law had prodded this mysterious woman, not Lucifer's pitchfork. One glimpse of Tree and she had run from the church. Her comments in the confessional, however, had been prophetic. Innocent lives were indeed at risk, and terrible things were happening. Yet, why had she said that only I could help her?

After I deleted the message, it struck me. A *silver van*, like the one in the church parking lot. I heard a noise from the next room.

"Hello? Who's there?"

"In here," a woman answered softly.

I spun around and charged into the living room. The gaunt, red-haired woman sat on the couch. A chill washed over me.

"That Irish lady's a damn pit bull, Father, but she's right. You really shouldn't leave your doors unlocked."

"Can I help you?"

"You can." Her face was drawn, her eye sockets deep as sinkholes. She nervously fingered a manila envelope. "The question is *will* you?"

"What do you want from me?"

"I want you to save my life."

Sallow skin draped her skeletal frame. Twig arms poked from her tattered, short-sleeved blouse. Her jeans were ragged and the toe of one scuffed shoe had separated from the sole.

The defiance left her eyes. "All I'm asking for is a chance to live," she said, her voice fading to the tremble of a frightened little girl.

Stunned, I searched for a coherent response. "How can I help you, my child?"

"Oh, I'm not your *child*." She waved the envelope. "I'm your sister. We need to talk."

I was so shocked by her words that I collapsed into the chair across from her. When I leaned forward, a peculiar odor assaulted me—a sweet but musty ammonia scent. My years in the hospital had taught me that the terminally ill sometimes have a distinct aroma called *fetor hepaticus*—the breath of the dead.

Was I imagining it? Unsure, I moved toward her and inhaled. She cringed and slid away on the couch, warding me off with a pencil-thin forearm. She looked as fragile as a hand-blown glass figurine.

I cautiously accepted the manila envelope she offered, opened it, and removed a notarized birth certificate dated thirty years earlier. It documented the uneventful delivery in Louisiana of a healthy, seven-pound baby girl to a Josephine Land.

My mind reeled. "I … I don't understand."

"That's my birth certificate. I'm Justine. Josephine was my mother. Read all the names."

And there, under "Father of Child," I saw my old man's name. My jaw dropped.

"Welcome to my world, Jake. Check out the pictures."

I tapped the envelope and two photos of my father tumbled out. In one, he stood next to a heavy-set, ruby-haired woman holding a baby. The other showed him playing saxophone in a honky-tonk, a young girl with a mop of red curls clinging to his knee.

Justine tapped one of the pictures.

"Our pappy was keen on breeding kids, just not on raising them. He disappeared when I was six. Never heard from him again." Her Southern drawl was similar to my father's. "My last recollection of that gin-soaked piss-pot is the taillights of the taxi as he drove away."

The mere thought of my father made my stomach queasy, and my brain started burping up sour, undigested memories. I studied the photographs. Although I had little doubt that she was my younger half-sister, the implications of our relationship were less clear.

"Okay, so we're related. Why'd you track me down? And why," I checked the name on the birth certificate, "Justine, are you afraid of the police?"

She dismissed my questions with a wave of her hand.

"I'm sick and I'm broke. I needed cash and wheels to get here from N'awlins, so I borrowed money from my aunt—and stole a van. Been living in it ever since. That's why I spooked when I saw the cop in church. Desperate people do desperate things, Father." Her eyes met mine. "I won't apologize, and I sure as hell don't want your absolution."

"So, what *do* you want?"

She was a wisp of a woman and appeared harmless, but when she reached into her purse, I stood and stepped back.

Desperate people do desperate things.

Justine pulled out a frayed handkerchief embroidered with lavender flowers. She touched it to the corner of one eye, then kneaded it like bread dough.

"If it's money you need, Justine, I don't have much, but I'll do what I can."

"I don't want your money. Or your pity, or your love. What I *want* is your bone marrow."

"What?"

She lowered her voice.

"I have cancer. Leukemia. My blood type is rare, and I need a bone marrow transplant. Soon. My momma's dead and her sister, my aunt, isn't a match. God only knows where our pappy is, and I don't have any other kin. There's no one else. I need *your* bone marrow for a chance to live."

A tear rolled down her cheek. She wiped it with the hankie and gestured over her shoulder. I peeked behind the couch. A young boy, maybe four years old, played quietly on the floor with toy soldiers, his hair as red as hers. He needed a bath and a change of clothes.

She placed a finger to her lips and continued in a whisper, "I know it's a lot to ask, and I didn't want to drag you into this, Jake, but I got no choice. My boy, your nephew, needs a parent—something our dear old dad never was."

My world began spinning in the wrong direction, and I felt lightheaded. Every way I turned in this town, I collided with my past.

Justine wiped away more tears and blew her nose.

"The poor kid's been in and out of foster homes since I got sick. Now that I stole the van, Children's Services will try to take him. I can't let that happen. *Please*, Jake, help me. We're family."

Family. A strange sense of wonder and elation emerged from the depths of my inner chaos. I hadn't had a real family for decades. My parishioners and patients had filled that void to some extent, but I could certainly make room in my life for my sister and her son. I gazed at the boy. The idea of my nephew warehoused in an orphanage or shuttled between foster homes made the decision for me.

"And his uncle won't let anyone take him either, Justine. We'll find a way." I sat next to her on the couch. "Yes, of course. If I'm a match, I'll donate my bone marrow."

She squeezed my hand weakly, then lowered her head. "And if I don't make it, if the transplant doesn't work …."

I lifted her chin with my finger and recognized my father's silver-blue eyes sunken between her cheeks and eyebrows.

"Don't say that. Don't even think it. We'll get through this." I glanced behind the couch again. "Justine, what's my nephew's name?"

"Randall James. I call him RJ."

Chapter Thirty-Two

---·---

Tuesday, July 4, 7:30 p.m.

JUSTINE STOOD AND said, "Thank you, Jake. I was afraid you might say no. And I really hate to ask for anything else, but I'm flat broke. Could you lend me enough money to get a cheap room for a night or two? RJ and I been sleeping in the van, and we both need a bath and a soft bed."

I had no cash, but no sister of mine was going to stay in some flea-bag flophouse.

"I have a better idea. Upstairs we have two guest rooms with a shared bathroom that you're welcome to use. This place is like a tomb sometimes. I'd love the company."

RJ peered around the couch at me but kept his distance. He looked like a Raggedy Andy doll with overalls that didn't quite reach his ankles and a mop of unruly red hair. When I smiled at him, he stepped back and examined his sneakers.

I put an arm around Justine's shoulder. "Pull the van into the rectory garage and close the door. We'll figure out a way to return it without getting you into trouble."

It didn't take long to unload their meager possessions. I

carried her suitcases inside, threw their dirty clothes into the washing machine, and showed them to their rooms. Justine promptly cajoled RJ into the bathtub.

While they were getting cleaned up, I took the opportunity to download my email. I hadn't yet found the rectory's computer. The last place left to search was the fourth bedroom. I opened Father LaFontaine's door.

The blinds were closed, so I flipped on the lights. A 1948 Cleveland Indians World Series pennant hung on the wall, next to a Louisville slugger autographed by the team. Several religious tomes and two volumes on botany lined the bookshelf, along with works by Kant, Nietzsche, Freud, and Jung. Clearly, LaFontaine was a well-educated and complex man.

An open book of Thomas Merton's meditations rested, facedown, on his desk. I flipped it over and read the passages highlighted in yellow marker: "Who knows anything at all about solitude if he has not been in love? Love and solitude must test each other in the man who means to live alone: they must become one and the same thing in him, or he will only be half a person. Unless I have you with me always, in some very quiet and perfect way, I will never be able to live fruitfully alone."

Merton seemed to be speaking directly to me about Emily and the austerity of the priesthood. Was finding this quotation mere chance, or a sign from God? Since the Lord spoke mostly to saints, my guess was coincidence.

I returned the book to the desk and picked up an envelope addressed to Father LaFontaine from the Superior General of my Camillian Order. Curiosity got the best of me. I pulled a small penknife from my pocket, then hesitated. Jesus glared at me from a crucifix on the wall. I set the envelope down unopened and booted up LaFontaine's laptop.

When the screen blinked to life, I downloaded my email, which included announcements for medical meetings, a pep talk from the Camillians on fundraising, the AMA Newsletter, and spam for an all-natural male enhancement pill—a thoughtful gift for your parish priest.

After deleting the junk mail, I shut down the computer, stood, and noticed a black-leather attaché case in the open closet. God, how I wished I hadn't promised LaFontaine to destroy it. Better to have refused his last request.

I needed to spend time with my newfound family and didn't want to deal with the briefcase, so I opted for procrastination and headed downstairs to the kitchen.

As I brewed a pot of coffee and filled a tray with a selection of teas, Justine entered the room. Her eyebrows were painted on and the roots of her wet hair were rust-colored, with no sign of the vibrant ruby highlights I'd seen in the photographs. A few patches of shiny scalp peeked through, suggesting that she'd recently been through chemotherapy. Her leukemia had left her haggard and pale. I didn't need a microscope to envision her crazed white blood cells replicating, rampaging through her bone marrow, and pouring into her bloodstream.

She wore flip-flops, cut-off jeans, and a clean T-shirt with the New Orleans Saints team logo. I was fond of both football and saints, but had never rooted for any team other than the Browns. If my sister followed them, however, that was good enough for me. *Go, Saints.*

"RJ's already asleep. Went down without a fight. The last couple weeks have been tough on both of us, Jake. I knew you'd been transferred to Oberlin but I've never been out of Louisiana before. That's one long, painful drive with a four-year-old." She combed bony fingers through her thinning hair and managed a feeble smile. "I sure am grateful for the bath and the bed. Jesus, I feel like a new woman." She stopped and stared. "Sorry. It's gonna take a little time to clean up my language and get used to having a priest in the family."

I laughed. "Believe me, on a bad day you'll probably have to excuse *my* French. Can I get you a cup of coffee or tea? How about a home-cooked meal? I make a mean scrambled eggs."

"Just tea. I been off my feed for a while." She tilted her head to one side and chuckled. "It's mighty kind of you to worry about me, Jake, but trust me, I'm tougher than a two-dollar steak."

We adjourned to the living room and I inserted a Simon & Garfunkel CD into the player, lowering the volume so as not to awaken RJ. We had thirty years of history to bridge and began swapping stories from our separate childhoods. It was a welcome diversion from the shit-storm that had become my life since my return to town.

Whenever Justine referred to our philandering father, she used the same nickname that I had for him—*Dirt-bag*. Concise and accurate. If some irate, two-timed husband strung up our daddy from a tree by his thumbs, neither of us would have cut him down. Clearly, we both had anger issues with our old man; being abandoned at a young age did that to you.

I answered a few of her medical questions, remaining as positive as I could without lying, then touched on stories of my teenage rebellion, time in the service, and my reconciliation with God. I focused on humorous memories, saving my darker tales for brighter days.

She entertained me with a funny story about dating, then segued to her own wild-child youth. Her tone became somber when she described the fling with a married man that had resulted in RJ. The guy wanted nothing to do with her or a child. Instead, he gave her money for an abortion and shut her out of his life. Justine trembled as she described her struggles as a single mother. I took her hand and held it. She didn't pull away. Finally, out of words and energy, she finished her tea, stood, and hugged me. It was like embracing a bundle of twigs.

"Time for some shut-eye, Jake. Thanks for the chat and the hospitality. Goodnight." When she reached the stairs, she turned around. "And tomorrow, I choose the music. Maybe bluegrass, or at least something more current." She grinned. "I'm not as ancient as you are, big brother."

Big brother. I'd never been called that before. As I watched Justine trudge up the stairs, comforting the sick took on a whole new meaning and urgency.

After she had gone, I listened to the unnerving silence of the rectory and thought about her struggles and the long odds of her survival. Before the quicksand of melancholy could suck me under, I went up and dressed in my pajamas, recited evening prayers, and climbed under the covers. Although I was completely exhausted, my mind thrashed about like a sack full of cats. After tossing in bed for twenty minutes, I flipped on the light, opened Oran Burke's novel, and picked up the story where I'd left off the night before.

When the runaway slave splashes through a shallow stream, the hounds lose his scent. As his food stash dwindles, he resorts to eating berries. He travels mostly through the woods at night to avoid people, but the dense forest on a steep mountain slope slows his progress. When he hears horsemen approaching, he hides in a cave with several side passages. One weaves its way to the far side of the mountain, where he resumes his trek north toward a safe house on the Underground Railroad.

As the slave arrived at the icy waters of the Ohio River, my eyelids grew heavy and I dozed off.

I slept fitfully, surrounded by characters out of *Uncle Tom's Cabin* and apparitions dissolving into dark passageways. At one in the morning, the howl of bloodhounds and the crack of whips wrenched me from slumber. I read a few more chapters, finally plunging again into unconsciousness an hour or so later.

Chapter Thirty-Three

Wednesday, July 5, 6:00 a.m.

THE AIR IS thick with dampness and decay as I stagger through a pitch-black tunnel into spider webs, tripping over tree roots. Furry critters skitter around my feet. The walls press in. Hideous laughter closes fast from behind.

I crash through a bush into jungle sunlight, trip over a body in the mud, roll the dead soldier over—and see Emily's bloodied face. Cries echo from the tunnel. Hoa Nho emerges, pointing an accusing finger. She wails ... and wails ... and wails.

* * *

A CAR ALARM shook me from my nighttime purgatory. I was drenched in sweat and shivering. The clock on my nightstand glowed 6:02. My next Urgent Care shift didn't begin for eleven hours. I groaned, rolled over, closed my eyes—and again saw Emily's face covered with mud and blood.

I sat up, wide awake. *Devil's Passage* rested on the bed. I bookmarked it but couldn't take my eyes off the cover. In the middle of the night, in a dream or half-sleep, something about it had seemed incredibly important, but in the morning light the significance had faded away.

The pleasing thought of spending more time with Justine and RJ launched me from the bed. After morning prayers, I showered and shaved, then put on well-worn jeans, sneakers, and a T-shirt branded with the navy-blue X of Xavier University. How I longed for the laid-back college life.

Not wanting to awaken anyone, I padded softly down the stairs. In the kitchen, I brewed a fresh pot of coffee and began preparing a French toast feast for my new family.

Family. Since my ordination, I'd been certain that I would never have one again. Then my entire world had shifted on its axis with the arrival of my sister and nephew. It was a wish come true, a prayer answered that I had never even had the courage to put into words. Who could possibly understand the mystifying ways of the Lord?

I located the powdered sugar in the pantry and beat three eggs in a large bowl, adding cinnamon and vanilla.

With no sign of activity upstairs, I sat at the table, sipped my coffee, and replayed my meeting with Tree Macon. I couldn't accept his theory of two unrelated killers. The evidence pointed to Oran Burke. But Oran's hospitalization gave him an ironclad alibi for McDermott's shooting—or did it?

Like an inkblot test, the events of the past few days offered a thousand interpretations. But in this case, only one was correct. The solution had danced just beyond my grasp as I'd slept. I needed to seize it before Emily or someone else got hurt.

I'd spent much of the evening reading *Devil's Passage,* and as I considered what Oran had written, the inkblot took on an entirely new appearance—and the image it formed shocked me out of my chair.

Had his novel explained how a hospitalized man without a car could shoot a victim who lived miles away? The answer would take some digging, but I knew where to start. Flipping through the telephone directory, I found the Oberlin Heritage Center, scribbled down the address, and shoved the note into my pocket.

Justine and RJ walked into the room. My nephew carried a box of crayons and a pad of paper. She sported a large, deep violet bruise on her upper arm that hadn't been there last night.

"Mornin', brother. Mind if RJ draws some pictures on the table?"

"No problem." I dipped bread into the mixing bowl and laid it on the heated skillet. "Breakfast will be ready in about ten minutes."

Justine accepted a cup of coffee and sat next to her son to watch him scribble. RJ was lost in his creation, the tip of his tongue poking from the corner of his mouth. As I finished frying the French toast, I asked him what he was drawing.

"Mommy and you."

Me? So soon? Clearly, RJ was expressing a need, an emptiness in his life. I might not be able to replace his absent father, but I could be an involved uncle and a male role model for him. I sure as heck would do my best to fill the void.

I peered over his shoulder. Our budding Michelangelo had drawn the requisite house with a large front door and tiny windows under a big yellow sun. My likeness wore the large, navy-blue X on my T-shirt. Justine's figure had a mop of red hair and sticklike arms and legs that hit uncomfortably close to reality.

"Okay, everyone, breakfast is ready. Grab a plate and let's eat."

We relocated to the dining room so as not to disturb my nephew's masterpiece on the kitchen table. Justine pushed the food around her plate but didn't eat much, complaining of nausea. I wanted to examine her abdomen to be certain that her liver and spleen were not enlarging, but she was already so frightened that I banished all medical considerations.

Sometimes having too much knowledge scared the hell out of me.

After breakfast, we moved to the living room. Justine and I resumed our ping-pong volley of childhood stories, while RJ played with his green plastic army. When I mentioned my time in the service, he stopped and looked up but didn't ask any questions. That would come later, when I'd earned his trust.

As we talked, my mind kept drifting back to Oran's book and the question it had raised. The address of the Oberlin Heritage Center seemed to be burning a hole in my pocket. Finally, I said I had to run a quick errand. Justine appeared disappointed. I promised to be home soon so that we could resume our conversation before my evening shift at the hospital.

I called Colleen and explained that my sister and nephew had arrived unexpectedly and would be staying for a few days. Surprisingly, Colleen warmed to the idea and offered to make lunch for the three of us.

Next, I contacted the lab at the hospital and scheduled a bone marrow compatibility test. Then I called a physician friend at the Cleveland Clinic and asked him to recommend a transplant surgeon. He took my cell number and said he'd ask around and call back.

I left the rectory and hurried southeast toward the historical society, my thoughts alive with the unlimited possibilities that a family presented. With the college on summer recess, the sidewalks were nearly deserted. The air smelled of pine and roses, and the sun poured liquid-honey light through an azure sky.

I stopped at Talbot Hall, where my focus shifted from family to murder. Full-sized train tracks emerged from the earth in front of Talbot's stone spires, memorializing the town's role as a stop on the Underground Railroad. The symbolism was obvious. The direction of Oberlin's runaway train of death, however, was unclear. I hoped we would emerge soon from darkness into light, but feared that we were hurtling down through blackness toward disaster.

Two minutes later, I arrived at the Oberlin Heritage Center, a beautiful historic house with ornate gingerbread trim and high, arching windows. I mounted the front steps, entered through the leaded-glass front door, and explained that I needed information from the 1800s.

"Our executive director has more local history stored in her head than all the books in our library," the receptionist replied. "Her office is upstairs."

When I knocked at her half-open door, a woman dressed in a tan business suit waved me in and pointed to the one chair in the room not buried under books and papers. She hung up the phone, stood, and extended a hand. Her hair was short and dark, and she had the wiry build of a marathoner.

"I'm Pat Murphy. How may I help you, Mister …?"

"Jake Austin. I grew up in town listening to tales of Underground Railroad slave tunnels. Is there any truth to these rumors?"

"I'm afraid *tales* is an accurate term. The *truth*," Ms. Murphy said, "is buried in the dust of history. I've read extensively on the subject, and there is no evidence to confirm, or deny, the existence of tunnels here before the Civil War."

"You're sure?"

She nodded.

I wilted in my chair and studied the hand-hewn floorboards.

"The reality, Mr. Austin, is that our town welcomed black freemen and escaped slaves so willingly that they often walked the streets without fear. By 1860, they accounted for over twenty percent of the town's population. We've found only one secret room used to conceal runaways from bounty hunters. First Church may have had a tunnel at one time to a nearby home, and some say there was another near West Lorain, but none has ever been verified." Moving a stack of folders to the side, she continued, "Are you familiar with the Wilson Bruce

Evans House on Vine Street? The red brick across from Martin Luther King Park?"

"No."

"Wilson Bruce Evans and his brother, two African-American carpenters, built it in the 1850s. They participated in the Oberlin-Wellington Rescue of runaway slave John Price and were jailed for three months for violating the Fugitive Slave Act. Wilson Bruce enlisted and fought in the Union Army, and some family members participated in John Brown's raid on Harpers Ferry. I thought that if any house contained a secret tunnel, it would be that one. I've personally examined every inch of the basement and found nothing but a dank cellar. No secret doors. No passages."

Tales and rumors. *Damn*. I'd been so sure.

My head jerked up. "Do you have a list of homes that existed before the Civil War?"

"Better than that. We have in-depth records of all local historical buildings."

"Perfect. May I see the files on houses along West Lorain?"

Murphy checked her watch. "I have a little time before my meeting. Follow me."

She led me through narrow hallways, past tiny rooms so common in nineteenth-century homes, then down a creaky wooden stairway to a basement not intended for anyone over six feet tall. The low, unfinished ceiling revealed exposed insulation, plumbing, and air ducts. Rows of fluorescent lights flickered, illuminating faded walls. I bowed my head, ducked under a support beam, and sat at a small table.

She said, "On West Lorain?"

"Anywhere near Oberlin Hospital."

She unlocked three metal cabinets, thumbed through dozens of files, and set six manila folders on the table in front of me.

"These homes on Cedar, Hollywood, and Lorain date back to that era."

"Anything on the hospital property itself?"

She opened a different drawer and handed me another folder.

"Our files are not to leave this room, Mr. Austin. If you need to print a few pages, the copier is in the corner. I'll be back soon."

I thanked her and opened the first folder.

Chapter Thirty-Four

———•———

Wednesday, July 5, 11:00 a.m.

As I copied the last of seven pages, Pat Murphy came down the stairs. The sign on the wall above the machine read TEN CENTS PER COPY. I'd forgotten to stop at an ATM and was penniless.

"I'm afraid I'll have to pay for these later."

"That's okay," Ms. Murphy said with a smile. "But please consider a tax-deductible contribution to the Heritage Center."

"I'll do that." My consideration didn't take long. I would return and pay my debt, but with my vow of poverty, I needed a tax deduction about as much as God needed advice.

Thanking her, I vaulted up the steps and out the front door, retrieved Tree's business card from my wallet, and dialed. He answered on the third ring.

"Tree, it's Jake."

"Hey, glad you called. You were right. The syringe and insulin bottles in Dr. Byrd's office had been wiped clean. No fingerprints. None. Not even Byrd's."

"Then you won't find the killer's prints anywhere in his office either."

"Thanks, Sherlock. I'd already deduced that."

"Listen, Tree, I think I found a missing piece to that jigsaw puzzle we talked about last night. I'm at the Heritage Center. Where are you?"

"Not far. Stay put. I'm on my way."

A minute later, Tree slid his cruiser to a stop in front of the historical society. He rolled his window down.

"What ya got, Jake?"

"Remember what you said about Oran's alibi, that he couldn't have shot McDermott because he was in the hospital at the time? Well, I think it's possible he snuck out."

"Not a chance." Tree shook his head. "I told you at dinner, the hospital doors are locked and alarmed at night. Only way out is through the Emergency Room, and there's a receptionist and guard on duty. No way Oran waltzed out unseen."

"What if he didn't need to use that door? Check this out." I handed Tree one of the file copies. "They tore the old Decker house down to build the hospital." I poked the bottom of the page with my finger. "See, it says here that the Deckers were active in the Underground Railroad, so they may have had an escape tunnel for runaway slaves. I'll bet there's a passageway out of the hospital."

"You're joking. Have you lost your friggin' mind?" Tree groaned. "I'm up to my ass in bodies and don't have time for this kind of shit."

"Hear me out. Oran's doctor said they found him *sleepwalking* that night in the hospital basement covered with blood, as if he'd accidentally torn open his laceration, but ...."

Tree massaged his chin for a moment, then his eyes widened. "But back-spatter from a gunshot at close range could do the same," he said, completing my thought. "It's not too damn likely you could sleepwalk from a patient room down two flights of stairs to the basement without someone seeing you—

unless you were awake and avoiding detection." He flipped off his mirrored shades and stared at me. "But even if there is some sort of secret tunnel, the entrance would have to be hidden, or it would be common knowledge. So tell me, how the hell would Oran know about it?"

"Good question. Maybe he stumbled across an old document while researching his Civil War novel."

"And why would Oran go to all that trouble and do it that night? Why not simply shoot McDermott after he was discharged?"

"Because it gave him the perfect alibi, Tree."

"I don't know. That's a real stretch—but I guess it makes as much sense as anything else that's happened this week. I'll check out the hospital basement, black-light it for blood."

"I'll come with you."

"Like hell you will." Tree gave me *the look*, the same one Sister Very Nasty once gave me in school when she caught me sampling the altar wine. "I'm on it. You keep nosing around, Mr. Snitch. That's why the department bought your dinner."

Soldier, Doctor, Cleric, Snitch. My résumé was a damn novel title.

"And where do you suppose this imaginary tunnel of yours leads, Jake?"

"Maybe to one of these nearby houses. They were all built before the Civil War." I waved the other copies. "You might want to examine their cellars too."

"You gotta be kidding me. You think Oran slipped from the hospital, then snuck out of somebody's basement? What'd he do next? Hot-wire a car and drive out to McDermott's place? Come *on*, man."

Although the big man rolled his eyes, he took the pages and tore out of the parking lot, leaving a loud squeal and some rubber behind. Pat Murphy must have heard the commotion. She peeked out of a window, then drew the drapes.

Tree could scoff all he wanted. The jigsaw puzzle was

snapping into place. Sitting on the Heritage Center front steps, I dialed my phone and went after the next piece.

"Hi Em, it's Jake. I need your help. Have you read all of *Devil's Passage?*"

"It's not in Braille, but I've listened to the audio version." She sighed. "Heck, I've been involved with that novel since day one. I told you, I helped him revise the early drafts. Remember?"

"Oh, right. Sorry. Em, this is important. I've only read half the book. Is there any reference in it to poisonous mushrooms?"

"No, there's not …."

Crap. Another dead end. My mind went blank.

Emily said nothing, and the silence lasted so long that I thought my phone had dropped the call. "Em, are you still there?"

"Yes, I'm here." She paused. "Jake, I don't understand. How could you possibly know that? Oran used mushrooms in the original manuscript to kill a character. I convinced him to take that part out. There's no way you—"

"Destroying Angel mushrooms?"

"Yes, but how in the world …."

Bull's-eye.

"I'll fill you in later." My exhilaration lifted me off the front steps. I felt giddy and fist-pumped the sky. The puzzle was nearly complete. "Thanks, Em. Talk to you soon. Love ya."

As I hung up, I realized what I'd said. The words had spilled from my lips in my excitement.

Oh, sweet Jesus. What have I done?

I started punching in Emily's number, then stopped. What could I tell her? I couldn't un-say it. Maybe she hadn't heard me.

I could spin it anyway I wanted, but it was the truth. I still loved her and always had—even if I couldn't act on my feelings.

Explanations and apologies, however, would have to wait. If Emily was on Oran's hit list, then I needed to find enough evidence to put him behind bars.

Tree's skepticism about Oran emerging from the tunnel into someone's cellar and stealing a car was reasonable. There had to be another explanation. Then it struck me.

If there really was a tunnel, it couldn't lead far from the hospital. And if Oran knew about it, then ....

I rushed back into the historical society. Pat Murphy broke off a conversation with her assistant. She appeared unsettled, either by the frantic police visit, my agitation, or both.

"Ms. Murphy, I'm so sorry, but I need to see those files again."

She took a step backward. "I don't think ...." She put one hand on the telephone receiver, but left it in the cradle.

"I have to see them *now*. Please."

Her eyes danced around the room. She was clearly afraid and uncertain.

"This is important, part of a police investigation. Call Chief Macon, if you want."

Murphy began to dial, then hung up. "Okay, Mr. Austin. Let's go." She turned to her assistant. "Stay by the phone in case I need you." Translation: *Call the cops if this guy turns out to be a nut-case.*

Taking the phone book off the desk, I followed Murphy downstairs. Oran had not been listed as the owner of any of the historic houses near the hospital, so I flipped through the telephone directory until I found a listing for "Burke, Oran."

I pointed at the page. "Do you have any information on this address?"

Ms. Murphy thumbed through the file cabinet. A pipe in the unfinished ceiling rumbled above us. She picked out a folder and handed it to me.

"It's one of the houses you originally asked for, Mr. Austin. On Hollywood."

I opened the file and found Maryann Miller listed as the owner. Oran's mother? Her maiden name? Or maybe she'd remarried. I ran my finger down the page. Twenty years earlier, the house had been owned by ... Cameron Burke. Prior to that came a lineage of Burkes dating back to Jeddah, who'd built the house in 1852.

"Ms. Murphy, what do you know about the original owner, Jeddah Burke?"

"Not much, really. He was a minister, the fire and brimstone sort, big in the Temperance League and abolitionist movement. He rented rooms to black students at the college."

In my excitement, I tore the page from the telephone directory and shoved it into my pocket. Shocked by my destruction of Heritage Center property, Murphy gasped and jumped back, nearly tumbling over an open file drawer. I realized too late how unhinged I must seem, but there was no time to waste. I'd find a way to apologize later and get her a new phone book.

Throwing a *thank you* over my shoulder, I charged up the stairs and out the door into the crystal-blue morning, sprinting toward Hollywood Street.

Chapter Thirty-Five

---◦---

Wednesday, July 5, 11:30 a.m.

HALFWAY TO ORAN Burke's house, I stopped in the town square to catch my breath in the shade of the semi-circular Memorial Arch, where a young woman sat reading between two stone pillars. I dialed Tree's cellphone but got voicemail.

"Tree, I found two more pieces of the puzzle. Oran owns a pre-Civil War home near the hospital, and he's written about Destroying Angel mushrooms. He's our guy—I'm sure of it. Meet me at his place. Hurry."

I broke into a trot, wondering what our next move should be. The evidence was circumstantial, and my conjecture and theories wouldn't justify a search warrant. We'd need some sort of ploy to examine his cellar.

The sun was high in a cloudless sky, and by the time I reached Hollywood, my sweat-soaked T-shirt was clinging to my back. The quiet neighborhood looked deserted. I leaned against a shady oak and surveyed Oran's house from across the street. There was no suggestion of activity inside, and no sign of Tree Macon.

I dialed 911 and cajoled an operator into transferring my call to the police station.

Officer Martinez answered, and I told him that I needed to speak with Chief Macon. He was unimpressed with my credentials as Tree's friend. Martinez was the palace guard, and his job was to keep the riffraff away from the king.

"Doesn't sound like a 911 emergency, sir. I'll leave a note in the chief's office to call you."

"Please, Officer, this is urgent. Get my message to him immediately. He'll know what it's about. Have him meet me at—"

"I'll do what I can, Mr. Ashton."

"My name's Austin. Jake Austin. Listen to me. It's important that—"

Click. Martinez hung up. *Crap*.

I had no idea if Oran was home. Two trash cans on the tree lawn were filled to the brim, suggesting that he hadn't broken his normal routine or left town in a hurry. No cars were parked in the driveway, but the garage door was closed and windowless. If a tunnel existed, then he'd had access to his car and could have driven to McDermott's place and back. And if the gunshot had spattered Oran with McDermott's blood, there might be enough DNA evidence in the car to convict him.

No way had he been sleepwalking in the hospital basement and accidentally torn open his stitches. Not a chance in hell.

Worried about Emily's safety, I waited for Tree as long as I could, then strolled across the street and onto Oran's front porch. Two wooden rocking chairs nodded in the breeze, next to a dead potted plant. The drapes were drawn and I heard no sounds from inside.

Unsure how to proceed, I knocked. No response. If Oran answered, I could pretend to be checking on his health. I rapped again. Nothing. The doorbell produced no chime. I tried the doorknob. Locked.

Feigning nonchalance, I walked to the side door and knocked again. Same result.

I pulled the page that I'd torn from the telephone book out of my pocket, double-checked the street address, and dialed the number. I heard the phone ring inside, followed by Oran's voice: "I'm busy writing the next great American novel, so leave a message."

The doorknob turned easily. I smiled. Even without a Roman collar, a priest would not be suspected of anything but good intentions if discovered. And a priest didn't need a warrant to visit the grieving spouse of his dead parishioner—or to snoop around.

I gave the door a shove. It resisted. There was a deadbolt above the door knob and Oran had probably locked it.

Stepping back, I tripped over a large rock, nearly falling to the ground. I considered using it to break one of the small glass panes in the door so that I could reach in and unlock it, but discarded the idea, not wanting to convert my "priestly good intentions" defense into breaking and entering.

A nearby window was cracked open. I glanced around, saw no one, and shoved it hard. It didn't budge. Summer heat and humidity had caused the wood to swell and stick in its frame.

As I considered the rock again, the implication registered. Wood expansion. The side door might be *stuck* rather than locked. I turned the knob and nudged the door with my shoulder. It opened with a loud *pop*.

Justine and Colleen had been right. You shouldn't leave your home unlocked, even in a small town.

I peeked in and called out, "Hello? Anybody home?"
Silence.
I stepped inside and closed the door.

Chapter Thirty-Six

Wednesday, July 5, 11:45 a.m.

I PAUSED ON a landing between the kitchen and a closed door, possibly a closet, and listened. A window air conditioner rattled somewhere inside. No voices, footsteps, or other sounds.

Setting my mobile phone on vibrate in case Tree returned my call, I took two steps up into the kitchen and stood on a tile floor that had recently been scrubbed clean. A mop and bucket sat in the far corner. The scent of Pine-Sol partially masked decades of embedded cooking odors. Clean dishes filled the drying rack in the sink. I had never seen a bachelor's residence this spotless.

Soft morning light spilled from the window onto a well-worn table, illuminating a stack of mail, book-ended by salt and pepper shakers. I picked up the pile of stamped and sealed envelopes. The address of the telephone company showed through the clear plastic window of the first, the electric company through the second, MasterCard through the third.

Cleaning and paying bills? Not the behavior of someone who

intended to flee the police. Could I have misread the evidence and concocted a case against an innocent man?

The last envelope was addressed in Oran's jagged handwriting to Ms. Sheila Burke in Cincinnati. I wanted to open it, but placed it with the others in their niche between the salt and pepper shakers. I could do a computer search on her when I returned to the rectory.

Startled by a loud *whir* behind me, I spun around. The refrigerator had kicked on and was humming softly. It took me a moment to regain my composure before I crept into the small living room.

A well-worn leather recliner faced a boxy, old-fashioned television. An upright vacuum cleaner stood sentry nearby, still plugged into the wall socket. Oran and Nancy Burke smiled from two framed photographs on the mantle above a wood-burning fireplace. The distant aroma of blazing logs and cozy winter evenings lingered in the air. Knickknack shelves along one wall displayed a collection of Hummel figurines and ornately carved soapstone. With the drapes closed, however, the room was gloomy and depressing.

My nerves amped up with each step. At this point, my presence would be almost impossible to explain. I could always claim to be making sure that Oran hadn't collapsed again. The caring-doctor defense.

I peered cautiously around a corner into a hallway with three doors, two open.

The first was a small bathroom. The dripping faucet sounded like drumbeats in the stillness. I flipped on the light. The room was unremarkable, except for two full bottles of sleeping pills in the medicine cabinet, one prescribed by Oran's neurologist and one by another physician.

Was Oran stockpiling sedatives for a suicide?

I crept silently to the closed door, listened, and turned the knob with a trembling hand. It opened with a soft click.

A figure lay sprawled in a chair, its back grotesquely arched so that its head disappeared over the chair back, arms and legs dangling.

My breath caught in my throat. I jumped back, poised to run, but stopped. The figure was motionless. I slumped against the doorframe, my heart racing.

No dead body—just a shirt draped over the back of a chair with a pair of pants laid out below. *Damn my imagination.*

I walked into the room. The double bed was neatly made, its blue bedspread accented by two gold throw pillows, suggesting a feminine touch. A lemon scent danced in the air and a can of Pledge stood on the nightstand, next to a romance novel with dog-eared pages. On the book's cover, a bare-chested man cradled a scantily clad woman in his massive arms. The author was Oran's wife, Nancy.

A newer paperback, *Parisian Passions,* lay next to Nancy's novel, the author, Joanetta Carter. It rested on a handwritten book manuscript titled *French Fantasy*—with Nancy Burke's name on page one. A quick examination of the flowery script revealed that the only real difference between Joanetta's published novel and Nancy's manuscript was the title.

One more puzzle piece snapped into place.

No, I wasn't concocting a case against an innocent man. Joanetta's name had been mentioned in every news report since her lifeless body was discovered at the quarry, and the book and manuscript linked her to Oran.

I surveyed the bedroom. One dresser drawer stood ajar, completely empty. I opened the others—all bare. The closet contained only wire clothes hangers. A tower of large cardboard boxes rose from a faded beige carpet, each box sealed with masking tape and labeled GOODWILL in black marker.

I stepped into the hall and entered the last room, a study. Along the far wall, a white floor-to-ceiling bookshelf with all the books removed gave the appearance of bleached mastodon ribs. Six sealed cartons lay nearby, four marked DONATE, one KEEP—FIRST EDITIONS, and the last, FAMILY PHOTOS.

Packing up. Was Oran getting his affairs in order? His illness was serious, but his death wasn't imminent. Incapacitation would come first. What in the world was going on here?

A large display case with glass doors along the right wall contained two elaborately engraved crossed swords and several gun racks with muskets and pistols of Revolutionary and Civil War vintage. One shelf held daggers, ninja throwing stars, and a blowpipe. A crossbow and arrows hung below them.

The drapes were drawn and the room was dark. I pulled the chain on an old desk lamp and it cast a jaundiced light on two photographs.

In one, a smiling Oran Burke stood between Sean Penn and Katie Holmes. The other, a sepia photo in an ornate frame, showed a soldier leaning on his musket. He wore the uniform of a Union officer and a sword was slung from one hip. The rakish slant of his cap contrasted sharply with his solemn expression. Although the soldier's shoulders were broader, his face bore a striking resemblance to a younger Oran.

A ceiling fan spun slowly above me, producing a clicking sound as it stirred the turbid air. Screensaver fish swam across the monitor of a desktop computer. I tapped the mouse and a rectangular dialog box replaced the fish, demanding a password. I listened again for movement in the house, settled into the chair, and typed the obvious password possibilities: Oran's name, address, and phone number. Nothing worked.

I was about to type in the titles of Oran's novels when I heard a hum and something touched my side. My heart fluttered like a caged bird trying to escape. I whirled the swivel chair around and … was completely alone.

The hum repeated, and I grabbed my cellphone. The display showed the rectory's telephone number. Colleen, no doubt, calling about lunch with Justine and RJ.

I was as freaked out as a seven-year-old on a dark Halloween night, and my hands trembled as I tried the top drawer of the desk. Locked.

The bottom drawer contained our old high school yearbook. Large red Xs crossed out class photos of Barb Dorfman and McDermott. More disconcerting was the circle around Emily's picture, and the question mark slashed across mine.

Was Oran celebrating his kills? Was this a serial killer's hit list, or a scrapbook of his achievements?

Damning, but not proof of murder.

The answering machine light blinked the number two. Although I didn't want to risk the noise, Tree needed hard evidence. I pushed the play button and lowered the volume. One message was the hang up from my earlier call. The second produced a soft soprano voice: "Uncle Oran, it's Sheila. I have a question. Give me a buzz."

Adjacent to the answering machine was a sealed envelope labeled FOR SHEILA BURKE. I picked it up. Metal shifted and jingled inside. My fingers outlined two keys. One probably opened the upper desk drawer. It had to be locked for a reason. Snatching a letter opener from the desk, I was about to slice open the envelope when I heard a door squeak.

I dropped the envelope and leaped from the desk chair. With no exit at this end of the house, I crept back into the living room. A floorboard groaned loudly. I stopped, then stepped closer to the wall, where the support was stronger. Tiptoeing quietly into the kitchen, I realized that I was still holding the letter opener. *Crap.* I had to get out of Oran's home before I was discovered. I couldn't risk returning it to the study.

I peeked around the corner and stepped down gently onto the landing where I had entered. The closed door, which I'd originally assumed to be a closet, had to lead to the cellar, and to the tunnel. I'd never get another chance to find it.

I hesitated. Had I really heard a door squeak, or was I spooking myself again?

Tires crunched gravel outside and a car door slammed. Footsteps thumped on the front porch.

Sweet Jesus.

Slowly drawing back the sheer curtain on the side door, I peered out the window. The footsteps retreated from the porch and a mailman sauntered back to his truck. No sign of the cops.

I wiped the sweat from my brow.

Damn it, Tree. Where the hell are you?

Chapter Thirty-Seven

———•———

Wednesday, July 5, 12:05 p.m.

I HAD FOUND only circumstantial evidence so far: antique weapons, Nancy Burke's plagiarized novel, and victims' photos crossed out in a yearbook. Even if I had obtained the evidence legally, it wasn't enough for Tree to get a search warrant—but it told me I was right about Oran. Which meant there was a good chance the basement contained a tunnel. The circle around Emily's class picture, her unexplained hang-up phone calls, and the threatening note at the reunion also meant that I couldn't walk away. This had to end.

The hinges squeaked as I opened the cellar door into darkness. Unable to see a light switch, I placed my left hand on the railing and clutched the letter opener in my right, feeling foolish. Hell, I'd been in tighter jams than this overseas and certainly didn't need a weapon to overpower a sickly guy like Oran.

But on his turf, with his arsenal? I tightened my grip on the letter opener and continued down the stairs.

The fifth step groaned under my weight. *Shit*. Panic pushed

its way up from the pit of my stomach, and I swallowed hard
to force it back down. Motionless, I waited. The soft *whoosh* of
the gas water heater firing up startled me. I released a trapped
breath and took the last few steps down to the painted concrete
floor.

The basement, dimly lit by two small windows, smelled of
mildew and something pungent and foul, a combination of
ammonia and sulfur. In the far corner, a grow light above a
potted plant cast an eerie, green glow.

I saw no light switch near the stairs and moved into the
room cautiously as my eyes adjusted. Something brushed the
top of my head, and I whirled around before noticing a chain
dangling from a ceiling bulb. I yanked it, illuminating wood-
paneled walls, but no tunnel or door.

On my left, a sport coat draped the back of an old couch
flanked by two end tables with reading lamps. To my right,
a flashlight rested on a scarred workbench. An assortment of
tools hung neatly from wall hooks over the bench. A litter box
under it explained the foul odor.

Beyond the bench, a pair of muddy work boots stood beside
a wooden box on the floor. I walked over. The box contained
soil and a few mushrooms.

Work boots for a box of mushrooms? That made no sense.

But I knew exactly what was in the box. Having seen
only photographs, I stooped down. The Destroying Angels
mushrooms resembled tiny white umbrellas. As I leaned in for
a closer look, cool air tickled the hair on my arm. The windows
weren't open and there was no fan. I passed my hand across the
wood paneling and felt the draft again.

Standing, I tapped the wall using the same technique I
employed to percuss a patient's chest or abdomen, moving
from right to left, listening for pockets of air between solid
structures.

Three feet from the mushrooms, the sound subtly changed,
becoming lower and hollower. Examining the paneling inch

by inch, I skimmed my fingertips carefully across it until they found a board that was not quite flush. I slid them under it and pulled.

A door swung open, revealing inky blackness. Light from the cellar's ceiling bulb turned to smudges inside the opening. I could barely make out a few ancient support timbers that inspired no confidence.

I grabbed the flashlight from the workbench, flipped it on, and peered into the tunnel. The gluttonous darkness gobbled up the beam, the gloom so heavy, I could feel it. Holding the letter opener like a Bowie knife, I inched forward.

The dank smell of decay swept my thoughts back to Cu Chi, to that horrible piercing cry the Viet Cong soldier had released just before shooting Kenny—bitter, mocking, scornful— the sound of a man with nothing left to lose, the sound that echoed in my nightmares. I heard the gunshot, saw the fist-sized hole in Kenny's chest, felt again the lust for vengeance that had driven me into those dark passageways—and the panic of being lost in that maze, certain that I'd crawled into my own grave.

The rumble of a window air conditioner upstairs shook me back to reality. I took another step—directly into a spider's web. I swept the sticky tangle from my face and hair and cursed. Since Vietnam, I'd hated spiders almost as much as snakes. At least in the States, most spiders weren't the size of your hand.

Another step and the walls closed in on me. I trembled, causing the light to dance through the distant shadows. The passage narrowed ten yards ahead where the wall had partially collapsed. Hell, the tunnel was one-hundred-and-fifty years old, and a sneeze would probably cave in the whole damn thing.

I tried to advance, but claustrophobia grabbed me by the throat and my feet refused to move. Too many ghosts from the war floated in the gloom. One underground, near-death experience in my life was more than enough. I was done. Tree and the police could take it from here.

As I began to back out, a faint, high-pitched cry echoed from deep in the tunnel. I hesitated and heard it again, plaintive and agonal, followed by a thrashing sound. A child? A woman? Had Oran's disease driven him completely insane? Could he have taken Emily? No, she was safe, working at the snack shop—or was she?

It didn't matter *who* was in there; I couldn't abandon them.

Fighting my terror, I crept forward. Sweat poured into my eyes. A stone bounced off my back and dirt sifted down onto my face. Where the wall had collapsed, the remaining opening was narrow. I was a much larger man than Oran, maybe too large to fit through. My light revealed a right-angle turn in the tunnel on the far side, and I had no idea what lay beyond.

Placing the flashlight and letter opener on the ground, I tried to squeeze past. One shoulder was nearly beyond the narrowing before I got stuck. I heard the cry again and bulldozed forward with all my strength, but only succeeded in wedging myself tighter until I couldn't move at all.

Trapped. *Christ.* If Oran found me, I was a dead man.

I dug my feet into the ground and gave a mighty lunge. The sagging wooden beam above groaned loudly, and a dirt blizzard drifted over me—but I hadn't moved an inch.

Time to get creative. I'd dislocated my left shoulder making a tackle years ago and thought I might be able to make myself smaller by popping my arm back out of its socket. I twisted hard. It hurt like hell, but my shoulder wouldn't budge. The timber above, however, did. I heard it crack and more of the ceiling crumbled onto my head and neck. The dust blinded me and set off a coughing spell.

When I could breathe again, I looked around. Part of the wall had caved in, but not enough to pin me down—and the narrowing had enlarged. I was free.

I'd made a great deal of noise, however, and had lost the

element of surprise. The cry came again, closer this time. I heard a scraping sound, like the soft shuffling of feet on the dirt floor or a small body being dragged.

My mind said to keep going, but instinct pulled me backward, out of the hole, taking the letter opener and flashlight with me. I moved to the side and crouched behind a pile of dirt, ready to ambush Oran.

Time stopped. I tried to quiet my breathing and remain motionless. Finally, a gigantic Siamese cat backed through the opening, belly low to the ground, dragging a bloodied rat, which writhed and cried as it resisted. The cat didn't even bother to glance at me, as if it owned the tunnel.

What little courage I had mustered ebbed away. Oran might still be somewhere in the tunnel, but I sure as heck wasn't going to find out.

As I retreated, the muddy ground sucked at my shoes, clinging to me like the memory of Cu Chi. I stepped back into the cellar and tripped over Oran's filthy work boots.

Wait …. If Oran wasn't wearing the boots, then he wasn't in the tunnel. Besides, what reason did he have to return to the hospital?

I heard a loud *crack*, then a *buzz*. Fangs tore my flesh and fire sizzled up my spine like a lit fuse, cramping all my muscles.

As I collapsed, I caught the glint of the wires leading back to the Taser in Oran's hand. Then the back of my head hit the concrete, and everything went dark.

Chapter Thirty-Eight

Wednesday, July 5, 12:20 p.m.

MY EYES OPENED to swirls of gray and black. I had no idea where I was, what had happened, or how long I'd been out. Minutes … hours … days?

The room spun like a carousel through thick fog. My stomach heaved, vomit rising. I gagged, swallowed hard, and tried not to retch.

As the haze cleared from my mind, pain flared in my lower back, the muscles twitching. My entire body ached. I lay facedown on the floor, arms and legs hog-tied behind me. Ropes dug into my wrists and ankles. My fingers were numb and tingled from lack of circulation.

When I raised my head, the room whirled faster. I lowered my cheek onto the cold concrete, closed my eyes, and waited for the chaos to settle.

The clack of metal on metal forced me to look up. Oran stood at his workbench. He rotated the open cylinder of a revolver one click and slid in a bullet. My cellphone and letter opener rested on the bench next to the Taser, its wires no longer visible.

Oran guided another round into the chamber.

I thought about Emily, Justine, and RJ. The fear of never seeing them again swept the fog from my mind. I tried to roll onto my back, failed, and strained against my bonds.

Oran glanced over and closed the box of ammunition.

"Jake, Jake. What were you thinking?" He shook his head. "I must admit, I'm nearly as *stunned* as you just were," he said with a chuckle. "To figure things out so fast, you must have read my novel. A jock who reads? Imagine that." He snapped the cylinder of the revolver shut. "I'm sorry you broke in here today. Very sorry."

"Oran, please. Don't do this. I never hurt you."

I stared at the gun and mumbled an Act of Contrition.

Oran studied the revolver and grunted. "Oh, this? Trust me, if I wanted you dead, you'd already be room temperature."

His tremors were much worse than I'd seen at the hospital. Despite them, he managed to slide his pistol into a shoulder holster.

"True, you weren't unkind in school, Jake. You simply ignored me. The reason you're still alive, however, is because Emily cares about you, and I care deeply for her. She's my friend. Killing you would hurt her, and she's had more than enough pain." His face hardened. "She's the main reason I shot McDermott. That jackal preyed on the gentle people of this world."

Oran walked slowly to the couch and slipped the sport coat on, concealing his weapon.

"Some creatures are inherently dangerous. Scorpions, black widows, rattlesnakes. No matter how well you treat them, they'll try to hurt you. History is filled with people like that too. Stalin and Hitler top the list. Was McDermott a Hitler? No. There are shades of darkness. To burn in the same circle of Hell with the likes of Joseph and Adolf requires both evil and power. But as McDermott gained wealth and influence, he would have done more harm."

Oran limped back to the workbench. The big Siamese deposited the dead rat under the bench, sauntered out, and nuzzled Oran's leg.

"My friend here and I have something in common. We both kill vermin. It's nature's way, exactly as your god designed it." He reached down and stroked the cat's fur. "I may be a small man, Jake, but I won't allow predators to hurt the people I love. I hear McDermott's not doing well. He seemed pretty damn dead when I left him. Maybe I should've driven a stake through his heart."

His cackle sounded like something from a padded room in the psych ward, unhinged and otherworldly. Had he become this cruel over the years, or was his Huntington's disease making him deranged?

"Nearly everyone detested McDermott, Oran, me included. But how could you shoot him in cold blood?"

But I knew the answer, knew all too well the nearly irresistible power of rage and vengeance. In my mind, I saw the muzzle of my sidearm pressed against the Viet Cong's temple, my finger on the trigger.

"Don't give me that pious bullshit, *Father*. Do as I say, not as I do? Hell, you told me what you did in Vietnam. Talk about cold-blooded." Oran filled a bowl with cat food and set it on the floor. "Besides, my sainted wife taught me the Bible. 'Every tree that does not bear good fruit is cut down and thrown into the fire.' Matthew, Chapter Seven, Verse Nineteen. McDermott was a blighted tree. I couldn't let his toxic fruit continue to poison Emily or anyone else." Oran sneered. "Donating money to charities was probably the only decent thing he ever did, but I had to put a gun to the cheap bastard's head to get him to write the checks."

While he ranted, I arched my back and brought my hands and feet closer together, trying to feel for a knot I could untie, but my muscles refused to obey my commands.

"If you care so much about Emily, Oran, then why'd you

frighten her with hang-up phone calls and threaten her at the reunion?"

"What? I didn't. What are you talking about?"

"The note on our table said, 'Enjoy your evening, bitch! God knows it could be your last.' Why Em?"

"Damn, I forgot about that. I left it for Barb Dorfman. She was sitting next to Emily, and I assumed they'd have dinner together. At least Emily had the good sense not to break bread with that walking dung heap."

As Oran reached for an old rag, his arm writhed though a series of contortions. He waited until the spasm passed, picked up the rag, and waved it.

"McDermott needed killing, and you need gagging."

"Just one question, Oran." I had to keep him talking until Tree got my message.

He checked his watch, set the rag on the workbench, and crossed his arms over his chest.

"I have a few minutes before my ... appointment. Ask away. Makes no difference to me. Bob Dylan spoke the truth." Oran sang the ending of "Like a Rolling Stone" in a sad baritone. When he finished, he added, "That's me now, Jake. Since Nancy's death, I have *nothing*, and not a damn thing left to lose. And with my failing health, I sure as hell have no reason to conceal any secrets."

He stopped and looked down at me. "I'm dying of Huntington's disease. As a physician, you know what's in store for me. A painful, demeaning death. I refuse to go out like that folk singer, Woody Guthrie, a wheelchair cripple in a nuthouse."

"I'm sorry, Oran. I really am."

He waved my sympathy away with one hand.

"At first, I withdrew to the shelter of literature and poetry. Warmed myself with the words of Henry James and Yeats. Then, one night, as I read Dylan—the other one, Dylan Thomas—I stumbled across his famous villanelle, a truly inspired poem.

As an erudite graduate of Oberlin High," he snickered, "I'm sure you know it."

Oran turned away, and began to recite, "Do not go gentle into that good night" from memory. Halfway through, he stopped and whirled back.

"The point is, Jake, I recognized how frail my deeds have been, how little lightning my years on this planet have sparked, and how few wrongs I've righted. I vowed not to go gently into my grave. I vowed to *rage*."

His exertion having taken its toll, he slumped against the bench, breathing hard.

"My body's failing me, and I knew my mind would betray me soon, so I had to act quickly. When Cathy Meeker asked me to speak at our class reunion, I hesitated until she started naming classmates who'd RSVP'd—including Barb Dorfman, all the way from New York. Delivered as if by Providence into my hands."

"Why Barb?" Staring up at Oran sent my back and neck muscles into spasm. I laid my face back down on the cold, hard floor. "And why kill Dr. Byrd?"

"Ah, so you know about Byrd too. You continue to amaze me." Oran tilted his head to one side. "Are you dying to hear my confession, Father? Good for the soul, is it? What a load of crap."

He slammed his fist on the bench, and nails rattled in a tin can like a tambourine.

"I took out McDermott for Emily, and for me. Barb Dorfman and Byrd were for my wife. Nancy and I worked and scraped to grow our meager savings. Barb used her friendship with Nancy to wheedle her way into our lives as our financial advisor. That vulture invested all our money in risky schemes that paid her the highest commissions. Nancy and I knew nothing of finance. We trusted her. When everything crashed and burned, Barb simply walked away with her cut. No explanation, no apology."

Oran picked a wrench off the rack and hurled it across the

room. It hit the couch and bounced away, clanking against the concrete.

"I should've paid attention, should've protected Nancy and our money—but I was too damn busy writing my novel."

He picked up a screwdriver and turned it over in his hand.

"Barb told Nancy to consider our loss *a learning opportunity*. Opportunity, my ass. The bitch ruined us. By the time we'd sorted things out, Barb had moved to New York, and no lawyer or prosecutor would take the case. Some bullshit statute of limitation thing, and a bunch of mumbo-jumbo about unstable market conditions."

He flung the screwdriver, impaling the couch. Stuffing leaked out like eviscerated bowel from a large gash in the cushion.

Oran's volatility terrified me. Sweat dripped from my face. I cringed when he grabbed a claw hammer from the rack and examined it as if he'd never seen one.

"The financial stress hit Nancy hard, Jake, though not as hard as the betrayal of her friendship. We used to invite Barb to our home for dinner. One night she accused us of not caring about the planet because we ate meat—and we felt *guilty*. As if Barb cared about anything except money and herself."

Even though I expected Oran to throw it, I winced when the hammer missed the couch, splintered an end table, and shattered the lamp on the cellar floor.

"As a writer of murder mysteries, I wanted to dispatch those who had ruined my life in ways suitably matched to their transgressions. So I prepared a special garnish for the reunion and added it to Barbie's dinner." Oran pointed to the wooden box containing the mushrooms. "Now that holier-than-thou vegan is eating dirt and fertilizing the damn veggies. How's *that* for poetic justice?"

His laugh ratcheted up to caustic.

"Barbie was the only one scheduled to die Saturday, but one never knows when opportunity will raise its hairy hand to knock. My unexpected admission to the hospital gave me the perfect alibi and access to the tunnel, so I seized the opportunity to shoot McDermott. Carpe Diem, or should I say, *Carpe devils.* I'd planned a more interesting death for McDermott, but time was short, so I had to make do with watching him suffer as he emptied his checking account of his greatest love."

Oran walked unsteadily to the secret passage, put the work boots in the tunnel, and shut the door with a click.

"Thought I'd closed that completely before you came downstairs. Good luck finding the release latch."

Oran's neck began a serpentine writhing motion. I used the distraction to try to rock onto my knees. With my legs and arms tied behind me, however, I flopped back down and smashed my forehead against the concrete. Skull-cracking pain gave way to twinkling lights.

When his muscle spasm abated, Oran said, "If you're going to continue to struggle, I can't be responsible for your injuries. Be a good boy and behave."

"What about Dr. Byrd?" The memory of his face in a pool of vomit transformed my fear into anger. "Why him?"

"What do you think this is, a TV show where the defendant jumps up and confesses to the jury? I'm not some idiot actor, and you're sure as shit not Perry Mason," Oran scoffed. "Well, why the hell not. Someone should know the truth. It's not like I'm ever going to trial."

He dragged a stool out from under the workbench and sat.

"After Barb's betrayal, Nancy developed chest pain. Byrd ran EKGs, stress tests, a heart catheterization, and found nothing. The *genius* diagnosed her symptoms as heartburn due to stress. Medication didn't help, so he admitted her to the hospital and shoved a scope down her throat for a simple look-see at her stomach—and rammed it through an ulcer that had been developing for months."

A tear rolled down Oran's sallow cheek. He picked up the rag from the bench and wiped it away.

"In the chaos, Byrd panicked and injected Nancy with a medicine she was allergic to—which he would have known if he'd read her chart or checked her wristband. She died instantly from a drug reaction."

Oran dabbed at another tear.

"After I buried Nancy, I vowed to bury Byrd. I sued him for twice his malpractice coverage, turned down a huge settlement offer, and took him to court, hoping to ruin him. His slick defense lawyers, however, dazzled a jury of my dimwitted peers. Although the evidence of Byrd's negligence was overwhelming, the jury found him not guilty."

He blew his nose and threw the rag on the workbench.

"On one hospital visit with Nancy, I'd seen a pharmacy tech deliver Byrd's insulin supply to his office refrigerator. Door-to-door service for the great man. Success in life, Jake, is all about attention to details," Oran added, pleased with his insight. "I laced his Scotch with sedatives he'd prescribed for Nancy, pointed my gun at him, and ordered him to drink. When he passed out, I injected him with his own insulin. It seemed appropriate that Byrd should die of a medication error, don't you think?" The corners of his lips tried for a smile. "Even if the fridge had contained only a ham sandwich, I'd have found another way to kill him. Fourth of July was my independence day from Dr. Byrd."

Oran patted the revolver under his sport coat.

"Been nice having this heart-to-heart chat, but it's time to dispatch one final devil for Nancy. I guess in that regard, we're both in the same business, eh, Father?"

Another murder? *Dear God in Heaven.* Where were the cops? I had to stall.

"Oran, there are medications for Huntington's now. And who knows what stem cell research will bring? Don't throw your life away. You may have years left."

"Not good years. You know that. And without Nancy, who

cares? Time is slipping away, and I won't spend my last few days in jail or drooling in a wheelchair."

"You've read about Huntington's, right?" When Oran nodded, I chose my next words carefully, hoping that they wouldn't be my last. "The disease can cause confusion, disorientation, make you do things—"

"My goddamn mind is just fine. You think I'm crazy? I know *exactly* what I'm doing." Oran advanced on me. "It's a death sentence for me, whether Huntington's or the State of Ohio executes me. Those four devils needed to be hurled back into Hell. What's one more?"

Barb Dorfman, McDermott, Byrd, and what I'd seen upstairs indicated the fourth was Joanetta Carter. Now, he was going after a fifth victim.

"Oran, you're being blinded by your grief over Nancy's death. Life isn't black and white. It's—"

"You're wrong. Things are either right or wrong, good or evil. We Burkes have understood that for centuries. My great-great-granddaddy, Jeptha, knew there was no *maybe* about slavery, no *upside* to tearing this magnificent country in half. He enlisted, rose to the rank of captain, and rode through swarms of musket balls into Confederate lines until the South fell to its knees in surrender. He died a few years later, defending his sister's honor in a duel. He did what needed to be done, and so do I."

Jeptha. The photograph of the Union soldier in Oran's study.

"You have reason to be proud of a man like that, but what would Jeptha say if—"

"Stop! Enough! We're done here. I have things to do." Oran headed slowly up the cellar stairs. "Have a nice life, Jake."

"Damn it, Oran, *don't do this.*"

Chapter Thirty-Nine

———◆———

Wednesday, July 5, 12:35 p.m.

"Damn it?" Oran stopped. "You really shouldn't swear, Father, though I'm glad you did." He hobbled to the workbench and grabbed the rag he'd used to blow his nose. "I nearly forgot your gag." He inspected the rag, dropped it, and pulled a clean, folded cloth from a drawer.

"One last question, Oran. Please."

"Don't push it." His voice rumbled like thunder. "You're stalling, and I have unfinished business."

"Just explain the tunnel. I have to know."

"Ah yes, of course." Oran glanced at his watch. "I still have a little time … to kill." He leaned against the bench. "My older brother and I found the tunnel when we were kids. The cellar often flooded back then, so adults rarely came down here. It became our indoor playground." Oran gestured toward the hidden door. "There used to be shelving covering the entrance. One day, I accidentally tripped the release latch. Next thing you know, we're in a cave. The tunnel had collapsed twenty feet in. Mother would never have let us use it, so we didn't tell her."

Oran shoved his hands into his pockets.

"After reading about slave tunnels in school, we dug and reopened the passage. It led to a rickety ladder with an old wooden door above that we couldn't budge. It took weeks to get it open. I tapped the door with a broomstick, while my brother wandered outside till he heard me. Turns out, the hospital loading dock steps had been built over the hatch. We crawled under the steps and found it covered with dirt, near a basement window."

Oran's eyes drifted upward into a memory.

"I snuck into the hospital and unlocked the window. We'd occasionally make what we called 'commando runs,' stealing small stuff. I guess we were junior tunnel rats." Oran stood again and combed his fingers through thin, graying hair. "Over time, we reinforced the walls. I hadn't been in the tunnel for years and wasn't sure if it had caved in or would collapse on me. Sadly for McDermott, I squeezed through."

"And your brother?"

"We each had a fifty-fifty chance of a normal life, yet we both drew the short straw gene from our father. My brother suffered bravely and left behind a wife and daughter. Luckily, I couldn't have children. My niece and I were tested together for Huntington's. She's negative, thank God. I told her I was too."

"Sheila?"

Oran's hands fisted. "How the hell did you know that?"

"Her name is on an envelope upstairs."

"Ah yes, of course. Well, one good thing came out of my illness. I took out a large life insurance policy before I got tested for Huntington's, so there's no exclusion for preexisting conditions. Sheila gets that, plus my book royalties."

He twirled the rag from both ends until the center thickened into an effective gag. I tried to keep the clock ticking.

"What about your father, Oran?"

"Died young in a mining accident, before his defective gene could attack him. I do remember stories about his mother and grandfather. Both died in their forties from *the twitches*, as they called it back then. Folks in town used to whisper about the Burke curse. All that bizarre family history finally made sense when the gene for Huntington's disease was discovered ten years ago."

The bindings were shredding my skin, and my hands burned like fire. I flexed my fingers and groaned. "Oran, my wrists …."

"Sorry about your discomfort, Jake. I tried to tie you to a chair, but you're too damn heavy to lift. Instead of loosening the ropes, let's try this."

Oran grabbed a pillow from the couch and slid it under my head. He twirled the rag into a gag and looked down.

Come on, Tree, I can't buy much more time.

"You said you took out *four* devils. Who was the fourth?"

"Doesn't matter."

"It does to me, Oran. I'll need to explain everything to Emily … and the folks in town."

Oran shrugged. "Why not? Joanetta Carter."

I knew the answer, but launched the question anyway. "Why her?"

"Q and A is over, Jake."

Oran put a foot on my back, shoved the gag into my mouth, and tied it behind my head. He crossed the room with a shuffling gait, then stopped.

"Ah, what the hell. Might as well tell you. Joanetta and my wife belonged to the same book club. Nancy had scribbled out the rough draft of her second novel. She was a two-fingered typist, and it would have taken her forever to type the manuscript. She hired Joanetta to transcribe it into a document on the computer."

Oran sat on the steps and tapped his fingers together.

"After Nancy passed away, I asked Joanetta for the manuscript. She denied having it. Next thing I know, this rookie, wannabe writer's book is released by a major romance publishing house."

Oran gave a derisive snort.

"Two plus two equals *plagiarism*, so I confronted her. Joanetta said the manuscript was crap and called Nancy a hack writer. She claimed that her revisions had saved the novel, which made it *hers*. Then this charming young woman, with her colorful tattoos and equally colorful language, suggested that I have intercourse with myself."

Oran's eyes narrowed to slits.

"I had no physical evidence that Nancy had written the book because Joanetta had the manuscript, and with my Huntington's, I didn't have time for lawsuits. Joanetta's lifestyle kept her strapped for cash, so I offered to stop by her apartment and pay her to add an acknowledgment about Nancy in the next printing. She agreed. Problem was, I wanted her to understand what a vile piece of shit she'd been before I finished her. But she was young and agile, and I wasn't sure I could subdue her." His lips slowly curled into a smirk. "Did you see my weapons collection upstairs?"

I nodded.

"I used my blowgun, hit her right in the chest." His strangled laughter could have corroded metal. He pointed to a far corner, where a plant sat under a grow light. "Curare, of Amazon poison dart fame. Interesting drug. Paralyzes the body, but the heart keeps beating, leaving the victim wide awake and completely conscious." He paused. "Which allowed me time to explain to Joanetta that plagiarism was akin to kidnapping a writer's child. Nancy's child and mine. And that by doing so, she had indeed fucked herself."

Oran shook his head.

"Curare's effects are, however, hideous. I can't quite shake the memory of Joanetta's facial contortions, as if hundreds of grubs were writhing beneath her skin. Or the gurgling sound she made as saliva pooled in her throat when she could no longer swallow."

Oran stood slowly and with difficulty.

"Joanetta had been a varsity swimmer in school, prideful of her awards. She belonged to a private club, and the condescending bitch told me that she swam every day so she wouldn't get fat … like Nancy. That insult sealed her fate. With her anorexia, it was easy to drag her skinny ass to the quarry to drown. Then I took her computer and Nancy's manuscript, and dumped her car near McDermott's house, just to make his life hell." He checked his watch. "Now, if you'll excuse me, I have one last score to settle. Take care of Emily for me, Jake."

Oran leaned heavily on the handrail and disappeared up the cellar stairs.

Chapter Forty

---·---

Wednesday, July 5, 12:45 p.m.

Lying on my belly, arms and legs hog-tied behind me, I arched my back and again tried to roll up onto my knees. The result was another face-plant, but I missed the pillow and hit the concrete. Blood poured from my nose, making it hard to breathe with the gag in place.

I flopped onto my side, wriggled over to the workbench, and tried to force the gag from my mouth by scraping it against the wooden bench leg, tearing skin from my cheek and smearing blood into one eye. The gag didn't budge.

The Siamese cat had disappeared behind the couch, but the rat lay under the bench, two feet from my face. Was I imagining it, or did its hind legs move? I squirmed and twisted until my head was farther away.

My cellphone buzzed above me. *Dear Lord, let it be Tree.* After a few seconds, the vibration stopped.

I wanted to kick the bench leg and knock something to the ground that might free me, but the way I was bound, I couldn't generate enough force.

Rolling onto my back, I studied the workbench, hoping for inspiration. None came. Completely exhausted, I gave up and let my knees slump against the bench leg.

Wait ... I couldn't *kick* with my feet, but I could rock my legs from side to side.

I repositioned and swung my thighs from right to left like a battering ram. My knee collided with the thick wooden leg. Pain shot up to my hip. I heard a thud and a rolling sound above. Sliding so that my thigh muscles would take the brunt of the impact instead of my knee, I swung my legs again. An old coffee can rumbled off the edge of the workbench and crashed down next to me in a hailstorm of screws and nails. I needed something sharp enough to cut my bonds, but the rim of the can was rolled and dull.

I tried again and the Taser tumbled down, striking me on the chin with the force of a Mike Tyson right hook.

Son of a ....

I scanned the room for other ideas. The wrench and hammer that Oran had thrown were on the floor but useless, and the screwdriver was out of reach, embedded in a couch cushion. The scattered chunks of broken ceramic lamp appeared too thick to cut the ropes, and its light bulb had exploded into tiny fragments.

Frustrated and defeated, I closed my eyes, too tired to move.

Brakes squealed and gravel crunched in the driveway. Heavy footfalls tromped up the porch steps, followed by knocking at the front door.

"Oran, its Tree Macon. Please open the door, sir."

I tried to yell, but barely managed a strangled moan through the gag.

Louder knocking. "Police. Open up, Mr. Burke!"

A fierce pounding. "Jake, you in there?"

I couldn't let Tree walk away. Rolling onto my side, I writhed toward the hammer, fragments of shattered light bulb and lamp tearing at my flesh. My fingers found the handle, and with a painful flick of my wrist, I swung the hammer and sent the coffee can rattling into the wall. Then I beat out a jackhammer rhythm on the floor.

I heard a loud thud upstairs, then another.

Come on, Tree, use those size-thirteen boots of yours.

A third thud, then the crack of splintering wood as the door gave way.

"Police! Oran, come out with your hands up." Tree's voice was no longer muffled. Floorboards in the living room groaned under the big man's weight. "Jake, where the hell are you?"

I banged out a reply with the hammer and groaned loudly.

Tree raced down the stairs, his gun raised. He surveyed the cellar, holstered his weapon, and cut my bonds with a jackknife.

Like a ragdoll's, my arms and legs flopped onto the concrete. The room spun again and my stomach lurched.

"Holy shit," he said as he untied the gag. "You okay?"

I nodded.

"Well, you look like crap. I told you to stay out of this. You're my snitch, not police." Tree turned toward the stairs. "Where's Oran?"

"Gone." I crawled onto the couch and plucked a piece of glass from my calf. Blood blossomed on my blue jeans, forming a purple circle the size of a quarter.

"What the fuck happened here, Jake?"

I began to explain, but when I mentioned the tunnel, Tree raised his hand and stopped me.

"Whoa! What tunnel? We couldn't find one in the hospital basement."

"It comes up under the loading-dock stairs outside, near an unlocked basement window. That's how Oran snuck out to shoot McDermott."

"Those windows are tiny."

"And Oran's a half-pint-sized guy."

Tree's expression relaxed. "That half-pint sure did a number on you, soldier boy. Looks like he used your face as a punching bag."

"Not funny. He Tasered me. The guy's a walking time bomb."

I massaged my throbbing back muscles, then pointed to a basement corner.

"That box contains the mushrooms that poisoned Barb Dorfman." I swung my finger in an arc across the room. "And the plant under the grow light is curare. Oran used it to paralyze Joanetta Carter. She stole Nancy Burke's manuscript and published it as her own. When Oran confronted her, she called Nancy fat and a hack writer. He's all about payback. I think Oran's mind is going."

Tree circled the room. "So where's this tunnel, Jake?"

"Behind that wall." I pointed. "But I don't know where the release lever is."

"Well, I do." Tree tapped the wall. "Here?"

"About three feet to the left."

The big man grabbed a sledgehammer from the workbench and swung it like John Henry, shattering the wood paneling and reopening the tunnel entrance.

He peered into the darkness. "Well, I'll be damned."

"Tree, you have to stop Oran. He bragged about the murders, and said he had one more devil to slay."

"Who?"

"I don't know. He didn't say." Blood trickled from my nose into my mouth, producing a pungent, metallic taste. I spit a red glob on the floor, pulled a handkerchief from my pocket, and used it to squeeze my nose to slow the bleeding.

"Think, Jake. Who else did Oran hate!"

"When his malpractice suit failed, Oran killed Dr. Byrd to avenge Nancy's death." With my nose pinched tight, my voice sounded like I'd inhaled helium. "He could be after the hospital administrator, Harvey Winer, or the lawyer who lost his case."

"Good. That's what I need." Tree scribbled in his notebook.

"Who else? How about the threat at the reunion? Could Emily be in danger?"

"No, Oran sees himself as her protector. He left the note for Barb Dorfman. She was sitting with Emily before we arrived. Oran assumed they'd have dinner together."

Tree flipped the page and wrote something. "Didn't Emily's father collide with Byrd's killer in the hallway? Maybe Oran's afraid of witnesses."

"Not a chance." I unclamped my nose. "He's dying from Huntington's disease and doesn't care about witnesses. If he did, I'd be dead. He won't live long enough to be executed. But he *despised* McDermott. Maybe one of McDermott's scumbag friends somehow wronged Oran."

Tree thought for a second. "McDermott didn't really have friends, just contacts who fed his collection business. His old drinking buddy, Natuzzi, pissed off everybody he met, but he's doing three-to-five in the Grafton facility."

"Natuzzi's out," I said. "I saw him at the reunion, sitting at McDermott's table."

"Wonderful, more shit flushed through the legal system. Natuzzi's such a huge turd, I'm surprised he didn't clog up the prison's sewer on his way out. If Oran shoots *him*, it'd be a public service." Tree pointed at the basement window. "You get a look at Oran's car?"

"No. I was eyeballing the cellar floor."

Blood ran across my lips, down my chin, and dripped onto my T-shirt. I pinched my nose again.

Tree jerked the police radio from his belt, flipped a switch, and brought it to life. "Martinez, its Macon. Put out an APB on Oran Burke for aggravated battery and suspicion of murder."

My head snapped up. "Tree, he's got a revolver."

Macon pressed the button on his radio again. "He's armed and dangerous. And run down his plate number and car description. Station a uniform at his house on Hollywood in case he comes back. And don't let anyone in till I get a search warrant." Tree paged through his notebook. "Tell Lorain PD to send someone to St. Joseph's Hospital. I want protection for Irv and Emily Beale, and the administrator, Harvey Winer."

Static, a squeak, then a muffled protest. Tree cut Martinez off.

"Yeah, yeah. I don't care if they don't like it. Tell 'em we'll square up the cost later. Find out who Burke hired as a lawyer for his lawsuit against St. Joe's, and lay some protection on him too. Burke's gunning for someone, but I'm not sure who."

Tree clicked off. "I'll handle Natuzzi and you, my friend, will go to the ER. I'm calling EMS."

"Come on, Tree." I unclamped my nose and shoved the handkerchief into my pocket. "I have a few cuts and a bloody nose. You beat me up worse than this on the football field."

"Don't care. I want you checked out. Now."

"Fine, you win. I'll go to the Emergency Room, but I'll walk. It's less than fifty yards away. Let EMS handle the real emergencies. Now, go do your job."

"Okay, okay. Listen Jake, if anyone asks, I heard you hollering for help. Got it?" He snapped the radio back onto his belt. "That's why I kicked the door in. Let's not give some defense lawyer and the ACLU assholes grounds to throw out evidence."

"God knows I *was* yelling, but the gag made it sound more like humming."

"Oh, and one other thing," Tree smiled, "don't go to the hospital through the damn tunnel."

"You're just no fun anymore."

Tree bounded up the stairs, leaving me alone. Limping to the bench, I grabbed a clean rag, wet it at the utility sink, and wiped blood from my face.

Going to the Emergency Room was a waste of time for me and for hospital personnel. All I needed was a shower, antibiotic ointment, and a few Band-Aids.

I plucked a shard of glass from my forearm, applied pressure with the rag, and hobbled back to the bench. My foot accidently kicked the Taser on the floor, and I picked it up and turned it over. I'd never seen one before. The Taser wasn't much bigger than my cellphone and weighed about the same—a toy compared to the weapons I'd handled in 'Nam—but it had knocked me on my tail and nearly got me killed.

I stared at it, then gasped. Oh, *crap*. Fingerprints. *Tree's going to kill me.*

My dizziness flared again. I clutched the workbench to steady myself and decided to call in sick for work. I hated to leave Urgent Care shorthanded, but Harvey Winer would understand, especially when his police protection arrived. Hopefully, he wouldn't rat me out to Lucci. I didn't want "slacker" added to the bishop's growing list of my shortcomings.

Lucci …. The thought struck like a lightning bolt.

Father LaFontaine's description of Nancy Burke pinballed through my mind: *a devout Catholic. Couldn't get an annulment. Couldn't marry in the Church. Oran never forgave Lucci.*

Oh, sweet Jesus. Oran was going after the bishop.

I grabbed my cellphone from the bench and speed-dialed Lucci's office number as I clambered up the cellar stairs.

Chapter Forty-One

———•———

Wednesday, July 5, 1:00 p.m.

THE BISHOP'S TELEPHONE rang and rang. Finally, a recorded voice informed me that his office closed for lunch from noon until two. I didn't know Lucci's private number and had no way to warn him about Oran.

I slowed to a walk halfway to Sacred Heart Church, dialed Tree Macon's mobile, but got voicemail.

"Tree, it's Jake. Oran's after Bishop Lucci. I'm sure of it. His secretary's gone to lunch and I can't reach him, so I'm heading to his office. Meet me there and send backup."

I sprinted to the rectory, hopped into the old Toyota, and turned the key. The car answered with a weak whirring sound—a battery death knell.

The radio and headlights were off, but a faint light glowed from the glove compartment where the door hadn't latched completely. I snapped it shut and tried again.

Whir.

I slapped the steering wheel and considered my options. Colleen always walked to work, and I couldn't wait for a cab to arrive. If the cops caught me speeding in Justine's stolen van, I would never get to the bishop in time, and she might be jailed before her bone marrow transplant. Could I risk that? What other choice did I have?

Thy kingdom come, Thy will be done ….

As I gazed at the rectory's detached garage, pondering whether to put my sister's freedom and life in danger, I cranked the engine one last time. The whir became a faint grinding … a sputter, a shudder … and then the car rumbled to life.

I shoved the stick shift into first gear and swung onto West Lorain. The tires chirped as I hung a hard left onto Route 58 and stomped on the gas pedal. The engine roared, but the speedometer barely edged higher.

Dialing 911, I asked for the police station, got Officer Martinez again, and updated him on the threat to Bishop Lucci. Tree must have given Martinez a tongue-lashing for ignoring my earlier call, because his attitude toward me had changed considerably.

"I'll contact Chief Macon at once, Dr. Austin."

"And Officer, track down Bishop Lucci's cellphone number and let him know he's in danger."

"Yes, sir. Will do."

"Also, have the Cleveland police send a patrol car to Lucci's office."

"Chief Macon will have to make that call and request their assistance."

I hung up, sped through two yellow traffic lights, dodged a pothole the size of Akron, and careened onto the Route 2 entrance ramp toward Cleveland.

Redialing the bishop's phone number resulted in the same recorded message.

The drive to Lucci's office seemed endless. Asphalt slipped slowly under the car. A dump truck flew by me in the left lane. My speedometer was creeping slowly toward sixty when the "check engine" light flared bright orange.

Dear Lord, keep this scrapheap rolling a few more miles.

As I crawled past cornfields, strip malls, and back into a residential area, the check engine light began blinking, warning me to pull off the road immediately. Instead, I swung right onto an exit ramp, stripping more rubber from the bald tires. The Toyota shuddered, and steam poured from under the hood.

I ran the first stop sign, rolled cautiously through two red lights, and screeched to a halt in front of the Diocese building. A cloud of oily black smoke engulfed me when I opened the driver's door and jumped out.

Only a few cars dotted the parking lot at lunchtime, but no police cruisers were visible.

I entered the building and dashed through the empty lobby past the four life-sized ceramic saints, my footsteps echoing in the silence. Hoping the elevator would get me to the penthouse faster than the stairs, I summoned it and waited. And waited.

I'd given up and was scampering toward the stairwell when the elevator doors parted. I drew a deep breath, entered, and tried not to panic as the doors slammed shut and the walls closed in.

The elevator inched upward as slowly as Church doctrine changed. I punched the button again. *Come on, damn it.* When I finally arrived, I listened before cautiously cracking open the door to the bishop's suite. The anteroom was unoccupied.

A sign on the receptionist's desk read BACK AT 2:00 P.M. The appointment schedule on her computer screen showed ORAN BURKE—MEMORIAL CONTRIBUTION in the 1:30 slot. Lucci, the consummate fundraiser, must have agreed to a meeting with Oran before his office reopened. Anything for a donation.

I placed an ear on the oak doors leading to the bishop's inner sanctum, my face inches from a carved figure of Jesus staggering under the weight of the cross. My legs became rubbery when I heard soft voices inside.

For one second, I thought, *What am I doing? I have family now. Why risk everything for Lucci?* But only for a second.

There was no turning back. My hesitation had cost a life in the jungles of Vietnam. Kenny Babcock had died in my arms. I couldn't allow that to happen again.

I reached into my pocket to silence my phone but yanked out Oran's Taser instead. I must have shoved it into my pocket when I realized that the bishop was the target, panicked, and dialed his office from Oran's cellar. Although I knew nothing about Tasers, it was all I had.

I found my cell in another pocket and pushed the button to shut it off. It played the phone company's advertising jingle. *Crap.* I shoved the phone under my armpit, smothering it until it went silent.

Muffled voices continued in the next room. Making the Sign of the Cross, I snatched an ivory-handled letter opener off the desk, turned the brass knob with a trembling hand, and eased the heavy door open.

Chapter Forty-Two

Wednesday, July 5, 1:40 p.m.

I PEEKED IN, saw no one, and stepped inside Lucci's cavernous office. Two brandy snifters on the bishop's desk rested next to a crystal decanter filled with amber liquid. His violet zucchetto skullcap lay on the floor near his chair.

I heard Lucci's quivering voice to my right. "Dear God in Heaven, help me!"

I tightened my grip on the letter opener, raised the Taser, and peered around the corner into an alcove.

The bishop sat in an open window facing out like an enormous Humpty-Dumpty, legs dangling into the five-story abyss, fingers laced behind his head in prisoner position. Warm air flooded in against the air-conditioned cool. His robes and purple sash fluttered in the breeze.

Oran Burke stood with his back to me, his revolver aimed at the bishop's spine.

Lucci whimpered, "Please, Mr. Burke. Have mercy! I didn't understand." A litany of Hail Marys poured from His

Excellency's lips between sobs. "I'll do anything you want. *Anything.* I beg you."

"Beg? That's rich. How many times did I beg? Hell, Father LaFontaine pleaded with you, but you ignored him. My sweet Nancy begged for your help till she ran out of breath."

"The *Tribunal* made the decision, not me. I'm not permitted to—"

"Enough with the Catholic mumbo-jumbo. You didn't even *try* to help Nancy. No more damn excuses."

Oran placed the palm of his left hand against the bishop's upper back. Lucci cried out. Oran's gun hand trembled, and I prayed for a full-blown spasm so I could grab his weapon.

"Nancy married a drunken wife-beater at sixteen. She needed to be shielded from him, Lucci, not told to make her marriage work. Though, protecting kids has never been a priority for the Church, has it?" Oran's voice dropped to a raspy hiss. "You *knew* what a Catholic wedding meant to Nancy—and like Pontius Pilate, you washed your hands of her, as if she were filth."

"You're right. I see that now. I was misguided." Lucci wept. "Have mercy on a foolish old man. Forgive me, *please.*"

"Forgive? You expect absolution? Say you're sorry and *poof* … it's all good? This isn't a goddamn confessional, and I'm *not* a forgiving man."

Oran's neck writhed through a series of spastic movements, but his attention stayed focused on the bishop. As I raised the Taser and eased into the alcove, I thought I heard a siren in the distance.

Lucci's prayer was stuck in an endless loop. "Holy Mary, mother of God, pray for us sinners …. Holy Mary, mother of God, pray for us sinners …."

Oran growled, "Say all the prayers you want, you callous, arrogant son-of-a-bitch. If there is a God somewhere, He sure as hell won't forgive *your* sins."

I crept to within six feet of Oran. His neck spasm stopped.

The only sounds in the room were the ticking of a mantel clock above the fireplace and Lucci's new stuttering prayer: "Deliver us from evil …. Deliver us from evil …."

"The only *evil* in this room is you, Lucci. You're not a man of God, just a sadistic bastard who bullied his flock of devout sheep into submission."

A gust of wind inflated Lucci's robes into a giant sail. He wobbled on the windowsill like an oversized Weeble toy.

"Time to finish our experiment. The Church says angels can fly." Oran snickered. "If you're an angel, you'll soar. If you're a devil … *splat.*"

A siren wailed in the distance. Oran inclined his head to one side.

"Ask not for whom … the siren tolls, Lucci. It tolls for thee."

Out of time, out of options. Pointing the Taser at Oran's back, I held my breath, steadied my hand, and pulled the trigger.

Click. A soft, pathetic *click.* My heart flip-flopped.

Oran whirled and aimed his weapon at me, but kept his left hand on Lucci's back. I gazed into the black void of the gun barrel. It loomed large and dark and deadly.

"Well, I'll be damned." For a moment, Oran looked puzzled, then his lips grew thin and bloodless. "You really are a pain in the ass, Jake. Too bad you didn't reload the Taser."

I released the stun gun and it clattered on the hardwood floor.

Oran's right hand trembled again, his revolver quivering wildly. A large metal poker leaned against the fireplace. If I could grab it, I would only get one swing. Did I still possess the killer instinct to crush a man's skull? But it was a fool's errand. Even with Oran's tremor, at close range I had little chance of reaching the poker alive.

A carousel of faces rotated through my mind. Emily, Tree, Justine, and little RJ. *God,* I wanted more time with them.

I shifted the letter opener to my right hand.

"I didn't kill you in my cellar, Jake, because of Emily … and because you appear to be a righteous man. Make no mistake, though, if you try to stop me, I *will* shoot you." Oran aimed the revolver lower. "A gut shot is a very unpleasant wound, as I'm sure you know, Doctor."

"Don't, Oran. There's been enough killing."

"We're one body short of *enough*. What difference does it make whether I fry in Hell or an electric chair for four murders or five? Or in your case, six."

"I called Tree Macon. The police are on their way."

Multiple sirens sang their urgent song, getting louder by the second. Oran's face contorted with malicious glee.

"The cops? Perfect. Thanks, Jake. You think of everything."

His eyes turned icy and he released a piercing sound, somewhere between a cry and a snarl, cold-blooded and bitter.

I had seen those eyes, heard that sound, years ago in the jungle—from a man with nothing left to lose.

"Father Austin?" Lucci sobbed. "Do something. Help me, *please*."

"Oh, there's not much he can do, Bishop," Oran said, his features stony. "For the second time today, the good Padre brought the proverbial knife to a gunfight." He gestured with his pistol. "Drop it!"

What I needed was a guardian angel, not a letter opener. As I released it, I saw motion to my left, then heard a deep voice.

"No, Oran. You drop *your* gun, and put your hands up. Now."

Tree Macon stood in a crouch behind a small metal filing cabinet that barely protected his lower body, a two-handed grip on his weapon. Sirens wailed, tires screeched. Cruiser lights flashed through the open window, painting the ceiling in blue and red.

"Game's over, Oran," Tree said, his voice calm and firm. "Drop it."

Oran glanced over. "Wrong game, asshole. This is chess, not football." He poked Lucci in the back with his finger. "Your bishop cost me my queen, and I'm going to take him off the board." Oran cocked his revolver with his thumb and aimed at my chest. "Lower your gun, Tree, or I'll take your knight too. You shoot me, I'll kill Jake. This is checkmate."

Tree never wavered. His weapon remained level, but his voice softened. "No, it's a stalemate, Oran. There's no way out. Don't do this. It's not worth it."

"Oh, but it is."

A stampede of footfalls echoed in the hallway outside of Lucci's office. Oran took his eyes off me and edged his pistol toward Tree. It shook violently. Tree held his ground, motionless.

Sadness swept across Oran's face.

"I'm sorry I dragged you both into this." Then, "See you in Hell, Bishop."

The same primal sound that filled my nightmares came from Oran's twisted lips again. In my mind I saw Kenny, blood bubbling from his chest. Fury rose up in me like a beast.

I sprang forward and grabbed the bishop's arm just as Oran shoved him. Bracing one foot against the wall, I pulled back with all my strength. Lucci's massive bulk continued off the sill. I strained against gravity, against fear, trying to stop a runaway freight train.

Gunfire exploded. My eyes burned. The room flared in colors too bright to be real, fading to crimson, then black.

Blinded, I felt the bishop pitch over the edge, his weight dragging me along. I tried to let go, but couldn't. Lucci's hand clutched my forearm with the death grip of a drowning man dragging his rescuer under water.

The bishop screamed. Tree shouted words I couldn't understand.

My shoulder slammed against the window frame. Sharp pain pierced my chest as it scraped over the sill. I couldn't breathe. My hips started across the ledge and my feet flew from the floor.

Christ, I'm going over.

As I cried out, something slammed into my legs, driving my knees into the wall. My body stretched like a rubber band until I was sure it would tear in half, then I snapped backward, crashing down into darkness.

Chapter Forty-Three

———•———

Thursday, July 6, 2:00 p.m.

Endless, black nothingness. I longed for light. My eyelids refused to open. They were heavy, weighed down, as if someone had put pennies on them.

That thought popped my eyes open. Murky shapes danced before me until my lids sagged shut. It felt like I was floating. I forced my eyes open again, blinked, but saw only fog and shadows.

A soft, rhythmic beeping throbbed nearby. Footsteps approached, receded, approached. Something gently squeezed the tip of my finger and refused to let go. Voices sounded muffled, like I'd slipped underwater. I wanted to speak, but my lips stuck together. When I reached out, flames ignited in my shoulder.

The footsteps faded again. Everything went quiet except for that incessant beeping and an irregular tapping sound. I caught the scent of something fresh and fragrant. Flowers … perfume? Newly mowed grass? Was I in a meadow?

The shadows slowly merged into emerald leaves, backlit

by an orange sun. A sparrow danced along the windowsill, pecking at the glass pane, then flew off.

I sighed, inhaled deeply, and my lungs filled with fire. Each breath drove a white-hot poker into my chest. My entire body ached. Pain flared again in my shoulder. I groaned and felt a gentle, warm pressure in my left hand.

"Ah, Sleeping Beauty is awake at last."

I glimpsed a beatific face lit by a luminous smile. An angel? But if this was Heaven, why did I hurt like Hell? When I turned my head farther, it objected, pounding my temples like bass drums.

"Or should I say, Prince Charming?"

Emily's voice. Was I dreaming? I stared, clinging to the lifeline of her smile.

Finally I whispered, "Awakened by a kiss?"

She squeezed my hand again.

"No, Jake, by a reduction in your medication. As you came out of your coma, you started thrashing, and the doctors sedated you so you wouldn't hurt yourself."

The sharp aroma of disinfectant prickled my nose, and my mouth tasted like filthy gym socks. A clear plastic bag on an IV pole dripped next to me, marking time, and a pulse oximeter hugged the tip of my right index finger.

"Where am I?"

"The Cleveland Clinic. EMS took one look at you and brought you here. You're going to be okay. It's Thursday."

"Thursday?"

"You've been unconscious for more than a day. I was so afraid …. We were all worried we'd lose you."

"What … what happened?"

"You don't remember?"

My head felt stuffed with cotton. I shook it, and boll weevils tap-danced across the inside of my skull.

"There were gunshots. Lucci was pulling me …."

"The bishop's in a room down the hall. When you grabbed his arm, you dislocated his shoulder. Probably on purpose, knowing you. I'm sure he'll forgive you, though. You saved his life."

"The window." Images floated back. "Lucci was dragging me out."

"You were draped over the sill. Tree grabbed your legs and hung on until the other officers could pull you both back in. He called it the toughest tackle of his career."

"And my eyes? I couldn't see."

"Your face was covered with blood. Oran's blood." Her expression saddened. "He's gone, died instantly when—"

"Is Tree okay?"

"He's fine physically, but he's struggling with Oran's death. It'll take him time to get over that."

I thought about the VC soldier who haunted my dreams, clutching a photo of his child as he died. I knew it would take Tree a lifetime to get over that one moment.

I tried to sigh, but pain trapped the air in my chest. I waited until it eased.

"I'm so dizzy, Em. So groggy."

"It may be the morphine. You broke your collarbone and ribs, and punctured your lung. It was completely collapsed. They removed your chest tube in ICU and transferred you here an hour ago."

The fingers of my left hand traced the unnatural angle of my right clavicle through the overlying sling.

Emily's hand wandered across my pillow until she found my face. I'd been to Hell and back, yet somehow her touch filled me with a warm glow. She smoothed the hair from my brow.

"You also banged that hard head of yours, Jake. You had a severe concussion."

"Like the Elyria game?"

"Except you weren't wearing a football helmet this time,

hero boy." Emily extended her cane and stood. "I'd better tell the nurse you're awake—and that you're a bit dizzier than you normally are. I'll be right back."

"No, wait. Don't go." I touched her arm. "Stay, please."

Emily sat, located the telephone on my tray table, and dialed Tree Macon. She gave him my status report and listened to his response, then said, "Are you sure you want me to show that to him?" She chuckled and hung up.

"Show me what?"

"Today's *Oberlin News-Tribune*. Tree read the article to me after he drove me here this morning." Her hand explored the top of the nightstand, found the newspaper, and unfolded it. She showed me the headline:

OBERLIN EXORCISM: PRIEST RIDS TOWN OF DEVILISH KILLER

"Oh, sweet Jesus. They've got to be kidding. *Tree* stopped Oran, not me. And he saved my life. Is he upset?"

"Upset? No, more like frightened. He's worried that this will inflate your already enormous ego." She grinned. "He told me to have a nurse pack your head in ice before it swells."

We sat quietly for a while.

"It's all coming back to me. Slowly."

"Then please help me." She wrung her hands. "Why'd Oran do all this? He was my friend, a good man. I don't understand."

I closed my eyes and took my time reconstructing events, beginning with Barb Dorfman's greed, Dr. Byrd's fatal medication error, Joanetta Carter's plagiarism and betrayal, and finally Lucci's callous dismissal of Nancy Burke's plight and Oran's simmering hatred of him. McDermott required no explanation.

"People always treated Oran so cruelly, Jake. His gentleness made him an easy target. That's no excuse for what he did, but

I guess I expected more compassion from the Church." Emily leaned in, a light floral scent drifting with her. She recited softly,

> So many gods, so many creeds,
> So many paths that wind and wind,
> While just the art of being kind
> is all the sad world needs.

"One of your poems, Em?"

"No. Ella Wheeler Wilcox wrote it around 1900, but it's still true today."

I searched through the fog in my mind for words to explain the inexplicable.

"Nancy's death and his Huntington's disease changed Oran. You were right, Em, when you said he was a nineteenth-century man trapped in this century. His world became as black and white as his stories. He saw himself as a hero wielding the sword of justice."

She turned toward the window light as if toward a memory.

"Oran once told me that he wished he'd fought alongside his great-great-grandfather in the Civil War." A tear trickled down her cheek. "As if that bloodbath was some glorious adventure."

"Oran's illness had begun to warp his reality, and his moral code demanded an eye for an eye. Even dangling the bishop from a window was a perverted, almost biblical, fall-from-grace metaphor. Who knows what Oran was thinking as his disease progressed?"

I didn't know if that was entirely true, but hoped the possibility would lessen her sorrow. If it was a lie, so be it. Sometimes there was righteousness in a good lie.

Emily lowered her head and wept softly. I wanted to comfort her, hug away her grief. Finally, she removed her sunglasses, dabbed her eyes with a tissue, and cleared her throat.

"Was I in danger? Would Oran have hurt me too?"

"No. He cared deeply for you." I had no reason to bring up the threatening note intended for Barb Dorfman, but added, "What I still don't understand, though, are the hang-up phone calls you received on the night of the reunion."

"Oh, that was Todd." She must have read the confusion on my face. "He's … a close friend. We were going to a poetry reading this weekend, and he was calling at the last minute to cancel. Every time Todd got my answering machine, he chickened out. He felt terrible and decided to apologize to me in person."

Todd? *A close friend*? That shouldn't have surprised or bothered me, yet it did.

"I don't get it, Jake. Why would Oran try to kill you and Tree? You two never hurt him. It doesn't make sense."

I thought about Oran's last minutes. When I told him that I'd called the police, and cruisers began to arrive, he had been … delighted.

"I don't think he wanted to hurt us, Em. He was looking out for his niece."

"Sheila? What does she have to do with it?"

"She was his only family, his heir, and the beneficiary of his insurance policy. If Oran committed suicide, the policy could be voided, but if—"

"If he placed you in danger and Tree shot him—"

"Then Sheila could claim the insurance. I think Oran committed suicide-by-cop. Tree and I just provided him with the opportunity."

Emily collapsed back in her chair. "Dear God in Heaven."

"Amen."

Emily sat motionless for a while before speaking.

"I met your sister this morning. *That* was a surprise. When Colleen reported you missing, Tree told them what had happened. He drove Justine and RJ here to see you when he brought me. You were unconscious and they couldn't stay long."

"Good Lord, I forgot!" My body tensed. "I need to get tested to find out if I can donate bone marrow to her."

"When your doctor met Justine this morning and heard the situation, he included your transplant compatibility test with your other blood work. You should know soon if you are compatible—that is, if you're up to it."

"Oh, I'll be up to it. Justine and RJ are all the family I have."

"Colleen sends her prayers."

Emily's voice was having a disconcertingly sweet and dizzying effect on me. Maybe it was the morphine.

"She says she'll visit tomorrow, Jake, and smuggle in some cheesecake."

Good old Colleen. The patron saint of blarney, cooking, and compassion.

Another silence followed. I took the opportunity to gaze at Emily, wondering for the thousandth time what kind of life we might have built together. Finally, she said, "I guess you're going to use the flimsy excuse of your coma to stand me up for the concert tonight. You haven't forgotten about the Youth Orchestra, have you?"

She feigned a scowl before laughing.

"Rain-check, Em?"

"Sure." Her amusement vanished and her brow furrowed. "Jake, do you remember what you said to me over the phone the last time we spoke?"

I felt the distant drumbeats of dread, then alarm bells sounded. I searched the depths of my turbid memory, came up empty, and shook my head.

"You said ...." She squeezed my hand gently, then pulled away. "You said, *I love you.*"

The mist lifted from my mind, and I saw myself on the steps of the Heritage Center, cellphone to my ear, words spoken in haste and excitement tumbling from my lips when she provided the final puzzle piece about poison mushrooms.

Thanks, Em. Talk to you soon. Love ya.

I should have felt enormous conflict and regret. I should have denied saying it, or spun my words into another meaning. There were as many kinds of love as there are stars in the sky, but what I felt was not mere friendship. This love was not serene and patient; it was restless and unrelenting.

"God help me, Em. I said it because it's true." A strange, warm calm flowed through me. Even if I couldn't act on my feelings, the admission was liberating. I reached out my hand. Emily's hand was waiting, and our fingers came together like jigsaw pieces. "I guess I've always loved you."

"Me … or the memory of me?"

"I see a lot of the girl I loved in the woman I danced with at the reunion. That was the happiest I've felt in a long time. It's been forever since I've … *soared updrafts* and *dreamt music.*"

A look of bewilderment, then her eyes widened.

"Was that … my poem from high school?"

"I carried it everywhere I went, Em, all those years. You were always with me."

"I was so scared for you and prayed for your safe return every day of the war. I missed you *so much.*"

Then why had she not written back to me? My letters to her from Vietnam had gone unanswered. Hell, I was only a kid, thousands of miles from home in the seventh circle of Hell, alone and afraid. The pain of her rejection still lingered. My lips began to form the question, but Emily's composure suddenly crumbled. I desperately needed to know the reason for her abandonment, but this was not the right time to ask her. I remained silent.

"It's just … I care about you even now, Jake, deeply, but …." She turned her head away. "But what do we do now? Where do we go from here?"

"I have no idea." I suddenly felt overwhelmed and exhausted. "First, I have to get Justine though surgery and put what's left of my family together." I touched her lips with my finger. "I cherish you, Em, but that knowledge, and my friendship, may be all I have to offer you now. I've made vows and … I hope you can understand who I've become, what I …."

A gruff "ah-hummm" came from behind us. Tree Macon filled the doorway.

"Hey, this is a hospital room, not a damn movie theater balcony." He grinned. "And you two aren't in junior high anymore."

Chapter Forty-Four

———•———

Thursday, July 6, 4:00 p.m.

AFTER TREE DROVE Emily home, I kept thinking about my rekindled feelings for her, and her critical question: *Where do we go from here?*

Since my ordination, I'd been certain of my calling. Now, with Emily back in my life, I was drowning in doubt. I decided to ask Bishop Lucci to place me on a *religious retreat*—a euphemism for a chance to get my spiritual act together.

A nurse came in and removed my IV. I requested a wheelchair. As she helped me into it, the floor tilted twenty degrees to port, then thirty to starboard.

"Are you all right?"

"I'm just a little weak." I plunked my bottom down in the chair. "I'll be fine, thanks."

"Please don't go far," she said, then added, "Oh, I almost forgot. The lab called. You're a good match for your sister's bone marrow transplant."

If I hadn't been so wobbly, I would have jumped up and danced a gig. As it was, I could barely roll the chair down the hall using only one hand and my feet. I was slowly tacking a zigzag course like a drunken sailor when DeQuan Kwame turned the corner.

"Mr. Kwame, what are you doing at the Cleveland Clinic?"

"DeQuan, Doctor. That is my name." He paused. "I have a wife and three children, and I sometimes work part-time here to … how do you say it? Help make the ends meet. I heard about your ordeal, and since I was here, I came to visit." He stepped behind my wheelchair. "Allow me to assist. Where are you going?"

"Four doors down on the left."

As he wheeled me, I expected a disparaging remark about witnessing my drug screening, but instead he said, "I am truly glad that you are still with us."

"Thank you, DeQuan. That's very kind of you."

"Not at all." He stopped outside Lucci's room. "What fun would I have if you were not around for me to tease?" He patted my good shoulder and strolled away.

Bishop Lucci was in bed, his halo of remaining hair a fringe of disarray. Without his regal robes and purple sash, he looked smaller, less intimidating. He must have heard the wheelchair squeak, for he opened his eyes, and of all things, smiled.

"Come in. Thank you, my son, for risking your life to save mine."

From SOB to *son*, a definite improvement.

I nodded, opting not to mention that I'd tried to let go of his arm as he dragged me across the windowsill toward certain death.

"I'm in your debt, Jacob. If there's ever anything I can do, just ask."

"There is one thing, Your Excellency."

"Please, call me Antonio. What do you need?"

I hesitated. How does a priest ask a man like Lucci to approve a spiritual sabbatical so he can sort out his feelings for a woman? The bishop seemed genuinely grateful, and I might never have a better chance to safely approach the subject, but he could undermine my ministry and my new life with one phone call.

"I would like a leave of absence from my duties at Sacred Heart—"

"Say no more, Jacob. Consider it done. You'll need time to recover, and I've heard about your sister's illness. Take as much time as you need. I'll inform St. Joseph's Hospital and your Camillian Order."

A gift from above, and I claimed it before he could take it back.

"Thank you ... Antonio." An honest and courageous man would have explained the misunderstanding, or at least mentioned Emily. Instead, I said, "I'm sorry to leave you and Sacred Heart shorthanded."

"Don't worry about the Church. We'll get by." He grinned. "We have for two thousand years."

I wished the bishop a speedy recovery and rolled away as fast as I could.

Chapter Forty-Five

———•———

Friday, July 7, 3:00 p.m.

I WAS DISCHARGED the next day, and an orderly wheeled me to the hospital entrance. Emily took my arm as I stood and waited for Tree to bring the car and drive us back to Oberlin.

She said, "I wish I could see RJ. Who does he resemble?"

"Picture a small tornado in tennis shoes. He has Justine's red hair and freckles, and silver-blue eyes like my father's … and mine."

A familiar voice interrupted our conversation.

"Jake, my darling. What in the world happened to you? Poor baby!" Tanya spoke in the same sultry, flute-music voice I remembered from the airplane. She glanced at Emily, mischief flashing in her green eyes. "It's wonderful to see you again though. I miss your company, Jake. When you're feeling better, we should have a drink … or something." She sighed. "Unfortunately, I'm headed to the airport. I'll call you when I'm back in town, and we can … get together again."

Emily removed her hand from my arm and stepped away,

confusion on her face. Tanya sashayed toward me and planted a loud kiss on my cheek.

"That's for your stunt on the plane, Father. Now we're even," she whispered, her chuckle both delighted and derisive. "See you around, Jake." Her high heels clicked briskly away.

Emily stood motionless, her lips a slash of crimson. "What the hell was that, *Father*? And please don't tell me she's a nun. I'm blind, not deaf and dumb."

I tried to crawl out from the hole that Tanya had dug for me, describing my plane ride and admitting that Tanya's performance was retaliation for my vanity. Emily said nothing. After I fumbled through another mea culpa, she burst out laughing.

"Listening to you babble those pathetic explanations is the most fun I've had in years." Tree pulled the car up. Emily took my arm again and we got in. As Tree drove away, she added, "You deserved everything that Tanya woman gave you."

BISHOP LUCCI KEPT his promise and arranged my leave of absence. In gratitude for my help in what he referred to as "The Incident," he also repaired the old parish Toyota and replaced its balding tires at his own expense. Although it would have made more sense for him to simply buy me a better used car, patching the old one probably saved him a few dollars. Vintage Lucci. The man was both a bishop and a bean counter.

I used my time off to get to know Justine better, hone my uncle skills, and clear the paperwork from my desk.

Shortly after my return to the rectory, my sister asked me to watch RJ. She drove off in the stolen van, returning by taxi an hour later.

"What was that about?"

"Keeping my butt out of jail, Jake. I parked the van in the Amtrak lot so the police would think the car thief had escaped by train, then I made an anonymous call to them from a payphone. The van couldn't stay in the church garage, and I wanted to get it back to its owner."

Clearly, our old man had passed some of his genes for deviousness on to both of us.

I spent each morning on the telephone, trying to expedite Justine's hospital admission for her bone marrow transplant. Since my sling made it impossible to drive a stick shift, she chauffeured me every afternoon to visit Father LaFontaine. His skin grew more yellow and his frame more skeletal every day. Bolstered by his robust faith, however, Henri remained upbeat, except when his beloved Cleveland Indians went into a summer swoon. We spoke about church business, baseball, and other mundane topics, avoiding all talk of his pancreatic cancer, my near demise, and the topic I most wanted to discuss—his briefcase. I considered broaching the subject several times, but as our friendship grew and his health deteriorated, I could never bring myself to burden him.

The Hospice staff, angels without wings, waged their endless war against pain and suffering, keeping Henri comfortable until he quietly passed away.

The day after his funeral, the swelter abated and Justine took RJ to the park.

As Colleen finished setting the table, I joined her in the rectory dining room. "Stay for supper, Colleen. Please."

"I cannot. I've a Legion of Mary meeting," she said. "By the way, Father LaFontaine's family collected his belongings while you were out today."

I slumped onto a chair and cradled my face in my hands. I'd failed to perform Henri's dying request. Another promise broken, another friend forsaken.

Colleen tapped me on the shoulder.

"Have you gone deaf, then? You've not heard a single word I've said."

I opened my eyes. "Sorry. What?"

"Father LaFontaine asked me to give you some things. I put

them in your bedroom closet." She turned to leave. "I'll see you tomorrow, Father."

I was up the stairs before the front door closed. The autographed 1948 Cleveland Indians World Series pennant from LaFontaine's room was draped over his black leather briefcase in the corner of my closet, next to the signed team baseball bat.

A door slammed downstairs. "Uncle Jake, Uncle Jake, we're home! The park was *sooo* fun."

My promise to Henri would have to wait. This was family time.

We ate supper and spent the evening playing Chutes and Ladders. My nephew cheated like the devil, but I was empowered to absolve him. Justine felt ill and retired early, so I read RJ two stories before bed and tucked him in, then took the attaché case down to the living room.

It was locked. I was unsure what to do. LaFontaine's request had been unambiguous.

Destroy my briefcase. Don't open it. There's nothing illegal or dangerous inside.

With no church doctrine or rule to guide me, this was purely an ethical dilemma and a matter of conscience. I was on my own. We'd been friends only a short time, but nothing about Henri gave me any reason to question his integrity or morality. The last thing I wanted to do was violate a fellow priest's trust and break a deathbed promise. But that's exactly what I did.

I wedged my penknife in, popped the locks, and opened it.

Sorry, Henri. The Church had swept too many sinister secrets under the Vatican rug. I refused to be part of a cover-up.

The case contained a packet of handwritten letters secured by a rubber band and a small photo album. In several snapshots, a younger Henri LaFontaine, dressed in street clothes, had his arm wrapped around a smiling woman's waist, holding her close. Judging by hairstyles and clothing, these pictures had been taken many years ago. In one photo, he kissed her cheek. Another showed the woman with her hands folded in prayer, her face caressed by the white veil of a novice. In the last, she wore the black habit of a nun.

I recognized her. She had run weeping from Henri's hospital room a few weeks earlier, clutching an airline ticket to Seattle, mumbling something about being "lost without him." I wanted to believe that this woman was merely a church colleague, a cousin, or his sister. Henri's secrecy and these pictures, however, suggested otherwise.

Beneath the photo album was a single red rose, pressed flat and dried. Emily had given me a similar boutonnière when we were high school juniors. Maybe Henri had worn this on his tuxedo at his prom. Had they been lovers? When and why did they part? I would never be certain, and wasn't sure I wanted to know.

I picked up the letters but hesitated. I knew all too well that not all forms of love involve physical intimacy. I'd heard LaFontaine's confession several times, and he had never acknowledged having an affair or breaking his vows. Still, I removed the rubber band and examined the dates on the envelopes. The most recent was postmarked one month before I'd arrived. I removed the letter and read.

Sister Christina wrote about her concern for LaFontaine's health and her continued prayers for his recovery. She was having difficulty getting permission to fly to Ohio but hoped to visit him soon. The letter was short, sad, and loving. Nothing more. I began to open the next envelope but stopped.

The implication was clear. Henri and I had three things in common. Unattainable baseball championships, unattainable women, and a collection of portable memories. I had my manila envelope, and Henri had his briefcase.

Secrets, yes; sinister, no.

Wish you'd told me, my friend, I thought. *I could have used your advice.*

I opened the fireplace flue, lit some kindling, and fed the flames with Henri LaFontaine's letters and photographs.

As the last flickering blue shadows from the fire danced across the wall, soft music floated down from upstairs. I went back up for a chat, but Justine's door was closed. I stole into RJ's room, listened to his quiet breathing, and whispered a short prayer of hope and gratitude. Then I returned to the living room, settled into my recliner, and pondered the many ways my life had changed since I'd fled Oberlin decades ago.

My father's abandonment and my mother's alcoholism had left me an angry, unsupervised teen. I had directed that anger at the world through the sanctioned violence of football and military service, but also inwardly with drugs, booze, and reckless behavior. And I'd driven away the one person who truly loved me. Emily.

My mentor in the seminary had suggested that sending me to war might have been a wake-up call from God, a chance to remake myself in His image. I'd scoffed at the idea but now suspected he was correct. Out of desperation, I had grabbed on to my faith like a life preserver, abandoning the self-centered boy within only to create a work-centered man, still hollow at his core. Over time, however, I'd become certain of two things: Emily was gone from my life forever, and the priesthood was my true calling.

Enter Emily at the reunion, unmarried but divorced.

Humans make elaborate plans—and God laughs.

The last few weeks had changed everything. I'd begun to effectively merge my two professions at the church and hospital, ministering to both body and soul. And although I'd failed to protect Kenny in Vietnam, I'd overcome my fear and hesitation and saved the bishop's life. Justine and RJ had satisfied my deep longing for family, restoring love to my duty-filled existence. And in Emily and Tree, I had rediscovered true friendship.

Although the ghosts of my past still haunted my hometown, I no longer had any desire to flee. Like my high school's new mascot, the phoenix, I might just rise from the ashes of my youth here.

Once, my life had seemed cursed. Now, I saw it as blessed. God certainly did work in mysterious ways.

My mind drifted back to Emily and the quote from the book on Henri's desk.

Who knows anything at all about solitude if he has not been in love? Love and solitude must test each other in the man who means to live alone.

I couldn't "logic" my way through my feelings for her. I needed time for the dust storm of my past to settle and to help my sister through her illness before I could even consider the future.

I watched the last few embers in the fireplace flicker and die, closed my eyes, and smiled, knowing that my DEROS had finally arrived. I was home at last.

Photo by Ed von Hofen

BORN AND RAISED in the Cleveland, Ohio, area, **John Vanek** received his bachelor's degree from Case Western Reserve University, where his passion for creative writing took root. He received his medical degree from the University of Rochester, did his internship at University Hospitals of Cleveland, and completed his residency at the Cleveland Clinic.

During the quarter century he practiced medicine, his interest in writing never waned. Medicine was his wife, but writing became his mistress and mysteries his drug of choice. He began honing his craft by attending creative writing workshops and college courses. At first pursuing his passion solely for himself and his family, he was surprised and gratified when his work won contests and was published in a variety of literary journals, anthologies, and magazines.

John lives happily as an ink-stained-wretch in Florida, where he teaches a poetry workshop for seniors and enjoys swimming, hiking, sunshine, good friends, and red wine.

For more information, go to www.JohnVanekAuthor.com.

Keep reading for an excerpt from the 2nd
Father Jake Austin Mystery

MIRACLES

Chapter One

————•————

Monday, July 24th, 2002, 9:30 a.m.

WHY DO YOU test me so, Lord? You've already shaken my world like a snow globe. Please don't let my sister die! Wasn't my time in the fiery hell of war enough? True, that forged me into who I am today, and led me to You and the priesthood. I do all that you ask of me at the hospital and the church, and do it gladly. You have my entire life and my heart. Isn't that enough? Sweet Jesus, don't take Justine from me and orphan my nephew. I beg you. He's only four! Please don't crush his tiny spirit the way mine was ground to pulp as a child. Have mercy on our makeshift family! I ask this in your name. Amen.

In the wistful stillness of an empty Sacred Heart Catholic Church, a plaintive meowing aroused me from my prayer and meditation. Without looking, I knew it was Martin Luther, the tabby that kept the church free of mice. I'd named him that partly because his stripes formed a perfect "M" on his forehead, but mostly because, like his namesake, he loved the Church even though he detested her rules. My furry Martin particularly hated the rule that required him to stay in the basement with his water bowl, food, and litter box.

Having once again pulled a Houdini and escaped from what I called the cellar *cat-acombs*, my resident heretic sauntered over and deposited a dead mole at my feet, peered up at me, and purred. I should have named him Rascal.

My cellphone rang, displaying the number of the hospital.

I pushed up from the padded kneeler and dropped onto the oak pew. Except for Martin Luther, I was alone in the church nave. The few faithful who'd joined me as I offered morning Mass had scattered like seeds in the wind.

I accepted the call, morphing from a mender of souls to a healer of bodies.

"Austin."

"Marcus Taylor here. Hope I'm not disturbing you, Jake."

I'd been praying that he would call me today. Hope mingled with the faint scent of incense in the air. I gazed at the crucifix above the altar and crossed myself, my heart upshifting and pounding in my chest. Dr. Taylor was the chief of staff at St Joseph's Hospital, and I desperately needed his help.

My turbulent past had swept me from a bloody overseas war, where I'd served as an Army medic, into medical school as I searched for inner peace. When I failed to find serenity healing the sick, I'd returned to my Catholic roots and entered a seminary. I was an anomaly. Although some Protestant ministers served both as physicians and clergymen, only the Camillian Order of the Catholic Church had welcomed my dual role. When I wasn't managing Sacred Heart Church, a small parish in the town of Oberlin, Ohio, I'd been assigned to work part-time at St. Joseph's, a nearby inner-city hospital that cared for many of the indigent in Lorain County.

"I'm glad you called, Marcus. Please tell me you have good news about my sister's bone marrow transplant. Justine and her son have been staying with me at the rectory and I'm watching her slip away more every day. She can't hang on much longer."

"Sadly, no. I've contacted some colleagues at the Cleveland Clinic and I'm waiting to hear back, hopefully today." He cleared his throat. "I know you're not officially back to work at the hospital yet, Jake, but I have a situation on my hands and could use your help."

A recent encounter with a serial killer had left me recuperating from broken ribs and a shattered collarbone. I'd just completed a three-week leave of absence from the parish; however, I was still on sick leave from the hospital. Nevertheless, I was not about to say "no" to a friend and coworker who was trying to save my sister's life.

"Sure. Whatever you need."

"EMS brought in a comatose one-year-old boy this morning, Jake. Might be a SIDS case averted by an alert parent."

Sudden Infant Death Syndrome. I'd practiced internal medicine for years before entering the priesthood, but had absolutely no expertise in dealing with crib deaths or children in comas. I had no idea why Taylor, the chairman of Neurology, would called me instead of a pediatrician or another neurologist.

"Okay, Marcus. How can I help?"

"It's touch and go. The child's teetering on the brink and his parents are coming unglued. They're Catholic, and I was hoping you could sit with them for a while and offer some spiritual support and guidance."

"Of course. I'll be there as soon as I can."

As I hung up, something touched my thigh. Martin Luther hopped onto my lap and nuzzled my arm, covering my black cassock with cat hair. He was an affectionate little critter. No wonder my nephew kept begging me to move Martin into the rectory with us.

I stood and slid the dead mole under the pew with the toe of my shoe, intending to remove it later. Cradling Martin with one arm, I genuflected, returned him to the cellar, and headed to the rectory.

Chapter Two

Monday, July 24th, 9:45 a.m.

OUTSIDE THE CHURCH, the eastern sky was the color of claret and birdsong filled the air like a distant children's choir. Heat-devils, however, swirled across the asphalt parking lot, and Ohio was already as hot as a blast furnace. Fortunately, a strong northwest breeze kept the treetops dancing and flags snapping, making the swelter bearable.

Entering through the backdoor of the rectory, I explained to Colleen that I had to run an errand and hoped to be back in time for lunch. She was the part-time housekeeper and my Girl Friday at Sacred Heart Church. Colleen told me that my sister felt better this morning and had taken her son to the playground for an hour, so I brushed the cat hair from my cassock, jumped in the parish's old Toyota, and drove to the Emergency Room at St. Joseph's Hospital in Lorain.

Like most inner-city ERs, the place was jam-packed and chaotic. The triage nurse directed me to a small waiting room reserved for families in crisis.

I knocked softly and opened the door.

A uniformed police officer whipped around in his chair and pointed a finger at me.

"Get out!" he growled. When he noticed my clerical collar and cassock he added, "Ah, give me a few minutes, Father. Be done as soon as I can."

I closed the door and leaned against a wall in the corridor, where I remained for almost half an hour, wondering what the heck was going on. When the officer finally emerged, I knocked again and entered the room.

A woman in her late teens or early twenties sobbed softly as she teetered on the edge of a couch, her elbows on her knees, head down, eyes fixed on the floor. She wore a tight-pink halter top above a bare midriff and low-riding shorts tight enough to stop the circulation to her long, tan legs. Unaware of my presence, she ran her fingers through jet-black hair, highlighted by a pink streak on the left. Her fingernails were painted in neon colors. Large gold loops dangled from both ears, flanking full, cupid-bow lips.

A man with bronze skin reclined against the couch cushions, his head cantilevered onto the sofa back, his eyes glued to the ceiling. Below a barrel chest, his beer belly was wedged into a wife-beater T-shirt stained with sweat. Red boxer shorts peeked out above filthy cutoffs. His heavily tattooed arms were thick but flabby. His left hand gently massaged the back of the young woman's neck.

They struck me as the odd couple—a scantily clad Snow White oozing pheromones, comforted by Dumpy, the eighth dwarf.

The door clicked closed behind me and their heads snapped to attention. They both sat up.

I approached them and said, "Dr. Taylor told me that a terrible thing has happened. May we talk for a while?" Two nods. "I'm Father Jake Austin from Sacred Heart Church."

The man extended a callused, moist hand. He was also young, though his face had lost the angles of youth. One glance told me that his life had been hard.

"*Gracias, Padre.* I am Miguel Hernandez." He wore the wrinkled forehead of a worried man. "I go to Mass at Sacred Heart sometimes."

The young woman tried for a smile without success. "I'm Martina, but everyone calls me Tina."

I'd seen Miguel at church. Never Tina. She was a striking woman and I would have remembered. Unlike Miguel, she had no accent and did not appear Hispanic. Her complexion and facial features suggested a European heritage, maybe German. She had a mole on her left cheek, and except for her hair color, she reminded me of the actress who played Ginger on the old sitcom *Gilligan's Island.*

I pulled up a chair and sat. Miguel's body odor assaulted me, but didn't mask the smell of alcohol on his breath.

"Please, tell me what happened."

A long silence. Tina broke it.

"It's like a nightmare, Father." She fixed me with enormous ebony eyes made darker by copious eye makeup. "I had the day off from work, first time in forever, and we were watching some tube while our baby slept." Makeup followed tears down both cheeks like black jet contrails. "We got no air conditioning and the apartment's a damn oven, so I moved the fan from our bedroom into little Pablo's …."

When she said the child's name, she choked on the word. More tears. Her eyes grew puffy, as though she was allergic to the memory, and she rubbed them so hard I feared she might gouge them out.

Tina rested her head on Miguel's shoulder until she finally composed herself.

"I plugged the fan in, fed him, and he conked out, you know, sound asleep on his belly, snuggled up with his teddy bear. When I came back to check on him, he was real quiet … too quiet."

Her upper teeth slid over her lower lip, and it blanched when she bit down.

"I didn't want to wake him, so I bent over the crib rail," she said. Her voice was strangled and so soft that I had to lean forward to hear her. "I couldn't see his chest moving, so I picked him up. He was floppy ... like a rag doll."

Tina became formless, dissolving into the couch.

Visions of my nephew building sand castles on Huntington Beach and chasing a Slinky down the rectory steps flashed through my mind. He was the closest I would ever have to a child of my own. The thought of seeing him gray and lifeless on a stainless-steel morgue table chilled me to the core. I ached for this young couple.

Miguel said, "I called 911. Took 'em forever to get there." Miguel swallowed hard. "I tried the CPR stuff you see on TV but didn't know what the hell I was doing. I mean, Pablo was blue! And he's so tiny, I was afraid to push too hard on his chest." He cradled his head in his hands. "*Diós mío. Ay!* What a dumbass I am."

He moaned, then suddenly raised his head and stared at me.

"Where the hell was Jesus when my baby couldn't breathe? Huh? Tell me that, *Padre*! How can God let this happen?"

I had no answer. I'd asked the very same question when my mother died in a house fire and when my friends were killed in the war. Although I'd learned to accept the Almighty's passive silences over the years, I wasn't happy with the arrangement.

Reverting to my seminary training, I pontificated about faith and the Lord's incomprehensible plan, expounding with enough conviction to almost convince myself. The words sounded hollow and tasted bitter. I gave them the best that I could muster, wilting a bit with every time-worn phrase.

When I'd run out of platitudes, Tina said, "Help us, Father. The nurse sent us in here. They're working on him, keeping him alive, but ... we need to be with our baby. Soon."

"I'll see if they're ready for you."

"Push 'em hard. We been here a long damn time," Miguel said. He stood, his face still flushed with anger. "And you can tell me why that cop treated us like *basura*, like garbage, like this nightmare is our fault. What the hell was that about?"

"I have no idea, but I'll try to find out." I felt I'd helped them so little that I added, "Do you want to speak with a hospital grief counselor?"

Tina shook her head.

Miguel looked down and took a deep breath. "Sorry I went off. It's not your fault. We'd rather stick with you, *Padre*, if that's okay."

"Of course." I wrote down my phone numbers and gave them to Miguel. He extended his hand again and thanked me *for all I'd done.*

Some days I hated my job.

From John A. Vanek and Coffeetown Press

———•———

Thank you for reading *DEROS*. We are so grateful for you, our readers. If you enjoyed this book, here are some steps you can take that could help contribute to its success and the success of this series.

- Post a review on Amazon, BN.com, and/or GoodReads.
- Check out John's website (www.JohnVanekAuthor.com), email him at John@JohnVanekAuthor.com and ask to be put on his mailing list.
- Spread the word on social media, especially Facebook Twitter, and Pinterest.
- Like John's Facebook page (JohnVanekAuthor), and Coffeetown's page (coffeetownpress).
- Follow John (@JohnVanekAuthor) and Coffeetown Press (@coffeetownpress) on Twitter.
- Ask for this book at your local library or request it on their online portal.

Good books and authors from small presses are often overlooked. Your comments and reviews can make an enormous difference.

Coffeetown Press and its sister imprint, Camel Press, publish many wonderful mystery series. For more information, please check out:

www.coffeetownpress.com

and

www.camelpress.com